Herr Schnoodle
McBee

Herr Schnoodle & McBee

P. K. PARANYA

Five Star • Waterville, Maine

First Edition
First Printing: October 2006

Published in 2006 in conjunction with
Tekno Books and Ed Gorman.

Set in 11 pt. Plantin.

Printed in the United States on permanent paper.

Library of Congress Cataloging-in-Publication Data

Paranya, P. K.
    Herr Schnoodle & McBee / by P.K. Paranya.—1st ed.
        p. cm.
    ISBN 1-59414-412-5 (hc : alk. paper)
    1. Private investigators—New York (State)—Fiction.
    2. Dogs—Fiction.   3. New York (N.Y.)—Fiction.
    I. Title.   II. Title: Herr Schnoodle and McBee.
    PS3616.A73H47 2006
        813'.6—dc22   2005033731

I dedicate this book to animal lovers the world over. Especially, it is dedicated to the founding mothers and the volunteers of Planned Pethood, a grassroots group responsible for spaying and neutering half the population of Yuma, Arizona, (the pet population, that is). And to the real Herr Schnoodle, my sweet doggie companion and my inspiration for this book.

1

Scrambling over garbage cans, Alexander McBee climbed up on the dividing fence and dropped, bent over, breathing hard.

McBee's heart pounded. He felt the exertion in every muscle of his body. "Barely forty and you're unfit as hell," he muttered when his breath caught up with him again. He didn't think of himself as lazy. He just didn't believe in sweat.

His first case in a month and already screwing up, but what the hey . . . he was trying, wasn't he?

"Hey, jerk! You tailing me?" The hoarse whisper sounded alarmingly close to his ear.

McBee pivoted, ready to get in a few licks until he recognized the voice of the sleazy bookie he had followed for days. So much for undercover.

"Yeah, I'm following you."

It was hard slowing his gasps to somewhere near normal, noting the other fellow was not even breathing hard.

"What the hell for?" Blackjack snarled. "I paid you a deposit and you screwed up the big bucks. You were supposed to watch Marie, not me, you jerk!"

Private-eye work could get complicated. When *had* he decided to switch from shadowing Marie to watching her husband?

"Lay off the name calling," Mac said, with what he liked to think of as cold menace in his voice. When he finally managed to straighten up he stood at least a head taller than this creep. A definite advantage. The optimism didn't last long.

Blackjack flexed his arms. A switchblade fell into a waiting palm. The man tapped it lightly against the side of his own cheek in a calculated gesture of intimidation.

"I asked a question. Why follow me?"

Mac fumbled in his jacket pocket, drawing out a pack of photos, extending them without speaking.

The street noises funneled into the alley, but Mac's ears closed as if in a vacuum. The only sound coming his way was Blackjack shuffling the photos.

Suddenly a loud squalling tore the air between the two men, and they both jumped. Mac looked down to see if he still had his socks and loafers on. Both men grinned self-consciously as the cats quarreled in the Dumpster.

"What's this all about?" Blackjack hit the pictures with the flat of his blade.

Mac swallowed and tried to tower over the fellow. He decided towering was not easy with a switchblade close to your face. He dropped back on his heels and forced himself to relax.

"It means the cops have all the evidence they need to bust you for aggravated assault. I took the shots the last time you beat up Marie—and got statements from the neighbors. If that won't do it, I know about Babette, your tootsie you got set up on the other side of the city. Marie's going to take you to court, and you'll lose everything but your Fruit of the Looms."

"Tootsie?" Blackjack's gravely voice rose an octave in outraged disbelief. "Tootsie? Are you in some kind of time warp or something?"

McBee studied the ground a moment. Maybe he should quit watching those old detective movies on late-night TV.

He thought they'd help him get a feel for this profession.

"Whatever. You're missing the point."

Blackjack's scorn progressed to a mask of hostility.

"McBee, you're a dirty-dealing double-crosser. Marie's messing around on me. Everyone on the street knows that. I hired you to . . ."

"Yeah?" Mac interrupted the tirade before the little man could build up a head of steam. Where short tempers were the norm, the neighborhood regarded Blackjack's awesome temper with unparalleled respect.

The bookie's narrow, pale face showed puzzlement. "But why? I paid good."

"Yeah, well—here's your money." Mac extended a handful of bills, mostly singles, hoping Blackjack wouldn't bother counting it.

"Aw, save it for your old age, if you're lucky enough to have one," Blackjack muttered with uncharacteristic generosity. "Just answer my question. Why?"

Mac shrugged, not sure what to answer and waited, expression carefully blank.

Marie deserved something better than this worm, for sure. She had a boyfriend, true enough, a legless Nam vet who painted pictures. Weeks ago, he'd watched them together as she wheeled him through the park. Their devotion was unmistakable.

Mac had warned them of Blackjack's suspicions. He recalled the thrill of pulling the roll of thirty-five-millimeter film out of his camera and tossing it in the nearby litter can. He had seen that dramatic gesture at least a hundred times in the late movies and had always wanted to do it.

Blackjack raised his arm and the knife slid back into his sleeve. Mac wondered what a good sneeze would do to his sweat glands with the sharp end pointed up like that.

"Hell, I don't give a damn anymore what Marie does," Blackjack snarled. "She's lousy in bed, anyway. I'm heading for Vegas tomorrow. Make sure our paths don't cross again—jerk!"

Watching the wiry, thin man saunter off, Mac considered his evaporated fee. Owning a license—reading "Alexander McBee, Private Investigator"—hadn't put many groceries on the table so far.

His problem started when he flew into the face of family tradition to become a tax accountant after college. He should have given up and joined the police force as his father and grandfather expected he would do. Call it stubborn, call it overreacting; rebelling was the most important thing in his life at the time.

Talk about shooting yourself in the foot—he detested working with figures. He still hated to admit he'd chosen the profession his father would oppose the most.

He should be tooling around in a fancy car, preferably a shiny, red convertible—strictly low-profile, of course. He should have nubile lovelies standing in line for his attention. Excitement should lurk in every corner. Damn it, he'd *counted* on it happening! He watched reruns of *Magnum* over and over to capture that Mr. Cool persona.

The late afternoon turned to dusk as McBee ambled along the littered streets. In absentminded distaste, he kicked away the blowing papers that clung to his trousers. Last week a paper loaded with squiggly jelly from the donut cart had landed against his leg. He couldn't afford another cleaning bill.

When he passed shopkeepers in front of their stores, sometimes they nodded, but none spoke to him. McBee's glance flickered into a doorway and took in the snoozing wino, his thoughts not registering the details. Was he invisible like that man?

Sometimes he had the feeling he'd been invisible all his life. People saw him, spoke to him sometimes—but did anyone ever see beyond his baby blues? He didn't think so. His thoughts carried him beyond his usual walk and toward the docks, unmindful of the dark corners with suspicious lumps of humanity lying along the wharf. Spaced out with drugs or liquor, they, too, were untouched by his presence. He felt lulled by the lap-lap of the murky water as he kicked at a stray can to break the monotony.

Life chugged along in slow motion. This wasn't how it should be. Sure, he was better off than them. He watched a particularly repulsive bum cradling a bottle of dago red as if it were his only friend in the world.

But what the hey—that wasn't a fair comparison. McBee had poured his body and soul into this PI business and it was turning sour on him. He was running out of options.

Something made a low whine as the water slapped louder against the side of the barnacle-encrusted pier.

He took two neatly folded paper towels from his back pocket and laid them on the dock before he knelt and peered over the side. From the fog-shrouded streetlight he could barely make out a form in the flotsam and jetsam. He smiled at the words springing into his mind. Flotsam and jetsam. In high school they were his two favorite words for weeks until his family banned him from ever saying them again in the house.

The dark mass in the water struggled weakly. A rat? Nope. At least he hoped never to see a rat that big. He bent to get a closer look.

Good Lord! It was a dog!

His first instinct was to turn away. He was sure he'd

always been allergic to any creature with fur. They could make him sneeze or break out in ugly hives. If the animal still had any life left, it probably carried bubonic plague from all that dirty water. Mac imagined he saw the whites of the dog's eyes move. He turned away and then sighed.

Maybe he should haul the beast up and let it expire in peace. Nothing should have to die in water so thick you could dig it with a shovel.

Reaching down into the slime, Mac grabbed a handful of fur. His nose clogged with the stench of pollution. The damned animal weighed a ton as he hauled it in and dumped it on the dock. He glanced down at his once-neat suit. What a mess. First the jelly donuts, now this. So much for wearing a suit and tie. He should have ignored that particular suggestion from the PI correspondence school's list of commandments. It hadn't hurt Magnum to run around in tight jeans and baggy bright shirts.

McBee examined the soggy heap of fur on the dock with distaste tempered with revulsion. It looked like a huge porcupine with bits of floating debris and grease stuck to its coat. Mac bent closer, seeing the heavy rope wrapped around its neck. No damn wonder the dog felt heavy.

He poked the animal with the toe of his shoe, hoping it was beyond caring. No such luck. The tail flopped weakly, spraying a greasy film over the tops of his shoes and the one trouser leg still clean. With that effort expended, the dog's head fell back, and its eyes closed in weary resignation.

2

The trip across town took forever. McBee had to promise the cabby an extra ten for his trouble. He hoped the guy wouldn't notice the ruined backseat until after McBee had sneaked through the alley and up to his apartment from the back entrance. It seemed a contradiction that the property owner refused to allow pets when the lodging was barely fit for an animal to live in.

Thunder and lightning played against the outline of the city. What an appropriate evening to haul in the Son of the Lock Ness Monster, and what a time to discover a hidden bent toward foolish compassion.

As McBee sneaked past the landlady's door with his burden, he feared the dog was more dead than alive. An occasional twitch of the long tail let him know he wasn't carrying a soggy corpse into the bathroom.

Mac washed the dog as gently as possible with the strongest soap he had. It took the hottest water and three complete soapings to pry loose the oil slick embedded into the wiry fur. When finished, he wrapped the trembling animal in his best army surplus blanket and carried him out to the couch.

While the dog began to dry, his appearance didn't improve.

Mac had to shave parts of his coat in some places to get to the embedded tar. Underneath the shaggy, long hair appeared to be a layer of lamb's wool. Judging from the size of his comical face, big brown eyes and dots of gold eyebrows, hair stiff as a porcupine, the dog looked part schnauzer and . . . the other part baffled McBee. The bushy eyebrows, the triangle-shaped ears, the stiff jowl whiskers, he resembled a Gilbert and Sullivan version of a stern and proper Prussian general.

Schnauzer and poodle! That had to be it. What a combination.

"Guess that makes you a schnoodle, old boy." He touched the dog's nose but wasn't sure what he should feel. Should it be hot or cold? Was that important? Something like the old riddle of feed a cold and starve a fever?

"Tomorrow the pound, fella. No pets allowed in this building, even if I wanted to keep you—which I don't."

The creature thumped his tail with a little more vigor, slopping his tongue over Mac's hand.

When Mac opened a can of chicken noodle soup, the dog eyed it with disinterest. Finally, as if doing Mac a big favor, he slurped daintily from the bowl. Then he carefully licked his jowls, much as a cat might clean its whiskers.

Three days later the dog was still there. McBee told himself it was a sort of challenge, waiting to see which form his allergic reaction would take. Would it come as bloat, sneezing and maybe even a virulent type of hives, or all at once? When nothing happened, Mac still wasn't quite ready to stop the experiment.

"I gotta do it soon, boy." Mac had always talked to himself. It only made him uneasy if someone caught him at it. Now he had an excuse, another live being in the room—a comfort he never thought of needing—to be assured that he was not eccentric.

Walking the dog grew more troublesome. Mac tried to do it before the landlady crawled out of bed and at night after she turned out the light. Some day she was going to wake up early and then the jig would be up. Mac told himself he only wanted the mutt to gain a little weight, make a halfway decent showing at the pound so someone might adopt him.

Not that it mattered, of course. The schnoodle wasn't his responsibility. He'd gone as far as he could.

He glanced past his own image in the mirror to the shaggy face watching in the doorway. The dog never let Mac out of his sight. He sensed when it was time to go to the office and the mustache bristles drooped. The liquid chocolate eyes got a sad, lost expression that became harder and harder to forget once the door closed.

Mac paused in shaving, regarding the mutt thoughtfully for a long moment. "I suppose I could keep you a while longer. What's a day or two when I might stumble on some dope willing to take on an ugly mutt like you."

The dog grinned up at him, his lips stretched, showing white teeth.

He could never get him to answer to a command. Mac tried "come," "sit," first in English, then Spanish and then a little pigeon Yiddish he'd picked up in the streets. Nothing. Zilch. Finally, in exasperation, Mac shouted "Actung!" and clicked his heels together as he saluted.

Instantly, the dog stood at attention, his head cocked to one side in a comical expression of interest.

"So that's it. If I believed in reincarnation you'd be Prussian, a real authority figure, for sure. Something I've always avoided, I might add."

Mac scratched doggy ears.

"I don't feel comfortable calling you mutt or pooch. Mind, it's only temporary. I hereby christen you 'Herr Schnoodle.' "

The dog responded with a shrill bark of joy.

"Hey, hey. I said it was temporary, didn't I? Read my lips. T-e-m-p-o-r-a-r-y. Maybe I can find some sucker to take you off my hands, so I don't have to take you to the pound."

Three weeks later they were still together. Life had simplified for McBee, and he wasn't sure if he should be grateful or not. The landlady finally caught them sneaking out and offered her ultimatum.

It took almost two seconds to decide. Mac moved everything into his cubby hole of an office on the other side of town. He didn't own all that many possessions anyway. He'd rented the tiny office for nearly a year and hadn't met one tenant, if there were any besides himself. The building was owned by a out-of-state slumlord, and Mac mailed his rent to a post office box in Queens. He had never frequented the office at night so maybe that's when the renters scurried out of their holes.

This is cozy, Mac thought with smug contentment when they settled in the makeshift office/apartment. At first living in one room with a bathroom the size of a postage stamp felt claustrophobic, but hey, a lot less to keep clean and tidy. He stirred their supper on the hot plate and Herr Schnoodle watched with enthusiasm. No one had ever regarded Mac with such uncompromising adoration. It wasn't hard to take.

It was a while before he noticed something else. He was no longer invisible. Strangers spoke to him, women smiled, shopkeepers hovered between grins and glares—distrustful when Herr Schnoodle ventured close enough to lift his leg. Butchers saved bones and little kids stopped to pet the pooch.

McBee wasn't sure he liked this new status. An admitted loner, content with his own company, he didn't have to worry about someone he loved leaving him. Like his mother, then his father, then his grandfather. Who needed anyone when they were just going to check out on him anyway?

He especially hated it when people stopped and pointed, laughter in their voices. He forgot that a few weeks before he, too, had laughed at the schnoodle and called him ugly. Now he became indignant when anyone else did it.

Life was definitely changing for Alexander McBee.

3

McBee trudged up the narrow, twisting stairs, wondering when he was going to get a job. Was his father watching from someplace up there, laughing?

He had heard a kazillion times how he'd failed family tradition—the cop thing—before his pop went to join the "sky patrol," as he always called it. When his father died, it should have been a relief to stop hearing that same line, but it continued to echo through his brain.

He felt sure Pop would approve—if he could ever get a client. What was the good of becoming a bona fide PI with nothing to show but a dingy walk-up office?

The scratching coming from inside the door shattered his morose reverie. He wasn't alone anymore. Herr Schnoodle waited for him.

After their meal of overcooked TV dinners—you couldn't be too careful about organisms crawling over that frozen food—the two settled back for their usual quiet evening.

The dog lay peacefully on the couch, while McBee tilted back in his chair, crossing his feet on top of his desk as he had seen James Garner do a hundred times on television. He never tired of watching reruns of *The Rockford Files*, convinced that Garner's bumbling charisma would rub off on him sooner or later.

So far he'd perfected the bumbling part.

He frowned at the telephone and drummed the pencil against the scarred desktop.

The sharp squeak of his outer door stunned him for a

moment, and he leaped to his feet before whoever was out there could get away.

The lady facing him couldn't have weighed more than ninety pounds sopping wet. His grandfather would have described her as "no bigger than a cake of soap after Saturday night." Her lavender hair was shellacked into stiff obedience. The big guy behind her had to be either the chauffeur or a bodyguard. If she knew the neighborhood, probably both.

"Young man," she wheezed. "Get an elevator installed if you want to stay in business."

Mac nodded solemnly in response.

"I might as well admit it. I've been to other agencies. Either they wouldn't help me, or I didn't approve of them." She glared at the shabby room with obvious distaste, shooting a withering glance at him.

"Do you like cats?" she demanded.

He tried to figure out whether she wanted him to like cats or not. He smelled a fee involved here and determined not to mess this one up.

"Umm, yes. As a matter of fact, I love cats." Nothing ventured, nothing gained. He watched her wrinkles rearrange themselves into a satisfied smile.

Before Herr Schnoodle, he hadn't had feelings either way about cats or dogs. He probably didn't like them because of germs and fleas and all that fur. When he was growing up, none of his schoolmates ever had a pet, with the exception of an occasional lizard or snake kept in glass aquariums. Certainly no one had ever allowed him a pet, since he had this allergy to fur.

It was then the dog decided to investigate. Mac watched with apprehension as Herr Schnoodle checked out the chauffeur's trouser leg with painstaking care.

"What is *that?*" The squeak in the woman's voice told

19

Mac dogs were definitely not her favorite animals.

"He's . . . ah, he's my partner." Mac held up his palm in a gesture of conciliation, pedaling through his repertoire of excuses to come up with something plausible.

At her raised eyebrow he hurried on. "Oh yes, Herr Schnoodle is accredited, same as I am. We work as a team." Oh, dear Lord, he couldn't let his first client leave.

"Fine. Fine. I'll have to trust you. My Persian, Feathers, is missing. I think someone took him for ransom."

He glanced up at the man filling the doorway and a surprised a look of dignified humor crossing his face. It might have been a trick of lighting, lasting a moment. Mac turned his attention to the lady.

"Sit down, Madam. Tell me the details." Finding a missing cat was a far cry from riding in a red Ferrari with the breeze ruffling his hair and a blonde on the other seat— but it might buy a few more TV dinners.

Mac knew she would not grace his presence with an introduction. She motioned for her driver to hand over a card with her phone number on it.

For two days McBee turned up icky garbage cans galore, peering into strange receptacles with even stranger contents, but no cat. He and the dog searched alleys at night, but McBee could vouch for the old tale about all cats looking alike in the dark.

One night, on the way home from picking up his newspaper at the corner stand, Mac nearly bumped into Herr Schnoodle standing at attention like a bird dog. Mac wasn't sure how to respond until the dog drew him by the leash out toward the edge of the street.

"No, boy! You'd be fair game for every cab passing by," Mac cajoled, trying to reel him in, but the dog wasn't giving up his stance. McBee followed him to the manhole cover, which was slightly askew, as were most in the city. Grimacing with the thought of wasting money on his evening paper, he laid it on the street and knelt to listen. He heard a plaintive wail, unmistakably a cat.

Sighing, McBee tugged the cover aside and peered down. Luckily this was a side street with not much traffic, or both he and the dog would have been reduced to speed bumps on the pavement by now.

"Here, kitty, kitty," he called in the most ingratiating voice he could muster. "Here Feathers, honey bunny." Hell, how would the little purple-haired lady have talked to her cat? He was damned if he knew.

Suddenly a frizzy, smelly object leapt from the bowels of the dark hole and attached itself to his chest with tentacles which could only exist on a creature genetically altered.

Herr Schnoodle let go one of his ear-shattering barks which didn't help matters. Mac finally managed to grab the beast by all four legs and carry him back to the apartment.

He knew it had to be Feathers.

In the apartment, he cautiously let the cat free on the couch. The dog sat watching, tongue lolling out the side, not coming close, as if suspecting the cat might be from another world. Dirty, one ear torn from fighting and the biggest, most satisfied look on his round face, the cat amazingly began to purr.

For a moment Mac caught himself feeling a strange envy and it crossed his mind—probably the first and last freedom Feathers would have. He pushed the idea away hastily. He was not about to lose his fee again, no modern-day Don Quixote he, tilting at parking meters from a lofty perch on the midtown bus.

The cat had to go home so he could pay his rent.

* * * * *

That night to celebrate, they went to The Cave. The dog loved the place and snorted in ecstasy at what had to be weird smells from his position near the floor. He sniffed everyone's leg eventually, much to Mac's consternation, but Schnoodle seemed to accept the patrons without making a liquid comment.

Several weeks ago, the first time Mac had brought the schnoodle in, Harry the bartender hadn't known what to make of him so he prudently decided to ignore the dog. From past experience it probably didn't pay to make snap decisions in a bar such as The Cave.

Mac told Herr Schnoodle to sit by his feet but soon he wandered around, making himself at home. Most everyone petted him, some ignored him and the dog had the good sense to leave those alone. He refused to lie peacefully down on the floor, though. He whined and pawed until Mac helped him up on a stool. With a contented sigh, the dog stared happily at his image in the mirror while Mac sipped his beer.

When Mac spoke to a few of the regulars and turned back for a swig, half the beer had disappeared.

"Hey! What gives? Harry, you messing around?" It wasn't beyond any of them to play practical jokes, and they *did* have smirks on their faces.

"You kidding me? I got nothing better to do than fool around with your lousy beer?" Harry took a swipe at the bar with his rag that seemed an extension of his hand. "Keep your eye on the mutt, why don't you?"

McBee turned away, pretending interest in the bar stool at the other side of him. He slanted a look in the mirror to see all the patrons watching with interest. Jeez. What's going on here? He glanced at the schnoodle in time to catch him slurping daintily from the widemouthed goblet. As soon as he turned full toward him, the dog straightened up and gazed the other way in comical innocence.

"Boy, you're a piece of work. Here, turn around and face me, you rascal."

The dog swiveled his head around, shaggy ears flopping, whiskers betraying a suspicious foam. He swiped his tongue along his whiskers, licking his chops in satisfaction. His breath smelled like he belonged in The Cave.

After that, Herr Schnoodle always got his one glass of beer and all the pretzels he wanted. Many times some entranced customer wanted to buy him another round but Mac refused.

"Come on, you guys. How will it look to have to take the mutt to AA meetings someday? What will they call him, a hooch-pooch?" After that only newcomers tried anything.

Tonight, to celebrate their fee, McBee sat on his favorite stool, idly swishing his beer around the sides of his glass. As he watched, the golden liquid worked its way up from the finger-sized bottom of the glass with bubbles foaming to the surface at the widemouthed top.

He felt eyes on the back of his neck and knew it must be Smitty. Mentally, McBee always referred to the ferrety little man as Slinky. Someday he was going to say that name out loud. Without turning, Mac spoke.

"What's new?" He took a swig from his glass and motioned for Harry to set Slinky—ah, Smitty—up. The bartender slid down the beer and shot and the man slithered onto a stool.

"I might have something today," he whispered from the side of his narrow lips. Smitty sucked off the foam and then dropped the shot glass precisely in the middle of the stein. Boilermakers. Mac shuddered, wishing, not for the first

23

time, that he had never laid eyes on the guy.

He needed a snitch, all PIs seemed to have them. But how to find one? Nobody volunteered for the job. Maybe walk up to someone who frequented this bar and ask, "Wanna snitch for me?"

Not and live past Tuesday.

He didn't even remember how Smitty turned up. The idea of looking under a large rock was a thought. Mac hid a grin, knowing it would be hard to explain.

Neither spoke for a long moment. Mac's glance touched over the tables and booths in the semi-gloom, not lingering too long on anyone. Staring at patrons in this bar could mean very heavy overshoes and a very damp ending.

Even before his correspondence course was finished, Mac began searching in the city for a bar with the right ambiance. What a word for this dive. They didn't call it The Cave for nothing. A dark hole on a dark street on the dark side of town. It had been a jewel of a find; Mac was proud of himself for breaking out of his comfort zone.

To Mac's surprise, he found it quite cozy and the people not hard to take, once the new wore off and he learned the simple rules. Don't stare. Don't talk to anyone who doesn't want to be talked to. Above all, never open a conversation with an unencumbered female. She could be somebody's girlfriend. Somebody you don't want to mess with.

"What ya got?" It could be that Smitty went overboard a tad, looking mysterious and whispering all the time. That was the reason he wanted to call him Slinky instead of the more prosaic Smitty. Of course they were both new at doing this PI stuff.

For a second Mac wondered what his snitch's first name was. George or Cecil or Herman? Oh, Lord, he didn't want to know. Not ever.

Smitty leaned closer and let out a cloud of garlic and stale beer, topped off with sour wine. Mac tried not to shudder but wished for once that his sinuses had stayed in their usual semi-closed position.

"Bertoldi, he lost a bunch of expensive grocery carts lately." The thin, shadowy man took a swig and the shot glass danced a jig inside the big one. He belched out a deep sigh, and Mac quickly turned away before he got clobbered with the fallout.

"So?"

"Mr. B is offering a reward. A good one. He's mad as hell."

"How come I didn't hear about it?"

Smitty shook his head and a dank lock of hair drooped over his forehead. He tossed his head to clear it away and Mac moved back even farther. Who knew what might fly out of that? The thick coat of grease could hold anything captive but only temporarily.

"He don't want everybody knowing. 'Specially the cops. The schlemiel thinks they might be in on it."

Sure. Cops always make a fortune stealing grocery carts. Mac slid several bills toward him. "Thanks. I'll see what I can do."

Smitty licked his fingers and counted and repeated the process. Mac cringed.

For the next few days McBee checked the neighborhood but nothing turned up. He talked to Bertoldi and the grocer agreed to let him work on it, promising a generous reward.

It was a start. Even Magnum had to start somewhere.

Behind the store the excess carts piled up like abandoned wrecks. Why the big deal?

"Here's dozens of new carts. What does it matter if

25

someone steals a few of those?" McBee kicked at a three-wheeled wreck that tilted at a forty-degree angle like a wounded animal in its death throes. Parts of the basket were missing and many identical carts huddled in the corner all jumbled together. What a useless fence. It wouldn't have kept out a tank.

"I hate something stole from me!" Bertoldi sputtered behind his bristling mustache. Everything bristled—his eyebrows, his hair, his speech. "If punks tink they get away with someting like this, God knows what's next!" He crossed himself and sketched a blessing toward the forlorn-looking buggies.

"And keep that ugly animal away from my store."

Mac shrugged. "Suit yourself, but we work together." The shopkeeper reminded Mac of a cheap balloon and he waited for the explosion.

Why couldn't he get a simple, up-front case with normal clients?

4

Several days later, on one of their investigative walks looking for stray grocery carts, Herr Schnoodle insisted on going down a short street jutting off an alley.

"Hey, old boy, I don't like this alley business." Mac pulled on the leash, but the dog pulled harder.

Halfway down the block Mac bent over to flick the dust from his trouser cuff when the dog let loose one of his bloodcurdling barks right near his ear.

"Damn!" Raising up in a hurry, he bumped his head on something swinging above. In front of his blurred vision perched a narrow brownstone from the early 1900s, out of place in the refuse-strewn street. The city still contained hundreds of these old houses, many falling apart and abandoned.

This house sat alone as if in dignified resignation. The tiny yard contained brownish grass and two trees struggling for life alongside the steps. Metal flower boxes of every conceivable size and shape hung from the eaves, under the windows and from the gatepost.

Mac pushed impatiently at whatever had slammed into his head and saw the swaying chrome plant holder. He noticed that various parts of it resembled Mr. Bertoldi's grocery carts. Some kind of exotic orchid nested inside, fascinating him for a moment as he massaged his forehead.

"Beautiful, isn't it?" A voice like a scratchy old 78 record dropped down from the second-floor window.

Herr Schnoodle bounded up the steps and pushed open the door.

27

Mac stared up into the wrinkled, smiling face of a man old enough to have been chef at The Last Supper.

"Care to come in for a cup of tea? I will introduce the rest of my darlings."

Might as well, the dog was already walking around, captivated by the new smells.

Once inside Mac felt as if he had lost a half century. The room had that odd odor some old people get—musty sweet and cloying. He reached for his aerosol inhaler.

The parlor—the only possible name for it—was spotless but crowded. It could have been a museum. He ran his hand over the prickly horsehair covering on the overstuffed chair. The couch was the same and both wore crocheted doilies on their sides and backs.

Dozens of clocks lined the walls and covered the tables, all ticking and tocking at odd intervals, their sounds muffled by the furnishings and heavy Persian rug covering the floor.

"I recognize a fellow plant lover," the crickety voice came from the doorway.

An apparatus zoomed down toward Mac at an alarming rate. Motorized, judging from the speed of it, a seat attached to a rail on the staircase. The person sitting in it was in peril of launching into space when it stopped at the bottom.

But it didn't happen that way. The seat paused with a shushing sound and the little man calmly stepped off.

"I—I guess you might say I like flowers," McBee stammered. He hated flowers, considering them on the par with animal fur and dust balls under the bed, harborers of dirt and fungus.

"Allow me to introduce myself, young man. My name is Isaac Steinmetz."

Mac took the proffered hand gently, afraid of crushing the bird-like bones.

"My, what a lovely dog. Is he yours? Of course he is," the little man answered his own question.

Lovely? The man didn't look blind, but who else would call Herr Schnoodle lovely?

Mr. Steinmetz turned and led them through the house. Even with the heavy gray sweater the elderly man wore, his skin appeared blue from the dank cold that permeated every room, yet outside it was a mild autumn day.

The back porch was glassed in. It was the one place in the entire house that absorbed streams of lukewarm sun. Warehouses surrounded and dwarfed the brownstone.

Old Steinmetz began pointing out his orchids, first reciting their long complicated names and afterwards referring to them as Alfred, Wilbur, Mildred—each had a name.

"You live alone?" Mac interrupted once.

Halting his dissertation, the old man seemed sidetracked momentarily by the intrusion. "What? Alone? Oh, my no! Not with this family of mine." His gaze touched each plant with tenderness. "But, of course, in terms of human companionship, I—I suppose I am alone," he conceded. "Harriet, my beloved wife, went to that garden in the sky six years ago."

Mac was proud of the way the schnoodle stepped carefully through the crowded rooms, not touching anything.

"Aren't you cold?"

"Truthfully? Yes, but I'm more afraid my darlings will catch a chill. Social Security doesn't go as far as it used to. I have to cut down somewhere."

It seemed he must have already cut down on food, he appeared so delicate that a good wind would blow him away. Lucky he didn't raise Venus flytraps.

"Can I make a glass of tea for you? I poured some for myself and it's still quite warm."

Mac sat in the parlor and waited at his host's insistence. The old man wobbled back with a tray of crackers and tall glasses of steaming tea. Herr Schnoodle licked his chops but stayed at Mac's feet until he was offered a plate.

After a few minutes, Mr. Steinmetz reached over and tapped Mac's hand. It felt like a dry leaf brushing against his skin.

"You did not come here to look at my flowers, true? At first I thought perhaps you'd heard of them, but that isn't correct, is it?"

"No, I didn't come here for that." The sofa, low and uncomfortable, caused McBee's long legs to angle up like a praying mantis.

"Ah, well, life has its disappointments. We find the strength to overcome them." The gentle voice seemed filled with irony.

"I'll get right to the point, sir. You stole . . . ah, carried away some of Bertoldi's grocery carts, didn't you?" To look at the man sitting in front of him, he almost doubted it. With what hidden reserve of strength had he managed?

"Of course, of course, my dear boy. They were poor bedraggled things, of no earthly use to anyone. I saw a way to make them beautiful—and please my flowers." He sipped his tea, looking quite smug.

"But you can't do that, sir. The police—Bertoldi—it's against the law." In the face of Steinmetz's calm assurance Mac wasn't sure how to continue.

The old man looked unrepentant. "Then do what you must, Mr. McBee."

Mac was stopped cold. Everything should have been plain and simple. Why did things get so damned complicated?

He tried to think of how Barnaby Jones would handle this but his mind felt cluttered like the room he sat in. Maybe it was catching.

He still couldn't figure out how Mr. Steinmetz did it. Bringing the buggies here, turning them into hanging planters. He could never have managed it if they had been the newer, heavier ones made of chrome.

"I'm curious, sir. How did you do it? Move the carts, I mean."

Mr. Steinmetz shook his head. "I didn't do it all alone, but I don't want to get my friends in trouble. I brought them here myself, they weren't even locked up. I thought Bertoldi no longer wanted them and would be happy to have them taken away."

"But these hangers look welded together."

"There is an alternative school two streets over. I've met a few young men who attend a welding class. They helped me fashion the baskets. It is good practice for them."

A community project, probably involving the Crips and Bloods, for gosh sakes.

McBee struggled to stand, afraid the overstuffed chair had claimed his body forever. "Sir, if you'll excuse me, I have to think on this before I do anything." He took the scrawny hand. "Thanks for the tea, I'll keep in touch."

Mr. Steinmetz wilted. The wavering smile drew across his pale face in a slash of shiny false teeth. His eyes glazed. "I'm not worried for myself. It's my family."

The schnoodle pushed his head under the old man's hand, staring up at Mac with reproachful eyes.

Mac turned to look at the cluttered room, the plants poking out of every recess and tried not to imagine what would happen to the man's home if he were gone even a few days. What if authorities declared him unfit to take care of himself? Mac shook his head. The old guy wouldn't last two days without his "family" and his house full of memories.

Yet it wasn't his concern, was it? He had a job to do. Who needed complications? He liked things neat and tidy.

The cold wind blew up his trouser legs when he let himself out the front door. He ducked his head instinctively and looked up at the offending basket. A real work of art, he had to admit.

It took several days to think it over and to approach Bertoldi.

"You find my carts?" The grocer rubbed his thick fingers together in anticipation.

Herr Schnoodle sat waiting for his piece of sausage. Once Bertoldi thought to trick him, and instead of sweet sausage gave him hot, but the dog gulped it down, licked his whiskers and belched to show his appreciation.

Now Bertoldi's round belly jiggled under the large, soiled apron and his mustache parted with an anticipatory smile.

Oh boy. This wasn't going to be any piece of cake. Mac reluctantly told Bertoldi about Steinmetz. He had to, the PI code of honor and all that. Something like the oath doctors swore to, or lawyers.

He also decided he sure as hell wasn't going to let anyone touch the old gent.

After Bertoldi blew up, ranting and raving for a good quarter of an hour, he eventually simmered down. Sweat beaded his olive complexion and his eyes bulged. Mac didn't want to be responsible for causing his heart attack. Jeez, he wasn't doing too good so far.

On one hand, Mr. Steinmetz was threatened with jail since he couldn't pay any fines even if he wanted to. On the other hand, Bertoldi might have a stroke. Things could have turned out better, Mac conceded.

"Mr. Bertoldi, if you'll listen for a minute," Mac interrupted the next volcanic eruption. It took a while, but he finally persuaded the irate grocer to come and talk to Mr. Steinmetz.

The brownstone house wasn't far from the store, and Herr Schnoodle led the parade with dignified importance.

After the two men met, Mac tiptoed out of the parlor and closed the front door gently behind him, leaving them deep in conversation—about flowers.

Several days later Bertoldi told him, "I don't think I pay. You don't bring back my carts."

That seemed reasonable. Hard-nosed but reasonable. Mr. B wasn't known in the neighborhood for his good works and friendly disposition.

"Yeah, but I found them, didn't I? What happens to Mr. Steinmetz?"

The grocer was embarrassed. "We make a trade. He gives me baskets and beautiful flowers. I don't make trouble. He can have all the old carts." He clamped a hand the size of a ham on the back of Mac's shoulder. "You pretty good detective. Just kidding, I'll pay you. In salami and cheese. I give all you can eat for—let's see . . ." He squinted his black eyes, pulling eyebrows the size of large caterpillars down so they almost closed as he sized up McBee's slender form. "Maybe two, tree months—how's that?"

Well, it wouldn't pay the rent, but at least he and Herr Schnoodle would eat a few less TV dinners.

Maybe his luck was changing, maybe the dog was good for him. He wasn't forgetting it was the dog who nudged him down that street in the first place.

Still, Mac needed a well-paying *dangerous* caper. How else could he deserve that certificate on his wall?

5

One overcast afternoon McBee and the schnoodle lunched in the park.

Mac unwrapped his tuna sandwich, carefully keeping the wax paper around it. He could almost see germs floating in the air all over him. Some might call them dust motes but he knew better. He handed the dog a bone from a baggie he always carried with him.

"Some detective, pal. If I packed a piece, the holster would probably be filled with doggie bones." He never carried a weapon, but it made him feel important to talk about it. He could have if he'd wanted to.

They sat side-by-side on the park bench, watching the pigeons. If Mac had any fears the dog would give chase, he should have known that was beneath Herr Schnoodle's dignity.

"You feed those things to your dog? They're full of preservatives and dyes—the same junk we have to eat. A helpless, trusting animal deserves better."

Mac jerked his head around to stare at the next bench, trying to look through the person. He turned away, hoping to discourage conversation. It was the oldest tactic in the city and practiced by ninety-nine percent of the population. Never make eye contact. Herr Schnoodle gazed in that direction as if knowing the apparition would speak to them.

"Name's Apple Sally. That's so they don't confuse me with the other Sally, I guess." She got to her feet and pushed a squeaking shopping cart to his bench.

He flushed, embarrassed. Was anyone laughing at his predicament? No one even glanced in their direction. "Confuse you with what other Sally?" He knew he would be eternally sorry for rising to the bait and didn't know what made him do it.

The woman's small hands were covered with worn gloves with the fingers cut off. "The Salvation Army, dummy. Everyone calls it the Sally. At first when I didn't rem—didn't want to tell anyone my name—they all started calling me Sally 'cause that's where I hung out. Then it got confusing, and since I sell apples sometimes, they stuck on the apple part." Her words flew out in a rush, as if she were afraid he would depart before she got them said.

How had he managed to survive all these years without this wonderful information? He fixed his best icy stare on her short, freckled nose. That should have put her back in her cage.

She ignored his glare, reaching down to pet the dog.

"You're a bag lady, aren't you?" He'd lived in the city all his life, but never on this side of town until he opened the office. He had never spoken to any of the inhabitants. It wasn't that he thought himself better than them. It was the germs they all harbored. It gave him the willies thinking about the little beasts they carried around wrapped in their blankets and various layers of clothing.

He had noticed her around the streets, now that he thought of it. Sometimes she talked to herself, sometimes to the pigeons. "I've seen you in the park before," he said, when she didn't answer his question.

"I'll excuse your rude question as mere ignorance." She glared back at him behind rhinestone sunglasses that tilted sideways because of a missing earpiece on one side.

It gave her a strange, lopsided quality that made him feel

35

dizzy, putting him at a definite disadvantage when he had to tilt his own head to match hers.

"Oh, forgive me your queenship—I didn't mean to pry."

She took off the sunglasses and ran her fingers through bushy red hair.

He decided she resembled a mean Orphan Annie.

She pulled an old Stetson out of the cart and clamped it down on top of the coppery mass, as if wanting to hide. She couldn't have been a tall person. Sitting down on the park bench, her shoes didn't touch the pavement. She swung her legs back and forth as a child would have.

"Never mind," she said with lofty forgiveness, as if he truly had apologized. "I mean it about your pup, though. He's a beauty. You should take good care of him."

Mac's gaze searched her face for the sarcasm. No one but Mr. Steinmetz had ever called Herr Schnoodle a beauty. Not without falling over backward with laughter. She was serious.

"Well—what can I do about it? The doggie biscuits, I mean. He has a delicate appetite, eats picky." It was his one nagging worry about the mutt. Swallowing so much polluted water must have done something to his innards.

She reached down into one of several paper bags in the shopping cart and brought out a notepad and stubby pencil.

He watched as she bent to write and tried to guess her age, which could be thirty or fifty. It shocked him to think of her as younger than he. What had she done with her life and why? In spite of the weird getup and general air of scruffiness, she didn't look dirty. But she must have been wearing every item of clothing she owned.

She glanced up in time to catch him staring.

"You act like I'm a bug or something. Didn't you learn any manners?" Her tone was unruffled, conversational.

He refused to look away like a guilty schoolboy even though her green-eyed gaze made him uneasy.

Cat's eyes.

He gingerly accepted the piece of paper she thrust at him. A recipe for homemade doggie bones. "What do you think, old boy? I've never baked anything but TV dinners."

"Ninny. Anyone can throw this together. Go to that health food store over on Fifth and pick up some brewer's yeast and desiccated liver. They have most of the other ingredients, too. You'll see—he'll love it. What's his name?"

He liked the sound of her laugh when he told her.

At the office later, he made the biscuits in his little toaster oven, and the dog did love them. Mac tasted one and decided they were damn good. For the next few days he searched the park to tell Apple Sally but didn't see her again. Each time he sat on a bench he expected to hear the squeak of her shopping cart wheels.

The city streets had swallowed her.

He had other things on his mind besides Apple Sally. Business was so bad he would have welcomed a herd of missing Persian cats or even another case for Mr. Bertoldi. He was that desperate.

One evening an old friend of his father's visited him. Joe edged near to retirement on the force, and he looked worried.

Mac warmed up the coffee and absentmindedly offered him a plate of doggie biscuits. Herr Schnoodle let out one of his barks, a sharp protest that could have shattered crystal. Mac's plastic tumblers remained unfazed.

Silly hound, didn't want to share his goodies. Mac slid his hand over to retrieve the plate. Too late.

Joe chomped down on one and pulled the plate closer to his round stomach for safekeeping. "Say, these are good. Where'd you buy 'em?"

"Ah—wouldn't you rather have some cake?" He remembered a half of a Twinkie left in the refrigerator. That and a cup of coffee had been his usual breakfast before the schnoodle. Joe wouldn't mind that the cake tasted stale.

Mac eyed the schnoodle who lifted his leg at the side of Joe's trousers. Mac pushed the dog with his toe, hoping Joe wouldn't look down.

"I'll get right to the point, Mac."

It felt good having Joe call him Mac. Back in the old days he had been "Little Mac" to Joe and everyone in the precinct.

Mac had the feeling Joe wouldn't know the point if he sat on it. The old joke went on down at the station that Joe was so long-winded, by the time he read a perpetrator his rights, the perp was out on bail. Mac hid his smile behind his hand and tried to look serious, as the occasion seemed to demand.

"Ya see, my neighbor's missing. Carl Pensky. Been missing for weeks, know what I mean? We got an investigation going on in the department, those white-shirt-and-tie yahoos straight out of police academy. They're keeping it on the QT, might be a kidnapping. Thing is, the Penskys don't have any money, or they wouldn't be in our neighborhood in the first place. Know what I mean?"

Mac wondered when the conversation would get around to him. Not more than three biscuits later he found out.

"Being a PI—no strings to the department, you know—I thought you could check it out—as a favor to me. They found an abandoned car yesterday, Carl's fingerprints all over it—and his empty wallet. Go figure."

Mac reached to slap Joe on the back in affection, like Joe always did him. He couldn't bring himself to do it, not being a hugger and a toucher like some people were.

"Thanks for the vote of confidence, but if the department can't find a clue . . ."

"That's my point! They stumble around stepping on each other's toes, and meanwhile Carl's little woman is a basket case. She breaks down anytime anyone talks to her about it. If there's a ransom note, could be she ain't saying. Maybe she'd tell you, not being a cop and all. Know what I mean?"

"Aw, Joe—that's crazy thinking."

"Did I mention there's a damn good reward? The insurance company wants to find out if he's for sure dead and gone before they pay off the missus."

Mac brightened. "Well, maybe it's like you say. A new insight on the case wouldn't hurt. I can poke around."

During the next few days McBee scratched and poked without coming up with anything. The guys from the station put up with him good-naturedly, in respect for his father, he supposed.

On the third day he took Herr Schnoodle with him for company. Joe and two uniformed cops met him, pointing out the vehicle in question.

Mrs. Pensky drove up to have another look at the vehicle in the police compound. She shouted angry threats at the cops. Why weren't they doing something to find her Carl instead of standing around gabbing?

Schnoodle ran up to her, sniffing her legs. She gave a terrified shriek, which blended perfectly with the dog's high-pitched bark, setting everyone's teeth on edge.

That godawful bark was the dog's only shortcoming that Mac could see. If you didn't count peeing on people he didn't like.

Mac retrieved the trailing leash. "Want us to get thrown out of here?" He relaxed his hold, and the dog leaped into the backseat of the car. He sniffed all around until Mac became alarmed. Did he plan to flood the backseat with his sign of displeasure?

While everyone watched Mrs. Pensky as she continued to wail on about her husband and how no one did anything to bring him back, Mac climbed in the car to see what the dog pawed with such industry.

He used his tweezers, always in his pocket, to pick up the metallic gold barrette. Mrs. Pensky walked closer, peering into the car. When she spied Mac holding the barrette her eyes widened in alarm and her hand crept to the side of her hair in an unconscious gesture of exploration.

Herr Schnoodle nudged Mac's elbow with his nose.

Finally Mac understood. Schnoodle picked up her scent the minute she walked on the scene and matched it to the one in the car.

"We think you know about your husband's disappearance, Ma'am," Mac said in a flat voice straight out of *Dragnet*, one of his favorite oldies. "This is your hair gizmo isn't it? We can check if you have one to match at home. You said you'd never seen the car before." He tried for a blend of steely resolve in his voice. "Maybe you'd like to tell us about it."

Mrs. Pensky began to sob, but the cops just stared at her, unmoved by her display.

"I'm thinking Mrs. Pensky is counting on a big insurance check in her future. I'd imagine there might be someone to share it with her." He looked at Joe and felt warmed by the surprise and admiration he saw mirrored there.

"Fine, Mac. We'll check into her alibi a little deeper, ya

know? We can dig up her accomplice." Joe nodded to his men to read her rights and take her away.

After that it didn't take them long to break down her defenses. She and her lover had killed Pensky for his insurance.

That night Mac baked the schnoodle a huge supply of biscuits.

It looked as if he had a real partner now.

6

The very next day McBee spied Apple Sally sitting on a bench, legs curled up under her long skirt, feeding the pigeons.

"Hi! I've been looking all over for you." He was still jubilant over his first officially solved case. Herr Schnoodle caught his mood and danced around like a puppy.

The bag lady regarded Mac suspiciously for a long moment before answering. Apparently satisfied by what she read in his open face, she patted the bench beside her for them to sit down.

"What's with you two? You look pretty sparky today."

He put a hand lightly on her knee in his joy and she jerked away. Her coppery eyebrows rammed together in a frown, her generous mouth thinned in anger.

"Don't touch me—ever!" She clutched her worn carryall close to her chest, scooting to the end of the bench.

He held up his palms toward her in a placating gesture. "Hey—I didn't mean anything. I got a little carried away." He felt irritated to think she would suspect him of making a pass at her. What a crazy idea! He didn't even care to picture what sort of body hid beneath her layers of clothing. For a second he felt a sharp retort linger on his tongue, but her look of quiet dignity stopped him.

Maybe she had to protect herself any way she could.

"We just solved a big case and I—we want to celebrate. Never got to thank you for the biscuit recipe. Wanna join us?"

He felt relief along with irritation. What a jerk. He still

had a few good telephone numbers in his book. He could celebrate with a real woman. This ragamuffin wasn't even properly grateful for his ill-considered invitation.

"Where?" She scratched Herr Schnoodle behind the ears and the dog responded with a silly grin.

It irked Mac to know the rascal had taken to Apple Sally so quickly when he usually ignored everyone else. Of course, the annoyance Mac felt wasn't anything so childish as jealousy.

"You don't have to join us. No big deal."

"I asked where, didn't I?"

He could take her up to the office but changed his mind. Not that anyone would have noticed a bag lady in his neighborhood, but he couldn't drag home every street person he saw, could he? What if she came back uninvited?

McBee closed his eyes a moment, thinking about his previous apartment and his ex-landlady. He imagined Apple Sally squeaking along with her shopping cart, pushing it up the stairs—she'd never leave it on the landing—too valuable. Bumpity, bumpity, bump up the stairs and past the old witch's door. He grinned, his good humor suddenly returning.

"Why don't we have a picnic? You wait right here. I'll go get the stuff. We gotta celebrate our first job, eh boy?" He ruffled the dog's ears and received a sloppy kiss in return.

"We . . . ll, maybe. It's a bit chilly."

"Oh, excuse me, Your queenship. I forgot, you may have a dinner engagement elsewhere," he said. "Or it may be you are ashamed to be seen with us." She was covered up enough to withstand zero degrees, she couldn't be chilly.

She shot him a look that could have knocked off the flies on the mirror at Jake's Diner. "Smart-ass. I don't want anyone getting the wrong idea about me. I prefer to be left alone. I don't need friends or family or . . ." She broke off in confusion, as if saying more than she meant to.

He pretended not to hear the thread of vulnerability that laced through her words. "Hey, look. I feel the same way. I've been a loner all my life, and I prefer it that way, too. So don't worry, I'm not hitting on you, if that's what you're afraid of."

Damn it, this woman always put him on the defensive. Why did he let her get away with it? He stood up. "Ah, well. An idea—nothing important. I must plan to do something spontaneous again some day."

The sarcasm was lost on her. She grinned up at him, her teeth small and white. He had expected stumps and snaggles.

"Okay already. I'm not ashamed to be with two good-looking dudes such as yourselves. Let's celebrate. Me and the schnoodle will wait right here for you."

Mac opened his mouth to protest and swallowed hard. He never left the dog with anyone. What if she ran off with him?

Her expression was unprotected, open. It said, "Trust me, please."

Hell, it wouldn't hurt to trust someone—at least this once—he supposed. It shouldn't be hard to track them down if she ran away with the schnoodle.

When Mac returned with an armload of groceries he saw the two of them romping on a blanket she had spread on the ground. He wondered what held the ragged thing together. He set the bags of food carefully off the material, expecting to see armies of fleas or bedbugs or worse. Oh, what the hey—it was a celebration, wasn't it? He held his breath and sat down.

"Would I be intruding to ask where you live?" he spoke around a mouthful of hero sandwich. He gave the dog a slice of salami.

She nodded her approval. "Salami's good for worms if he has any. No worm alive could live with all that garlic."

They laughed. Somehow the unpleasant subject of worms wasn't off-putting, coming from her.

"I know this swell old man, see. He's the one said I could use this grocery cart and sells me apples wholesale." She fished around in the seemingly bottomless bag always strapped to her shoulder and hauled out a wrinkled piece of paper. "He even gave me this to show the cops. It says he is loaning the cart to me for as long as I want to use it."

She ate with obvious enjoyment, the soiled, fingerless gloves lay in her lap. Her hands were surprisingly dainty and pale, nails short and unbroken.

"And?" he prompted.

"Oh, where was I? Yeah, Mr. Olson, he lets me buy fruit kinda like wholesale. Real primo stuff—apples, peaches, nectarines—two-dollars-a-piece stuff. I sell them at the train station sometimes. It's a lot better for people to eat than junk they get out of those candy machines."

"Stop the music!" he interrupted. "You talking Olson as in 'The Swede'?"

She nodded. "Guess some do call him that."

He regarded her in a different light. The Swede had been right-hand muscle for the mob in his younger days. He was one of the few who left "the family" and lived. While he worked for the mob, he'd been the terror of the streets for welchers and people who didn't pay protection on time. He'd retired, but still held a lot of community respect.

"How long have you—ah, been on the streets?"

She laid down her half-eaten sandwich and folded her

hands in her lap, staring at him with a baleful glare. The sudden animosity shocked him.

"I don't ask personal questions, and I don't want some damn busybody prying into my life. You writing a book or something? A lousy sandwich don't buy you anything, buddy."

"Oh, jeez, will you get off it? I'm trying to pass some time with small talk. I don't give a damn."

"Hah!" Her voice sounded smugly satisfied. "I thought as much. You want to pick me over like a basket of used rags."

You ought to know, he wanted to come back with. He watched the pigeons and didn't speak.

She finally broke the silence.

"Hey, I'm sorry if I came on strong, but I keep to myself. It's called survival."

That was probably as close to an apology as he would ever get.

He looked at her with grudging respect. There was something more to this person than showed on the surface. A sorrow deep in her eyes, a look of undefined remorse in her expression when she wasn't on guard. What circumstances had turned her into a bag lady?

He didn't bother to wonder why he felt intrigued or any concern. Probably the first time in his life he had ever felt curious about anyone, and he wasn't curious about that, either.

"I assume you don't read the newspapers," he said, remembering what it was so important to tell her. "Two bag ladies have been killed lately, their bodies dumped in the East River. You want to be careful."

She paused momentarily in her petting of the dog. "Yeah, talk has been circulating the mission. I heard the

46

women whispering something about it last night. But one of the dead was a man, wasn't it?"

"Right. Dressed as a woman." McBee was going to contact Joe to see if they'd come up with any motives. He didn't need to worry about Apple Sally, she could take care of herself, couldn't she?

"I can take care of myself," she echoed his thoughts. "I stay on the lighted streets, don't hang around alleys, keep my nose clean and mind my own business." Not like some people, her expression spoke volumes.

Mac shrugged. He'd warned her. What else could he do? Maybe the killings were just a fluke, and let's face it, the police and public were not interested in a couple of dead street people.

They finished the lunch in companionable silence. Mac watched as she patted the dog, waved at him and pushed her cart down the street to be enveloped within the mass of humanity on the sidewalk.

A wave of worry swept over him. "Damn, Schnoodle, I can worry about not having anything to worry about. Pops used to say that about me."

He closed his eyes and let the sunshine filter down through the trees, warming his skin.

7

Jobs trickled in with a moderate degree of regularity. Joe sent most of them from his position on the force. None of the detectives wanted to admit using an outside gumshoe, as the older cops insisted on calling him. With Herr Schnoodle's help Mac solved several more cases.

Between jobs, late one night, McBee heard a knock on the door. The knock sounded so tentative he didn't hear it at first, but the dog growled low in his throat. Opening the door carefully, he left on the double chain until he checked out the intruder. Few strangers ventured into the neighborhood after dark.

"You McBee, the private eye?"

"Maybe." Couldn't the fellow read the lettering on the door?

"Got a little job for you. Can I come inside?"

"I suppose so. But careful of the watchdog, he's highly trained to attack on my slightest command."

The stranger stared at Herr Schnoodle with pointed skepticism as the vicious animal in question sprawled with his chin resting on his paws, eyes closed and snoring gently.

Mac wanted to kick him.

"I need this package delivered to a friend. He's leaving on the 4 a.m. flight to New Hampshire. That's why I come now—so's you'd have time to locate him."

"Why aren't you delivering it?"

The man shrugged his shoulders, like a snake shedding its skin. "Got no time. Besides, I owe him a favor and he

48

wouldn't accept it from me. Too proud." He patted the package lightly. "My dear mother baked this fruitcake especially for him. He loves 'em."

As soon as the man counted out some bills and disappeared, Herr Schnoodle raised his head and wrinkled his nose in concentration.

"Aw come on, you old phony. You're getting to be an awful snob. He didn't smell that bad. 'Course his aftershave wasn't anything to brag about but . . ."

Mac watched in amazement as the dog galloped around the room, barking and growling as if he had suddenly gone mad. He jumped on a chair and put his paws on the package, snapping at it but not touching it with his teeth. Mac had never seen him in such a state.

"Hey, buddy. That's a fruitcake. I'll buy you one if you want."

Herr Schnoodle pawed at the package and whined, his liquid eyes pleaded, struggling to convey a message.

"Shh! Be quiet a minute, will you?" Mac picked up the package and held it to his ear. The dog nearly went crazy.

It didn't take long for Mac to dial 911, and the bomb squad answered his call in minutes. They discovered the package held enough explosives to blow up half the block.

No wonder the creep paid him extra to make sure he delivered it on time.

Mac never did find out if they caught the guy, but he figured the cops could trace him from the fellow who was to have been the recipient of the deadly "fruitcake."

A few weeks later the airline sent him a little medal in the shape of an airplane. Attached to the medal was a small certificate stating "Private Investigator Alexander McBee has saved many lives by acting on his astute judgment and following up with swift action, unmindful of the danger to his own person."

Mac took Herr Schnoodle out for hamburgers that night.

One morning a few weeks later, Joe pushed Mac's door open and wandered in. Herr Schnoodle remembered him and his tail wagged slightly, but he growled low in his throat, probably also remembering his missing biscuits.

"Morning. Gotta extra cuppa?"

"Sure, you bet." Mac made certain the biscuits were hidden away this time. As soon as the schnoodle saw his biscuits were safe, the dog let Joe pet him.

They talked of this and that. Finally, Joe sighed deep somewhere down inside his gut, and Mac figured whatever the cop came for would soon emerge.

"You heard of The Gold Tiara—down on Fifth Ave?"

"You bet. Who hadn't?" It rated just under Tiffany in consumer extravagance.

"Someone robbed them the day before yesterday. Fellow took a diamond necklace. Thing's worth at least a hundred thou."

Mac waited.

The policeman scratched his thinning hair and then hastily arranged the wisps back over the bald spot.

"Remember the Count?"

How could McBee forget? Pop had talked hours with grudging respect and admiration about the dapper thief. But that had been so long ago, when both the thief and his father had been new at their work.

"Your father and me, we bumped heads with him a couple of times. Too many, in fact, know what I mean? He made fools of all of us at one time or another."

"Shouldn't he be about a hundred years old now?"

Joe nodded. "I figured he had to be either dead or up the

50

river by now. Know what I mean?"

"What's your point?" McBee knew it wouldn't do any good to ask, but he did anyway.

Joe took a long slurp of coffee and munched on one of the stale donuts from yesterday's breakfast before he spoke.

"We collared him outside the store, but he ain't telling where he stashed the necklace. I know he's got it. In the old days we had ways of making suspects talk, but now it's ACLU and Miranda, a damn shame."

"How'd it happen?" He knew his father's friend wouldn't know how to condense a story if his pants were on fire.

"Well, you heard your pop talk about how the Count dresses. This spiffy-looking dude walks in and meanders all around the jewelry store, looking at the best stuff. Hell, the clerk figures he had a live one, know what I mean? Seems the Count had been dropping in for days, getting friendly with this one clerk until he could call him by name. That's his MO."

Mac took another swallow of coffee and waited.

"Anyhoo, while the Count checked out this diamond jobby, an accomplice distracted the clerk with a phone call. When he turned around—guess what?"

"Our friend pocketed the necklace. What's the big deal? They caught him, didn't they? Just out of the store, you said."

"Patience, patience." Joe sucked on his teeth a minute as if needing to warm up to his story.

"He waited by the revolving door. He *waited* for us, for Chrissake." Even now the idea infuriated Joe.

"Didn't he have the loot on him?" Loot. Now he was beginning to talk like the old-timers. It rubbed off after a while.

Joe shook his head. "Nope. Not a trace. I mean we searched him with everything but a Geiger counter. Nothing. Slick as a pickpocket in church."

Mac digested the puzzle. Herr Schnoodle sprawled between Joe and his dog biscuit jar, never taking his gaze from the visitor, plainly saying he didn't trust him.

"What are you? Part elephant? You don't forget a damn thing, do you?"

"What?" Joe looked startled at the sudden exchange between McBee and the dog.

Mac felt embarrassed. He had become so used to talking to the mutt as if he were another human. Now he did it in front of people. He hoped Joe wouldn't spread it around the precinct.

"I don't get it, amigo. I sure don't," Mac said. "Looks like you got a terrific puzzle on your hands, but it's all insured, anyway. Glad you could drop around." He got up and took the cups to the tiny sink in the alcove called a kitchen.

"Not so fast! That ain't what I came here for, to gossip. I need your help. The mayor's office is pressuring the chief and he's down on us. A councilman's brother owns a share in the jewelry store. The necklace was on loan, it wasn't theirs. They were commissioned to make a ten-thousand-dollar copy of it so some high-society dame could wear it to her lah-de-dah functions.

"Besides, the chief says it's not covered by insurance since we caught the perpetrator and didn't reclaim the evidence."

"Well, then, for once you haven't finished your story. Why can't the cops wrap it up themselves? There couldn't be so many places to search, and besides, maybe the Count handed it off to an accomplice, the one who made the phone call for him."

"Good thinking, but no way. The clerks and manager were right there, before he even got out of the door, practically. The store doesn't want any uniforms around, not even plainclothes. Claims it'll hurt their reputation."

"You want I should help?"

Joe nodded happily. "Yep. Big reward, too, did I forget to mention that?"

Mac grinned. "I'll do it. The kind of case Pop always loved to solve."

The next day McBee and the schnoodle pushed through the polished brass door.

"A moment, sir. No animals permitted in here." The clerk strode toward them, glaring down her nose as if they might have something catching.

She was full of it. He had seen tiny poodles carried in by their owners. Loyalty aside, even he had to admit they were of a different species than the schnoodle.

"Bring out your superior. We're here on official business." It made him feel good to say that. He had seen everyone from Danno on *Hawaii Five-O* to Remington Steele utter those words. It made him part of an exclusive club.

The manager walked up and agreed they could look around. The clerks pointedly ignored the pair as they snooped. According to Joe's notes, the cops hadn't missed any clues that he could see. He showed the Count's dashing fedora to the dog, who sniffed it with some enthusiasm and then darted through the revolving door when a customer walked in.

As soon as the bushy rear disappeared, panic grabbed hold of Mac.

Was the dog going home? He would be struck by the first taxi that plummeted down the street. Mac rushed out so fast he turned the elderly lady in the other half of the door around twice before she stopped.

He skidded to a halt in front of the store where Herr Schnoodle patiently waited for him.

"What's the matter, boy? Don't you want to eat? We need this job to pay our rent."

The dog licked his hand as Mac bent to pull on his collar, but didn't budge from his stance. Mac straightened up and leaned against the drain spout. What perturbed the scamp? He usually loved to go on cases, getting as excited as a kid.

Mac rapped his fingers on the metal in exasperation. Herr Schnoodle barked and pranced around on his hind legs.

Tapping the pipe again, he watched as the dog went through his act once more. He gave the drainpipe a closer examination. It seemed to be the usual old-fashioned type made of galvanized metal, painted the same color as the ancient brick building. The historical society designated the two-story structure a landmark, the little sign on the side made that clear.

He followed the drainpipe as it flattened out across the sidewalk and ended abruptly at the curb. The schnoodle walked alongside but hurried back to the building as soon as they reached the curb.

Taking out his penknife, Mac dug around the pipe about eye level. Nothing. He remembered the Count was at least a head shorter, and he bent down to dig more persistently into the fragile metal.

He struck a soft area and pulled at it with the point of his knife, peeling off a piece of painted tape which revealed a hole the size of a half dollar. Very interesting.

He went inside to call Joe. He should be in on this, after all.

As soon as his father's old friend showed up, Mac asked him to go up on the roof with a pail of water.

"You kidding me? We'll get tossed out on our keisters."

"Not if they get the necklace back," Mac reminded him. Everyone from the shop trailed out to watch. The manager locked the door behind them, not trusting anyone.

"Okay, I'm up here now. What do I do?"

Joe stood leaning over the sidewalk, high on the flat roof. Herr Schnoodle growled low in his throat if anyone ventured close to the pipe. A crowd of onlookers had gathered around.

"Go to the curb, boy. Stay." He pointed to the street. The dog obeyed, standing guard with every hair bristling to let his audience know he meant business.

What a ham.

"Okay, I'm ready. Now pour," Mac shouted up at him. "Try not to slop it all over us."

Joe poured. After a minute Schnoodle gave one of his crazy barks and grabbed at something in the gutter. He came up holding a long necklace of sparkling diamonds clenched firmly between his teeth, a low, menacing growl coming from his throat.

Mac doubted anyone in the street would try to challenge the dog for the jewels.

"Good boy, good boy." He patted the dog and took the necklace.

Later that night he, Joe and Herr Schnoodle celebrated with steaks. They went to Anthony's, the one decent place in town allowing the dog to come with them. The food was good and plentiful, and Tony didn't seem concerned with the board of health. Probably owned half of them, Mac reflected cynically.

"But how did you *know?*" Joe persisted.

Mac shrugged and cut another piece of meat for his partner resting under the table. He couldn't tell anyone the truth. If word got out, the pooch would be fair game for every con artist in the city. How could he admit to everyone that the schnoodle solved most of his cases? How would that look? Did it matter to the dog whether he became famous or not?

Besides, it was a matter of pride. What PI wanted to admit his partner was the brains?

"I'm my father's son," Mac finally answered, knowing it was true at last.

8

McBee spotted Apple Sally in front of the St. Vincent de Paul's soup kitchen several days later.

Herr Schnoodle shivered with glee, wiggling his back so much he nearly knocked two winos off their unsteady legs.

Apple Sally bent to pet him.

"Where's your cart?" McBee asked. She'd take that like a snide remark, but he hadn't meant it to be.

She shot him a strange look. "I leave it with Mr. Olson at night. Lots of people would like to get it away from me, and I got to sleep sometime."

Each time they spoke, sparks of some kind went off. He had decided from the beginning she was a contrary person and nothing had changed his opinion since then.

"Ah—I—we are kind of at loose ends. Want to grab a sandwich with us?" These impulsive urges of his had to stop. Spontaneity was not on his list of habits.

She bristled visibly. "What do you think I'm standing in line for, to get a tan?"

"I asked a simple question. Do you or don't you?" He hated all the people in the line staring at them in undisguised interest. Didn't they have a life of their own?

She stepped out of line with obvious regret. "We were having chicken and dumplings today. Okay, I guess you can buy me lunch—no strings attached, though."

He almost laughed. He might have if he hadn't remembered the karate lessons she told him about. He wouldn't put it past her to toss him right here on the pavement in front of her friends. Hell, the only strings attached were the ones dangling from her jacket lining.

His forehead wrinkled in an effort to think where to take her. Some place no one knew him, for sure. From now on he needed to plan ahead when to pull this spontaneous stuff, things were getting out of hand.

They mixed into the noon-crowded street. He looked down on the cowboy hat she wore today and saw the perky red bow fastened to the top. It nestled in the crease and didn't show from the front or back. Strange. A hat with a secret.

"There aren't too many places I can take the dog," he began. Maybe she would change her mind and go back to the soup kitchen line.

"Have you ever been to One Eyed Jack's? I washed dishes there a couple of weeks. It's clean."

One Eyed Jack's. He tried not to shudder. What did she know from clean? "I guess it's okay. Will they let the schnoodle in?"

"Hah! They won't even notice him," she said.

That didn't help quell his misgivings.

"I used to see this guy come in with a parrot on his shoulder, and Joe has two cats in the back room on account of mice. No, they won't mind the dog."

They grabbed a table toward the back in the crowded, noisy room. The smells were tantalizing. He pushed Herr Schnoodle under the table, a safety zone from the stampede of rushing waiters. Mac took out a folded paper towel from his back pocket and Apple Sally grabbed his wrist.

"Alexander! You aren't going to wipe off the table and chairs are you? You'll get us thrown out of here. Or laughed out of here, I should say."

He had thought of it, but actually he was only prepared

to wipe off the silverware and the lip of his glass. Oh well, he knew that redhead's temper by now. Reluctantly he refolded the paper towel and put it back in his pocket.

Several of the regulars stopped at their table to talk to Apple Sally, and a couple of scruffy-looking characters waved at her.

She ordered the special of the day for both of them. Mac had to admit it tasted good. He refrained from asking what it was.

Apple Sally ate with a dainty precision, a napkin spread across the lap of her voluminous skirt, her left hand off the table. She kept sneaking tidbits to the dog.

"You don't have to do that. He gets enough to eat."

She hadn't removed her hat, but looking around he saw that everyone who came in with a head covering left it on. Probably wasn't safe to lay anything down. He doubted anyone would be remotely interested in her beat-up old Stetson.

"I want to feed him, do you mind?"

He shrugged. "Suit yourself."

Later they walked toward the park. She thanked him for the lunch in that matter-of-fact way he found so disconcerting. They watched the pigeons for a while, not talking. He felt comfortable with her, especially when they weren't speaking. Mac admitted his impatience with small talk and had very little to offer. His father had been the same and his grandfather, too. Maybe it was a mother's job to see that guys in her family knew how to make small talk.

Apple Sally pulled out a bit of food and unwrapped it for Herr Schnoodle. The dog gave a mighty bark that filled the air with pigeons for blocks around. She laughed at the schnoodle's amazement as flapping wings and flying feathers settled around them.

"Now you've cut it," Mac watched the two of them. "He may connect that awful bark with the flying birds. So much for peace and quiet in the park then."

"Ah, well. The schnoodle's expression was worth it. I can't imagine how a dog with so much hair on his face manages to come up with so many different expressions. It's positively uncanny." She sank to the bench, still laughing. "You never did say where you got him."

Mac considered a long moment. Inborn caution forbid him to discuss the dog's past with anyone. Someday someone might try to reclaim him if the dog became a well-known personality. Maybe he could make a trade-off.

"It's kind of personal. We could trade secrets."

She looked at him with suspicion deep in her cat eyes. "What's that supposed to mean?"

"I'd like to know a little more about you. What could it hurt? Then I'll tell you the Herr Schnoodle saga."

She took off her hat and beat the dust out of it against the park bench. Her hair shone copper red in the sun, making an irregular halo around her head.

"Why do you want to know? Why are you always prying? You *should* be one helluva good detective."

Should be—as if she didn't quite believe it. He shifted his feet uncomfortably and looked at the dog. "Can't say why I want to know about you. Maybe it's that I don't like loose ends. The more I see you, the more confusing it gets. One thing—you're hiding something, for sure."

"Aren't we all?" she countered.

A dark cloud scudded across the sun. Lightning flashed in the distance.

"Well? What do you say? Deal?" he prompted.

"I dunno. Why should my business be any of yours?"

He looked pained. "It isn't. But PIs develop a sixth sense

about these things—if they want to stay alive." He had always wanted to say that. "There's more to you than a run-down grocery cart and a cowboy hat left over from the gold rush."

She took off the broken sunglasses and nested them carefully inside the upturned hat. As if there were any more places on them to break.

"Look. It might be a relief to talk about it, but I got to be sure you won't spread it around the streets. The less people know about you out here, the safer." She turned her face away and wiped angrily at her cheeks.

She would regard tears as a sign of weakness. He wanted to pat her hand in much the same gesture he had learned to use with Herr Schnoodle, but he didn't dare.

"Come back to the office with me. It's getting ready to pour any minute. I'll pick up some donuts and make us some tea. We'll see how it goes. It isn't mere curiosity. I like you."

What made him say that? Saying stuff without thinking wasn't his style. It came as a surprise, but he did like this strange, unorthodox creature. He must be getting soft—first a dog, then a street orphan.

The rain started as they walked quickly toward his office.

Once inside, she shed some of her outer clothing, looking younger, more vulnerable without hiding beneath the baggy jacket and hat.

Watching her seated cross-legged on the thin carpet, munching contentedly on a cream-filled donut, he felt a strange protectiveness toward her. She was in trouble, he'd bet his last buck—if he had been a betting man.

Finally, when she had eaten and stirred her tea, she looked up at him. Her eyes always surprised him, they were so inconsistent with the rest of her—unexpectedly exotic.

"You should use honey in your tea. Sugar's bad for you."

He grinned. "This coming from a person who downed two jelly donuts?" After he said it he could have kicked himself, but she didn't take offense, only smiled and shrugged her shoulders.

"Come sit up here like a big girl," he teased. "At least the stuffed chairs are more comfortable than the hard floor."

Apple Sally looked around. None of his furnishings looked all that comfortable, he could read her thoughts.

She was probably right. He had outfitted his office in "Early Salvation Army." That sounded better than saying it was all he could afford when he started out. Maybe he could have refurbished it by now, but why spend the dough? He was comfortable.

"I think I'd like to tell you about Paul—and Eric, too. Promise on the schnoodle's head you won't tell anyone?"

He nodded. "Sure. But what could be so . . ."

She sketched the air with an impatient gesture, took a deep breath and began. He listened while the rain pounded against the window.

"I had a husband—and a son." She closed her eyes, her brow puckered with the struggle going on inside. "They—they're dead. Lost in an explosion. Our house burned to the ground and everything in it. I woke up outside in the front yard, lying on the snow. I remember the wind blowing so cold off the water. Oh God! Why was I left behind?" She bent her head into her arms resting on her lap, and cried in soul-emptying sobs.

McBee sat, stunned, afraid to touch her, thinking it might be the first tears since it happened to her.

Trying to picture this woman as a housewife, going to

62

PTA meetings, living in a normal house with a regular family, boggled his mind.

Herr Schnoodle pushed under her arms in sympathy. She patted his bristly head and managed a hiccup.

The silence of the room crowded in on them. The drumming of the rain at the windows and the tinny sound of Mac's cheap alarm clock ticking broke the stillness. Once in a while the small electric space heater turned on and off with a whisper. He poured her another cup of tea and handed her a paper towel to blot her face.

He hadn't expected any of this.

9

"Aren't you supposed to offer your handkerchief to dry my eyes?" She made an attempt at sarcasm, but he could tell her heart wasn't in it.

"Nah, that's old. Nowadays real men use paper towels. The bathroom's behind that curtain if you want to freshen up." The very idea of washing a handkerchief saturated with God only knew what kind of germs always made goose bumps on his arms to think of it.

What had he let himself in for this time? He didn't like to get this close to anyone—especially strangers. His father always told him you're born alone, you die alone, so everyone is a stranger in the long run. Still, McBee wasn't prepared to share his emotions with anyone.

Bad enough that the dog created a small chink in his reserve, he couldn't leave himself wide open to everyone. He learned that when his mother died and left them behind.

It was his own fault, though; he shouldn't have tried to pry into her business.

She picked up the tea and cupped her small hands around the restaurant mug. For a second she turned it into bone china.

"I bet you're sorry you asked me now, aren't you?"

He watched the dog lick her arm, searching for a patch of skin beneath the long, floppy sleeves of her shirt.

" 'Course not," he lied. "I had no idea—I don't know what to say . . ." He couldn't look at her directly yet, the pain in her eyes was too intimate—too much to share.

"Ah, well, I didn't expect Donahue, did I? I'm pulling myself together now. Apple Sally is tough and strong, she's a survivor."

He finally looked at her, grateful that her edge of sarcasm had returned. Had this been some crazy story she made up as she went along to get him off her back? He decided that was too cynical, even for him. Yet something didn't jell. She hadn't explained how she came to be left behind. You don't walk away from an explosion. He decided not to open that can of worms—at least for now.

"Did it happen here—in New York?"

As she shook her head, a guarded look entered her eyes. "No. A big city, though. With subways and an elevated train and docks, like here. I don't want to talk about that part."

"It's hard to believe you hit the streets afterwards. How did you survive those first weeks?" He thought of the roving gang of muggers, the street kids ready to fight at a crossed eye, the winos, and pimps. How'd she do it?

She smoothed back the hair that curled around her cheeks. "It was a nightmare at first," she admitted. "I fought off five-six attacks the first month." She pulled a stick with a wrapped handle from the scruffy old airline bag at her feet.

"Ever see a cattle prod? I hitched a ride one time, and a truck driver fixed me up with this. He told me if I poked a man in the right place he'd forget all about raping anyone."

McBee touched the weapon gingerly, turning it over in his hands and nodded. "That'll do it all right. Remind me to stay in line."

They laughed, easing the tension.

"I began to figure out my style of dress, whatever showed the least skin, I figured. I slept in the basement of a karate joint and did some cleaning for them. They taught me some moves to protect myself. I made friends with Mr. Olson. I think he must be in good standing with the right people because now no one bothers me unless he's a new-comer. I soon set 'em straight."

All of New York knew about The Swede who used to run numbers in the old days and now probably fronted for a book joint. The cops knew and liked him. Of all the floating debris in the streets, The Swede remained a slick of oil on top, keeping it steady and together. They left him alone.

"Looks like you got it all worked out. But you can't hide away forever. You must have relatives who worry about you."

She walked to the window. He moved toward her, standing close, but not too close. The fog rolled in on top of the residue of softly falling rain. Lights in the street below looked like a French impressionist painting. He loved that window, a miracle in an otherwise drab, ugly room.

"I don't think there's any family. I'd have felt the loss. I'm doing okay. You're looking at the real me—Apple Sally. No more, no less."

"Bat guano! I don't believe that for a minute. You don't know from one night to the next where you're going to sleep, or if you'll find anything to eat. It's a wonder you don't get sick with all those germs surrounding you."

She laughed, a trilly little sound that made him smile.

"Turn off your mother act, Alexander. I don't buy it. I'm satisfied with the way things are—for now. You don't know the streets like I do. There are decent people here, too, down on their luck. That's all the family I need." She put her hands on her hips and glared at him.

He looked at Herr Schnoodle who was watching them anxiously. Mac bent and absentmindedly fed the dog his

66

fourth dog bone. He always did that when something upset his orderly life. If he really went on a kick, the dog could balloon to a hundred pounds.

McBee liked the way she called him Alexander. No one had called him that since his mother and Pop, of course.

"How about dinner? It's still drizzling out there. I can hustle up some bacon and eggs."

"Thanks, but it's getting late. I didn't realize how fast the time went. I gotta get to my bunk before they close the door in the women's side."

She reached out her hand. He held it between his, marveling at its smallness. Sometimes she gave the illusion of height and bulk in her wrappings.

"Friends?" she asked.

He wrapped her in a bear hug. The top of her bushy head barely reached his shoulders. She didn't push away and they stood close for a long moment. He dropped his arms and stepped back.

"Friends," he agreed.

For the next week he didn't see Apple Sally anywhere on the streets. He hoped she was okay, not regretting her outburst too much. His whole perspective of her had changed, and he found the thought hard to digest.

Everything in him cried out to keep his distance, to stay uninvolved—but something about her story didn't set right. She was running away from something or someone. Of that he felt certain.

When he went to visit Mr. Steinmetz, the front door pushed open on the ancient brownstone. Mac let himself in. The old man toddled out of the kitchen, his expression lighting up to see Herr Schnoodle.

"Mr. Steinmetz, shouldn't you lock your front door?"

The old man shrugged narrow shoulders. "Why? What's to steal? If someone wants in, they will break a window." His face suddenly arranged the wrinkles into a smile. "Thank you for caring. I do lock it most of the time," he confessed. "I was busy in the back and forgot."

Mac sat down easy on the sofa. It felt a little like sitting on sandpaper. He motioned for the dog to sit. "It's okay if he comes in?"

Mr. Steinmetz peered down at Herr Schnoodle with near-sighted intensity. "Such a fine specimen. Of course he may come inside. He has more manners than some children."

The new feeling of dry warmth permeated the house, taking away the usual smell of damp vegetation mixed slightly with mildew.

"You have heat turned on?"

Mr. Steinmetz beamed. "Is it not wonderful? My darling family is so comfortable now, they bloom their little hearts out for me. Look!"

The room filled to bursting with blooming plants of every kind imaginable. It felt as if he sat in the middle of a science fiction movie where the plants take over and eventually wipe out the populace.

"But how . . . ?"

"Ah, you wonder how I can pay for heat now? My friend—if it were not for you." He dabbed a white handkerchief at the corner of an eye and continued. "Mr. Bertoldi and I—we are partners of a fashion. My young friends make the baskets, and he sells them in his store. That way my little family finds new homes when they grow too large for this one." His laugh sounded like dry leaves raked on a lawn.

"Bertoldi?"

Mac couldn't believe it. The storekeeper was a legend

that went even beyond this neighborhood. Rumor had it that he sent more housewives home with the sniffles and red eyes than their own mother-in-laws could have. He was loud, belligerent, domineering and stingy. Even the street gangs and the mob left him alone.

"Oh, he's such a dear, generous man. He gives me so much more than my share and thinks I don't notice. I accept his generosity because he enjoys his little subterfuge."

Mac's thoughts turned upside down and he patted Herr Schnoodle, feeling his tremor of uneasiness. The dog was thoroughly intimidated by the strange odors, the overabundance of furnishings and the teeming plant life in the room. He didn't budge away from the safety of Mac's leg. He hadn't seemed nervous before, must be the heat.

Mac refused the tea offered and stood to leave.

Mr. Steinmetz offered his hand. "Dear friend, please return to visit anytime. You will always be welcome in my home." Tears sprang into the faded blue eyes and Mac looked away.

Damn! His world began to spin out of control and it made him tense. The Mr. Anonymous invisibility had stood him in good stead all these years, leaving him naked and vulnerable without it.

"Now, now," Mac blustered. "It was a job—I was doing a job." He shook the fragile, blue-veined hand Mr. Steinmetz offered and left hurriedly.

He had another reason for hurrying. He couldn't wait to see the new Bertoldi, "terror of the tenements." Would it be total disillusionment?

Mac opened the screen door of the grocery store, the bells tinkling behind him. He sighed with appreciation. A person could almost make a meal from the smells of the sausages and salamis hanging from the rafters, the big rounds of white and yellow cheeses piled against the walls, the black olives swimming in oil and garlic. The grocer had open tubs of dry whitefish near the counter. Crisp, long, golden rolls of bread stood upright in a huge wooden barrel.

Mac left Herr Schnoodle outside. The dog had gradually learned to behave in more civilized fashion when it came to leaving his mark, but sometimes smells got too much for him to resist. This was such a place.

"Ah, Mr. Bertoldi! It's been a while."

"Not long enough. You come for more sausage and cheese? I bet you got your money's worth already. Not one sausage more. It would be cheaper to pay you cash."

Mac regarded the wide-aproned figure, the wildly moving hands and the mustache under the nose that quivered with indignation. Twice Mac had returned to collect some of the promised sausage and cheese. He figured that came to probably fifteen cents an hour—max.

Gazing into the familiar red face, he sighed with relief. How splendid that some things never changed.

10

The next morning a surprise waited when Mac returned from his walk with the schnoodle.

"My God! I don't believe it." The young woman stared at the dog with wide-eyed astonishment.

"Don't believe what?" His heart sank down into his loafers. An owner come to claim her lost dog? He looked at the curvy, blue-jeaned figure leaning against his office door and struggled to hold his runaway pulse in check. No, not even for her would he give up Herr Schnoodle.

"That's got to be the ugliest dog I've ever seen in my entire life."

Relieved, Mac considered briefly whether he should be offended and then hoped that the schnoodle would forgive him. This woman lit up the room. In such circumstances loyalty must take a backseat to hormones.

"He may be unusual-looking, but he's lovable."

The woman turned to him. Her eyes were dark, almost black, in shocking contrast to her pale blonde hair and golden complexion.

He fumbled with the key and then swung the door open, mindful for the first time of the skimpy furnishings. It had become more of an apartment than an office. The old beat-up schoolteacher's desk was the only remnant of the days before the dog. He wasn't sure why he held on to the ugly piece of furniture. Well, yes he was. How would he get rid of it?

"Your hair's real, isn't it?"

"Of course it's real. Isn't yours?"

"Jeez. You know what I mean." He waved her to a chair and sat behind his battered desk, striving for an aura of dignity.

She plunked a bulging camera case down on the floor beside her chair and wrapped a shapely leg around it as if the bag might disappear when she wasn't looking.

Such cynicism in one so young.

"My hair is unbleached, my mom is Puerto Rican and my dad a Norwegian sailor. I'm twenty-eight, unmarried with a steady job. That about does it for the resume."

He didn't bother hiding the flush of embarrassment that started from his collar and worked to his forehead. Had his interest shown so obvious?

"I guess that leaves only your name—and why we're graced with your company." He felt besotted by the promise of dark fires deep inside her eyes.

"I'm Darcy Rasmussen. From the *Union Globe*."

He struggled to hide a grimace. Most people referred to the paper as the "Onion Glob." The worst kind of rag with the publishers fending off lawsuits from coast to coast.

Everybody read it.

"And?" Mac's next question, why was she here, died on his lips. He couldn't think of a friendly way to say it without sounding rude.

She raised a slim, delicately arched eyebrow. Her nose had a delicious, almost imperceptible curve. She reminded him of a golden eagle he once saw at the Bronx Zoo. It had the same dark, searching eyes and the look of finely honed restlessness.

"My boss thinks there's a story here." She turned around the room which suddenly grew smaller by the minute. And shabbier.

"Story? Here? You have the wrong address. I'm Alexander McBee. Of course if you'd want to talk about it, I can fix us . . ." He started to say a cup of tea and decided it sounded too old-fogyish. What did a young woman of twenty-eight drink in the morning?

She answered his question before he could ask.

"I don't suppose you got the makings of a Bloody Mary around?"

He started to make a disparaging crack as he would have if Apple Sally had uttered those words, but something in Darcy's self-assured brass put the brakes on his normal early-morning crankiness.

"Sure. I could scrounge it up. But isn't it a little early . . . ?"

"Please, spare me the lecture. I was out all night—on the job. Trying to stay on the fringes of a rocker's orgy, getting all the names and details without joining in. Man, it's exhausting work."

She pushed her Ann Jillian–bob behind her ears impatiently.

His fingers itched to do it for her. "Yeah, tough."

He brought her the drink and watched as she sipped. Be careful with this one, something told him.

"Okay, now that the preliminaries are over, what makes your boss think you can dig into a story here?"

She shook her head. "He's got an instinct for that sort of thing. He noticed a little blurb in the paper about you, the Count, and the diamond necklace and it stirred him up."

Mac wondered how to discourage the story without running her off. He didn't want anyone putting two and two together and coming up with Herr Schnoodle. For one thing, it would be damned embarrassing to admit the dog could probably solve the cases without him. For another, and more important, the former owner might claim him. He could see the headlines, "Wonder Dog Solves Crimes!" Hell, some lowlife might even kidnap the schnoodle.

"Why don't you get a job working for a decent outfit?" he sparred for time to think.

She stared him down.

He looked away, unable to meet her scrutiny.

"I like it. It's exciting—something new every day. Why do what you do?" she countered.

"Hey, hey. Don't compare my work to that sleazy hunk of paper."

"Hold on a damn minute, Mr. Holier-Than-Thou! Since when does a PI rise above using bugs on unsuspecting people, snooping in garbage cans, opening people's mail and generally making an ass of himself?"

Mac felt the flush of exasperation flood into his hairline. Of course, he would have done all those things in his line of work. Magnum probably hadn't, Jim Rockford might have—but then Mac hoped to do a lot of things for his clients that he wouldn't be too proud of. That was what made a good PI, even though it wasn't in the manual.

"If it makes any difference, I think my boss is way off this time. I don't see any story here, but a job's a job." She shrugged her shoulders and everything rearranged in delicious abandon beneath her T-shirt. "It's a job, and I have orders to stick to you a while, and that's what I'm going to do."

True to her word, sometimes she stayed nearby as if they were joined at the hip, sometimes she disappeared for hours. Whenever he looked up, he caught a glimpse of that outrageous hair, shining in the sun, as she stalked him. It was nerve-wracking. In spite of his appreciation for her odd beauty, he longed for his privacy.

Joe called about another job and Mac turned him down, hating to do it. He could have left Herr Schnoodle out of the picture, he might even have solved it without his help. It wouldn't have been the same, though. He hadn't done all that well on his own before the schnoodle came along.

"Are you on a case?" Darcy demanded one morning. She began showing up later and later. Mac had mixed emotions about that.

He shrugged. "Could be. You're supposed to know all about me by now. You tell me."

She grinned. "For god's sake, McBee, you got to be the biggest *nebbish* in town. I've never been so bored in all my life." She yawned as if to prove her point.

"Good. Then why not pack it in and go chase someone else?"

Her forehead wrinkled into a frown. "I honest to God don't know why. Except . . ." She regarded him as if he had been a specimen under a microscope. "I think I'm beginning to like you—isn't that the absolute pits? You and that scruffy rag bag you call a dog—the strangest pair I've ever come across and believe me, that's saying a lot. Besides, the boss is rarely wrong."

Mac tried to hide his pleasure. "I thought we were dull?" He wasn't too proud to fish, obvious or not.

The compliment didn't follow. He should have known better.

"Yeah. In spite of that square jaw and chiseled profile, you are dull, no two ways about it. I'm taking myself off your case—for now." She reached into her camera bag and pulled out a card. "If anything ever happens in your life, call me. It'll be easier on us both that way."

He felt relieved, but let down, too. "Want to go to dinner some evening?"

"Why?"

"Never mind if you have to ask." He couldn't figure her and right now he didn't much care. He longed to retreat back into his privacy. He tossed her card on his desk. "Maybe you'll hear from me."

He knew that must have sounded like the hard-boiled Kojak, and he waited for the effect it would have on her.

She was already through the door, clacking down the stairway.

So much for that.

While Mac sat and mulled over where he went wrong with Darcy, the phone rang. Just what he needed, his first customer in weeks.

11

In the cab going across town, Mac watched Herr Schnoodle's expression of bristly interest as the driver maneuvered through the afternoon traffic. Having a dog made a dent in his wallet. He used to take the bus.

He closed his eyes and thought of that classy, red Ferrari of Magnum's. Well, hey, what would he do with a car in the middle of the city? Yet it was tricky to tail someone in a bus when the tailee rode in a cab. The damned bus stopped so often by the time he caught up, the cab usually was parked at the curb, empty.

When Darcy found out about him using a bus, she accused him of being cheap, but he knew better. He didn't enjoy spending money, was all. Cheap wasn't in the same category as conservative or frugal, surely.

Like today, for instance. Another divorce case. He hated them, but they were bread and butter. After the phone conversation, he had gone in to speak to Mrs. Treyhune. This divorce case was different, uptown all the way. The horse-faced lady knew her husband cheated on her, and she wanted to take him to the cleaners.

Mac twisted to look out the back window.

"Damn!" He spoke out loud and Herr Schnoodle swerved his head around in that funny double-take way that never failed to make Mac laugh. Mac barely noticed this time, busy hoping Darcy wasn't back there two cab-lengths behind. She was hard to miss with that bright cap of shiny blonde hair. He knew she would give her lifetime subscription to *Ms.* *Magazine* to know about this job.

The Treyhunes were top-drawer society—blue-blood Mayflower kind of old money.

He figured the old gal picked a PI from the yellow pages—a nobody, who would conveniently disappear from her life when he finished digging the dirt and burying hubby.

Mrs. T gave off about as much warmth as those blue diamonds in her dinner ring. One of her glances would have congealed all of the grease on his breakfast this morning.

He thought of Mr. Treyhune and almost felt sorry for the guy. Almost. How could anyone feel sorry for a man who had to be the all-time Mr. High-Liver? Mac traced him to four love nests. Maybe there were more.

Watching a different long-legged beauty meet Treyhune each night was quite an experience. The distinguished-looking elderly man disappeared for hours inside their expensive apartments.

To give the fellow credit, at his age he headed for a special niche in the *Guinness Book of Records*. Or a slab at the morgue with a massive coronary. Either way, he would die with a smile on his face.

Mac wondered if a secretary kept track of his "workload." Juggling the addresses and schedules could get hectic and Mr. T didn't look all that swift.

Mac signaled the driver to pull over to the curb. He watched for a moment as the dapper little man bounded into the foyer of a large condo, waving his umbrella as a conductor would a baton. Today Mr. T wore a disguise, a walrus mustache which didn't go at all with the long, brown wig peeping discreetly between his neck and shirt collar.

Mentally reviewing the photo Mrs. T had given him weeks ago, Mac thought the disguise overkill. The person staring back at him from the picture was clean shaven, gray and balding with rimless glasses—a proper Wall Street executive.

Did the little man take off his disguises when he made love to his sweeties? Did the women know the identity of their sugar daddy? Any of them might choose to blackmail him if he continued this charade. He was ripe for picking. It would be a favor, actually, to let the wife do it first.

Herr Schnoodle and McBee walked slowly toward a small park. Mr. T would be with this lady friend at least an hour. He and the schnoodle might as well get in a little snooze while they waited.

Looming condos shaded the park. A few carefully tended trees seemed superfluous, like miniature forms in a toy railroad setup. Mac and Herr Schnoodle sat on a bench. A maid in a white apron walked a little dog on a leash and another maid watched two children swinging. A quiet park.

Compared to the one close to his office this one was sterile and flat. How odd, this should have been the exact kind of park to appeal to his sense of order and here he was thinking it boring.

Apple Sally wouldn't have been caught dead sitting here.

Mac could just see the entrance to the condo from the angle of his park bench. He stretched and let the dappled sun sift down through the sparse leaves to touch his body. It felt good to relax and allow the bright gold and shadows shift the colors and shapes behind his closed eyes.

He awoke to Herr Schnoodle's low growl.

"Hi, McBee. Funny place to spend an afternoon, dozing on a park bench like an old rummy. Out of your own habitat, too, I see."

Darcy. She had to be the one person in the world the schnoodle detested and growled at. The feeling seemed mutual.

He stared up at her, the haze of daffodil-colored hair making a halo around her head.

"What are you doing here?" He beat her to the punch. She had planned to ask that question first. She made a fast recovery.

"Following you guys."

He hoped by some quirk of benevolent fate that Mr. T had sneaked out the back door a long time ago. The schnoodle had the habit of notifying him with a loud bark when the man hurried from the swinging lobby door. So far the only sound from the mutt was his growl when Darcy clicked up on her high-heeled boots. Wouldn't she love to sink her pearly whites into a case like this? It was front-page tabloid material.

"Why are you following us? Last time we talked, you had better things to do and didn't hesitate to tell me."

She drummed her long red nails on her camera case and pouted. "You're on a case, aren't you? It may be the one the boss is waiting for. He thinks you have ESP or some such nonsense."

"Because I solved a couple of mysteries? That's a PI's job, for gosh sakes. We all do it the same, uncover a few angles, work on hunches, follow leads—you know the drill."

"Oh God, deliver me from the clichés, McBee. It isn't necessary to convince me of your ordinary little life."

"Anyway, even if I had a case, and I don't, everything's in confidence. How many divorce cases would I get, for instance, if the people knew your rag was going to put them in headlines?"

"All I know is that your friend Joe at the south precinct thinks you're akin to the Second Coming. He's certain you have a direct line from there." She pointed at the sky.

"Darcy, listen to me a minute. I barely eke out a living

80

doing this. If I was so damn good would I live where I do?"

"I wouldn't put it past you," she laughed. "Frrrugal like the Scotsman you are," she rolled her *r*'s until he had to laugh with her.

Well, frugal wasn't bad, not enough to argue with her about. Maybe if she had said tightwad or stingy he might have taken offense. For all the good it would have done. Why did the extravagant wastrels get all the gold stars in life and when a guy tried to live conservatively, he became an object of ridicule? He had never figured that out, beginning with high school and his first date, which he had assumed was Dutch treat.

"Come on, let's not argue," she cajoled. Slipping the camera from her bag with practiced dexterity, she snapped a quick picture of a maid engrossed in reading a book to a child. "I take stuff on my own, too," she added.

"I guess. I can't imagine that paper wanting to print anything so pleasant."

She put her camera back in the bag and folded her arms across her chest. They barely reached.

"That munchkin I see you with once in a while—calls herself Apple Sally?"

He nodded, suddenly cautious. It was one thing for *him* to snoop into Apple Sally's past but . . .

"She's not a streety, you know. That intrigues me very much."

"What makes you such an expert?" he countered.

"Hah! I was born and raised here, right in Hell's Kitchen. I'm neither bragging nor complaining, just stating the facts. Take my word—she's not a street person."

"Aw, come on. Maybe she's from a different city."

"Street people are the same the world over. Were you aware some weirdo is killing off bag ladies?"

"Not exactly headline material, was it? I caught it on page six several days ago. No one cares."

"I guess not. But my point is, the last one murdered was a frizzy-haired redhead. Did you know that?"

A fist struck McBee in the solar plexus and he tried not to groan with the shock. "What?"

"That's why I'm asking about your little friend. Maybe someone doesn't like street women, and maybe he especially doesn't like red-headed ones. You'd better clue her in."

"How? She wouldn't think it had anything to do with her. She thinks she's invincible."

"Well, she damn well isn't. The last one offed was inside the mission over by the subway entrance."

A wave of relief flooded over him. "That's practically the other side of the city."

"Don't be obtuse. We're not talking about a rocket scientist here. The killer is obviously a wacko—unless . . ."

It wasn't like Darcy not to finish a sentence once she had the floor. He grew uneasy at her uncharacteristic hesitation.

"I said I didn't think she was a street person. One reason she's acting the part could be she's hiding from someone. Doesn't that make sense?"

Apple Sally admitted to a memory problem. And she didn't seem quite up-front when she spoke of Paul and her son. Like she was holding back. At the time he'd assumed it was lack of remembrance. Maybe it was more. He couldn't discuss it with Darcy, though. He wasn't ready to trust her.

"It makes sense, in a way. But I still don't see what you're getting at."

"Damn, McBee! You can be so dense. What if . . . just suppose a hit man was after her. He could have whacked a few bag ladies by mistake, but now he's zeroing in on specifics."

"God, that's far out, even for your imagination, Darcy. She doesn't strike me as being an ex–mob member or even a wife of one. Why else . . ."

"You haven't been paying attention. She's hiding something. She claims a memory loss—maybe, maybe not. It could be a screen to hide behind when someone gets nosy. There are lots of reasons for a hit. She could be a witness to a deal or overheard something."

"She did mention a fire." Omygod, he didn't want to tell any of Apple Sally's story, especially to Darcy.

"There! A fire. Perfect. Did anyone die? Was a big insurance involved?" Darcy paced back and forth in front of the bench.

Thoughts bumped around inside McBee's skull like marbles in a jar. He had been sensing danger for Apple Sally since he met her, but put it down to his natural ability to worry about anything and everything.

He stood and stretched. "Well, guess me and the schnoodle will be off." Darcy, for all her smart mouth, could be a help. She was streetwise, curious and knew how to dig for information in ways he was just beginning to experience. He had to think things out.

Her lovely face reflected astonishment. "Serious? You two were actually taking a stroll?"

"Of course. I try to show him different parts of the city—broadens his horizons."

"Bull . . ."

Suddenly the high piercing bark of the dog cut into her speech. Instinctively, McBee looked toward the condo entrance while Herr Schnoodle strained at the leash.

"Ah ha!" Darcy stood on her tiptoes to get his same view. He felt her shoulder brush his.

"So? Okay, but it's an ordinary case, nothing to interest

anyone." He sat down and patted the schnoodle.

"If it's so ordinary, why not tell me about it?"

He felt alarmed by the note of reasonable logic in her voice. How could he get rid of her without discouraging her altogether? Maybe he should ask her to dinner again, that would probably do the trick. But if she said yes, how could he fend off her curiosity? Impossible.

If she found out about Mr. T's secret life and printed it in that rag, he could kiss a handsome fee *adios,* plus he'd probably end up in court, being sued. Mrs. T stipulated that the job must be accomplished with finesse.

This was his opportunity to make an impression with the upper set—maybe work up a clientele of paying customers for a change.

He looked down at the dog and gave him another biscuit. Herr Schnoodle licked the back of his hand in sympathy.

"How come you don't like dogs?" He asked the question, stalling for time until he could come up with something better.

"Oh, they're okay, I suppose, although anyone with a brain prefers cats. Anyway, call that a dog?"

"Now wait a damn minute here."

She laughed and he noticed an eye tooth was slightly crooked giving her perfect features a delicate, endearing flaw.

"Dummy! I'm kidding. He's not bad, although I lean toward Dobermans. They're sleek and trim."

"Figures. Matches your disposition, too, I bet."

She wrinkled her nose.

"Well, gotta go. Me and the schnoodle have more walking to do."

While McBee waited for Darcy to cool off on the Treyhune case, he began to dig in on Apple Sally. She was hiding something, he'd bet his five-year-old, well-broken-in Reeboks on that.

After a week of phone calls between New York and Chicago and asking Joe to badger the computer expert in the precinct, Mac came no closer to Apple Sally's beginning than when he started.

Mac picked Chicago because she mentioned elevated trains. Was that the only city with els? He didn't know, having never been away from New York. Maybe Boston, since she mentioned snow and the wind off the water. Why couldn't she tell him everything? Was it really a case of not remembering?

He could take the train to Boston and check the microfilm records at the newspaper. What would he do with the schnoodle while he rambled around the country?

Since her visit, it seemed as if Apple Sally avoided him. He frequented some of her hangouts he knew about, but didn't ask about her. Streeties wouldn't give him the time of day, he knew that much.

One morning, when he wasn't expecting it, he spotted her sitting on a stair step. Herr Schnoodle raced him to plunk down beside her. For the first time in his life, Mac ignored the germy footprints he might be squishing under his behind.

"Where's your shadow?" she asked.

He fidgeted, trying to rest on the hard steps. "You noticed?"

"Hah!" She snorted. "Everyone on the street's noticed. The Rasmussen woman isn't one to disappear into the woodwork."

"I know, I know." He watched as Apple Sally tickled the schnoodle behind the ears. The dog laid his head on her knee, and if he had been a cat, he would have purred.

"He likes you. Do you prefer dogs or cats?" Now why

did he ask that silly question?

She licked her lips and responded seriously. "Dogs, I think, although I don't dislike cats. I remember we had a couple . . ." She broke off and looked down at her feet.

"How long do we have to know one another to be friends?" he asked. "Why shut down at the first mention of anything personal?" Did she know about the latest killings? Would it close her down more if he told her?

Her eyes stared at him blankly, as if seeing beyond his face. "I don't need friends. I don't need anybody or anything!" She started to rise.

"Okay, okay. Sit. You were here first. If you want me to leave, say so and I'll go." He stood, hoping she would at least motion him to sit again, but she continued to stare at Herr Schnoodle's left ear.

Mac looked down at the top of her head. Without her usual odd hat, her hair looked bright in the sunshine, covering her small head with hundreds of curls. He decided now was not the time to bring that to her attention.

"You should wear your hat. It—it keeps the sun away from your face." Maybe the hat would hide some of that telltale coppery mass from a wacko killer.

She looked up at the sky, overcast and dreary. "Hah!"

He thought of her wild sobbing and the story she had told him, the bits and pieces which she plainly regretted letting out. She was in some kind of jam. Why didn't he let it go? Months ago he wouldn't have given it two thoughts.

Darcy sensed something fishy with Apple Sally. Damned if he could figure it yet, and that bothered him. He hated loose ends. Sometimes it seemed as if she tried to talk about it.

Mac left her sitting on the step, feeling her stare on his back as he and Herr Schnoodle walked away.

12

One late afternoon in The Cave, Harry swiped the grungy-looking bar rag across the shiny surface in front of McBee.

Usually after the bartender performed that chore and turned away, Mac wiped the bar in front of him with a clean paper towel.

The bartender didn't go away this time. "Mrs. Rodriguez has been trying to find you," he said.

"Who's Mrs. Rodriguez?" The bar was dark and quiet, a lazy afternoon. McBee glanced around for some of the regulars. Not even Smitty lurked in the shadows, cadging drinks.

Harry shrugged. The cigar he kept in his mouth was never lit. Mac wondered if it might be a tattoo, but hesitated to get close enough to look.

"Don't know. Smitty came by, said she was looking for you. Something about her missing kid."

"Did he say where I can find her?" Getting information from Harry was like pulling alligator teeth. The bartender had plenty to offer, but was it worth the effort?

Harry nodded. "Yep. Smitty wrote it down." He pulled a scrap of paper from his apron pocket and slid it toward McBee.

Mac shielded his eyes from the bright sunlight as he left through the back door. "Don't pout, fella. I'll get a brewski later. Business before pleasure."

Herr Schnoodle expected a beer and pretzels, and he raised his leg alongside a parked bicycle to show his displeasure. The only problem was, a very irate man straddled the bike at the time.

"Watch that crummy mutt! He damned near took a leak on my trousers!"

"What'd you expect? You sat there so long the dog thought you were a fireplug." Sometimes McBee couldn't believe the mouth he was getting. The schnoodle had somehow liberated his lifelong inhibitions and it was great, even if he might wind up with a bloody nose or two.

Mac and Herr Schnoodle entered a run-down section of town. The graffitied walls reflecting so many street gangs they probably had to draw numbers to see which night they fought. Mac leaned down and snapped the leash on the dog's collar, ready for a quick getaway.

He had lived in the city all his life, but this corner of it made him uncomfortable. The first time he had ventured in with Smitty didn't help a whole helluva lot. His snitch had told him a little about the Rodriquez family then.

All the cops and the street people called this dead end area the "Bottleneck" ever since he could remember. It was Little Sicily, San Juan and Harlem all rolled into one mishmash of noisy humanity. To say he wouldn't be caught dead here at night would be a gross understatement.

Yet if Mrs. Rodriguez wanted him to find her son, he should check it out. Business is business.

He walked up two of the three flights of stairs briskly, thinking what good shape he was in. By the third flight he huffed and puffed, more from the smells, he assured himself. Cooked cabbage, hot peppers, soiled diapers, and wino upchuck impregnated the stairwells and walls, each odor fighting for supremacy.

He knocked on the door which opened cautiously, as if someone knew he was coming and waited.

"*Si?*"

Oh boy, this is going to be rough. He didn't know a

word of Spanish but *adios, mañana and taco.*

"Senora Rodriguez? My name's McBee. Alexander McBee."

The door squealed open and a little dark-haired woman watched him with round, black eyes. Everything about her was round. Round and short.

"You speak English?" he asked hopefully.

She nodded. "Little bit. Come in." Her sentences seemed round and short, too.

"Is it okay if my dog comes in? He behaves himself." He wouldn't have left him outside in the hall for anything.

The woman nodded again, locking the door behind them. "Sit? Cuppa coffee?"

The room was barren, the furnishings sparse, as if someone were prepared to leave any moment. He relaxed when he saw how neat and clean everything was. No self-respecting germ could exist here.

"No thanks. About your son?" Now she had him talking in bursts of small sentences. "Your little boy is missing? Have you called the police?"

For a minute he feared she planned to sit on the couch with him. He could imagine it tilt up in the air—a teeter-totter with him hitting his head against the light fixture overhead. Luckily she chose a chair in front of him.

"*Si.* I told the police. Two weeks go. They don't find him."

"Okay. I don't know what I can do, but bring me something he wore so my dog can get a smell of it."

She came back with a freshly starched and ironed shirt.

"No, that won't do. Something that smells like him. Pair of sneakers, maybe?"

She came back with a pair of ratty tennis shoes that had half the dirt from New York embedded in them. She looked embarrassed. "My boy Jesus, he say no wash these. Boys think he sissy." She managed a weak smile.

Smitty told him the boy was ten. They came to the United States a year ago, from the slums of Puerto Rico. An uncle sponsored them but died soon after they arrived so she and the boy stayed on.

He knew she hadn't called the cops. Mac had lived in the city long enough to know people like her would distrust authority and officials of *immigrado* even more than she feared for her boy's safety.

"Have any idea of why he might run away?"

She wrung her hands and tears sprang into her eyes, rolling down her chubby cheeks. "I need to go to hospital." She rubbed her stomach. "Jesus—Jesse thinks he is in the way. When we come here, my son don't want name Jesus. Say kids tease him, change to Jesse." She sighed and her bosom puffed up, reminding him of the pigeons in the park. "Neighbors say ask for welfare. Someone say if I do, they take my son away. I don't ask."

He reached to pat her hand. "Tell me what he looks like."

"My Jesse, he is this tall." She held up her hand. "Very skinny. I feed him, make him eat, but he is like a . . . a stick. He does not smile, his teeth are . . . are ugly." She put her head down, and Mac knew she felt shame.

"Does he go with any gangs?" Mac shuddered, thinking of sashaying down the alleys trying to question the Crips or the Bloods.

She put her hands to her mouth. "Oh, no! Not my Jesus. Never. Not home in Puerto Rico, not here."

"Okay, okay," Mac said in a hurry, trying to hold back the rest of her outburst before it got sticky. "How about friends? School? Was . . . is he into sports?"

She shook her head. "My boy, he does not make friends easy. He has a little . . . what you say . . ." she gestured toward her shoulder, helplessly lost in the language.

"A chip? He has a chip on his shoulder?" Oh great. An illegal kid with bad teeth and mad at the world. Peachy.

"Please. Do not ask questions at school. I have told them I am sick and he must stay home to be with me."

Mac wondered if he even went to school. Maybe the school authorities didn't know about the deceased sponsor.

"I can't promise anything, Mrs. Rodriguez, but we'll do our best. Sure you don't want me to go down to the station and try to explain this to them?"

"No! Oh, no! Find my boy. People here say you good man. Honest man. Find my son." She buried her face into her apron and sobbed. Never able to cope with female tears, he let himself and the dog quietly out of the door.

Smitty lived somewhere in this neighborhood. He had to be the one to have filled poor Mrs. Rodriguez with false hope.

Well, nothing to do but begin. He held on to the paper bag containing one very used sneaker. Herr Schnoodle kept nosing it with obvious curiosity. First he had to get hold of Smitty and narrow down some of the local hangouts for kids Jesse's age. One look around and anyone could see the futility of knocking on doors. No one would tell him the day of the week.

"We'll go back to The Cave, old-timer," he said to Herr Schnoodle who strained against the leash. No doubt the Bottleneck made him uneasy, too. The dog wagged his tail and darted a liquid glance back over his shoulder but didn't pause in his haste to be gone.

Once in the bar, Mac waited for Smitty. The man would find him when he wanted to. Mac hoped it was soon, he didn't want to spend his entire evening here.

"What's new, McBee?" a puff of warm air attached to a voice slithered up and rummaged along the hairs on his neck.

"I wish you wouldn't do that. Do you have to sneak up on a guy?" Mac groused.

If he watched too much television, then this character watched too many old movies. He was a hybrid, a cross between a nasty Humphrey Bogart and a mellow Lon Chaney. With all his signals crossed, he stuck to his own inward script. He never varied his routine, always speaking from the corner of his mouth, always whispering sibilantly enough for an entire room to take notice, and always tiptoeing up on a person. Other than that, the fellow was probably normal—for this part of town.

"What's with the Rodriguez boy?" Mac signaled for Harry to give Smitty a drink.

"This one's on me. You don't owe me nothin'," Smitty said, his Adam's apple bobbed as he drank. Finally, he wiped his mouth on his jacket sleeve and continued.

"The kid ain't bad. Mrs. Rodriguez, she's too tight on him. Scared he'll get mixed up in one of those gangs. They're close, those two, got no one else." He took another drink and pushed his glass aside, patiently waiting for another.

It bugged Mac that this guy always left at least an inch of a drink in the glass. Smitty obviously didn't have a steady income, sometimes he relished that first drink as someone else might a T-bone steak. Yet he always left some in the glass. A status thing, Mac decided.

Anyway, now didn't seem the time to mention Smitty's shortcomings, so Mac ordered another drink for him. The guy might brag that the drinks were on him, but Mac and the bartender knew better.

"So, where was I?" Smitty ignored the napkin at his elbow and wiped the drink residue from his mouth with the back of his hand.

"Why the kid ran away, etcetera," Mac prompted. He glanced at Herr Schnoodle over on the next bar stool.

Damn! Someone had slipped up and given the mutt another brew while he had been yakking. He reached over to take it away and the dog growled a warning, putting his paw over the top of Mac's hand.

Schnoodle nosed the goblet away and then nosed his pretzels to the other side, just in case. Mac laughed and let it be. If the dog fell off the stool, he could look forward to a dilly of a hangover the next morning. Did dogs have hangovers? Why not? Fair is fair.

"So, Mrs. Rodriguez . . ." Smitty continued as if he hadn't been interrupted, "she's got problems. Tumor or something. Gotta go to the hospital and her job cleaning offices could be kaput. Then they don't eat or pay rent on that fleabag apartment. The kid's bugged and thinks if he runs away she can make it on her own with welfare." He took a deep breath and swiveled his head around to shoot a glance over his shoulder. As if anyone cared to listen to their conversation.

"You must have some ideas. Is he trying to get back to San Juan? Do you think he might be . . ." Mac couldn't finish about the boy maybe lying dead somewhere under a pile of trash.

"Nah, he ain't dead or nothin' like that. He's got plenty of moxie. He'll take care of himself okay. His mother is worried, and she won't go to the hospital until he comes back."

Mac was impressed. In all his dealings with this fellow he had never thought of the man having warm feelings about anyone. After all, he barely tolerated the schnoodle.

"Start with Bertoldi, the grocer," Smitty whispered hoarsely. "He's been missing some stuff. Might be the kid's hanging around there."

Not the grocer again. How many bad-tempered people lived in this city, anyway? Did he have to run into them all?

Mac turned his head to make sure the mutt wasn't getting another drink on the house. When he turned back, Smitty had disappeared. His three glasses lined up neatly, testaments to his presence, an exact inch of liquid left in each.

Helping the dog down from his stool, McBee felt a stab of pride in the way Herr Schnoodle handled himself. Everyone watched and pretended not to. Mac never allowed him more than half a brew and he had at least one and a half today, but barely staggered. A last-minute lurch toward a customer's tempting trouser leg gave him away. Mac snapped the leash on and pushed open the door, sucking in the night air.

He used to be hesitant about staying at The Cave after dark. He still wasn't sure if he was being foolhardy, but what the hey.

13

Early the next morning McBee opened the door of The Cave, letting it hit his heels softly as he entered. He looked around and wondered if the people sitting in the back booths were actual cardboard cutouts that Harry rigged up to look busy. No matter what time of day or night he came in, it seemed as if those same people sat talking.

He took a coffee and waited. Smitty always knew when he was there. After ten minutes and no one showed, Herr Schnoodle began to nudge him with his nose. "Come on, it's too early for a brew. I'm drinking coffee, see?" he reached for a couple of stale pretzels, pushing them toward the dog.

The door opened and a shaft of sunlight penetrated the gloom. Mac didn't turn around to look, sure Smitty stood behind him. He was wrong.

The dog growled low in his throat. The strong scent of Spaceman's aftershave enveloped the room. Word was the Spaceman preferred to drink it rather than wear it, and the schnoodle wasn't used to Old Spice breath.

The fellow sat down on the next stool and Mac turned slowly, not wanting to come face to face with the smell too quickly. "How's it going?" He never had learned the man's name and hesitated to call him "Spaceman," although everyone else did.

Mac remembered seeing the dried out junkie lying underneath a pile of cardboard in an alley. The cops had busted him for possession, and being his first arrest, he was offered the cure and took it. Or so Harry the bartender said.

Then the halfway house dumped the Spaceman back into the streets. The man offered to help Mac in the underground whenever he might need it, swearing he would stay straight.

Just what Mac needed, another oddball snitch.

"I'm doing fine, doing fine," the Spaceman's voice grated—like spinning car tires over gravel.

They sat for awhile not speaking. The Spaceman never drank from the bar, not even freebies. He must prefer his own weird concoctions.

"Word's out you're looking for Jesse Rodriguez."

Mac nodded. How did these things get around so fast?

The schnoodle nudged him for another pretzel, wanting a beer. Mac had a fleeting picture of himself and his partner attending AA meetings.

"Not now, fella. Not now."

"How about trying the Salami King?" The Spaceman twirled slowly around on his stool. Luckily, he didn't do it all the time. Mac had this problem about undue motion, sitting in a rocking chair made him seasick.

"The Salami King?" The man probably referred to Bertoldi. No one in the streets liked the grocer, but they respected his awesome temper.

Both Smitty and Spaceman had mentioned Bertoldi in connection with Jesse. It was a start.

"Soon as I get my case wrapped up—the paying one—I'll lay a couple of bucks on you," Mac offered.

"Thanks," the Spaceman said with quiet dignity.

Mac and the schnoodle headed down the street toward Bertoldi's. Mac's thoughts traveled in the direction of Treyhune, his one paying customer whom he had temporarily forgotten.

The Treyhunes should be first on his agenda. If he could wrap up this case without Darcy's interference that would solve the rent problem for this month. Then he only needed to worry about the Spaceman.

A PI had to have sources. Someday he might need more information than Smitty could provide. It came out cheap enough to pay for Spaceman's rent at the Y and give him a few bucks for groceries. A couple of bucks a month, no big deal.

That brought him up short. A couple of bucks—no big deal? What was he getting to be, a blithering spendthrift? His father would have had a big laugh at that one. He accused his only son of being as tight as the bark on a tree.

The last time he trailed honey-boy Treyhune, the man had done some strange things, strictly out of character. What was he up to? If Mac didn't let the wife know something soon, Darcy might sniff it all out and beat him to the punch. It was just a matter of time until she turned over the last rock and the bugs crawled into daylight. If she knew Treyhune hid a modern-day harem right under his wife's long nose, supermarkets would blast the news at every checkout counter in America. Damn it, he needed this gig.

He sighed as he thought of the points he'd make with Darcy if he let her in on the whole scam. The temptation lasted a brief eternity before he brushed it away regretfully.

Mac tied Herr Schnoodle to the fireplug in front of Bertoldi's store and waited for the kids to discover him. It didn't take more than three minutes. Did they use tom-toms or what? The kids loved to "take care" of the dog and in no time at all, dozens laughed and played around him.

At first, like his master, the schnoodle had been grumpy and short with the kids. Later, he began to glory in the attention, forgetting the dignity he seemed to think was required of a PI's assistant.

Mac went inside and waited until Mr. B finished with the two customers. It was late afternoon and he closed at seven.

"Hello, my friend," the grocer greeted him.

Mac turned to look behind him to see who he spoke to.

The grocer was probably relieved that Mac didn't want any more free sausages and cheese. "How's Mr. Steinmetz? I haven't visited him lately."

The hard look folded into unaccustomed lines of cheerfulness as Bertoldi rubbed the pickle juice from his fingers onto his apron.

"Fine. Fine. Everything fine for little man now."

This was the closest the man would ever come to saying thanks. Fine with him.

"Word's out you're having problems with petty stuff, someone swiping apples, an orange or two." How could he tell? Did he count every pile several times a day?

"Petty?" Bertoldi's voice rose so that the hanging salamis vibrated like wind chimes in a breeze. "What you mean petty? No stealing is petty. You gotta nerve!" He calmed down with effort when he noticed several customers start to enter and dart away.

McBee took a deep breath. It took a lot of guts to continue the subject after that outburst, but he had no choice. He sensed the Rodriguez boy's trail started from here.

"Okay, okay. I'm talking fruits and vegetables—not stealing from your cash drawer with a sawed-off shotgun stuck up your nose. Get the difference?" he waited for the next explosion.

Mr. Bertoldi frowned. "Oh."

Oh? Was that all? Waiting for the explosion, this mild "oh" felt the same as when you ate the bottom from your ice-cream cone and, waiting for the thick cream, it turned to a slow, watery trickle.

Mr. B related at great length how diabolical and crafty this network of thieves worked, convinced at least a dozen hardened criminals were trying to put him out of business. At the beginning of the day he knew exactly how many salamis hung outside against the window. He even knew the count of his oranges and tomatoes. At the end of every day he always came up short.

"Did you ask any of your customers or the kids outside if they saw anything?"

Bertoldi stared at McBee as if he sprouted two heads. "You kidding me? Them *gindolas* don't see nothing, don't know nothing and don't say nothing."

"Mind if I check around?"

The big man shook his head. "Help yourself. But this time I don't pay. I never called you, remember?"

He hadn't paid the last time, but Mac grinned and walked outside to get Herr Schnoodle.

Nothing seemed out of the ordinary in the back, just the usual clutter of junk the grocer couldn't bear to part with. Suddenly the dog let out one of his piercing barks.

"Oh come on, it's a pile of rags. Probably full of creepy bugs."

The schnoodle barked again. It was his "I won't give up until you look" bark.

McBee kicked at the rags and pulled up a piece of cardboard to kneel on. The pile looked hollowed out, as if a small body had wiggled into the center, making a nest. A cat probably. He examined it closer, but saw no animal hairs on the dark material. Unfolding the paper bag he'd carried all day, he gave the dog a sniff of the sneaker.

Herr Schnoodle plopped down and rested his chin on his folded front paws as if to say, "Yep, this is it."

Did Jesse sleep in back of the store, stealing enough to

eat? Why did he hang around so close to Bottleneck territory and yet far enough away so that no one from there would likely spot him?

More important, how did he sneak food right from under the watchful eye of Bertoldi?

"Looks like we're bunking here tonight, amigo." If an animal slept here instead of Jesse Rodriguez, then he would only be out a night's sleep in a battleground of germs, bugs and rats. But Mrs. Rodriguez had only twenty-four hours left to find the boy before her surgery.

Mac didn't tell Bertoldi he and Herr Schnoodle planned to sleep on the premises. Could be for nothing and the grocer would probably charge him a night's rent if he knew about it. Taking his master handy-dandy key ring from his pocket, one of the free gifts from the PI school, Mac quickly undid the dinky lock on the shed door. Heavy wooden slats made up the door so that he could get a hand through once he entered and relock it behind him.

A stuffed chair that even mice had given up on languished in a corner. Herr Schnoodle promptly showed his disinterest by lifting his leg on the side of it. Cases of sour red wine and a large tin of soda crackers lined the back wall. At least they wouldn't go hungry or thirsty, although the mutt preferred beer. Mac opened a stack of newspapers near the center of the pile and pulled out some to scatter on the floor and the chair. He wouldn't be comfortable, but he'd be reasonably unsoiled.

At eight p.m. he heard Bertoldi come out the back door and rattle the lock on the shed to check it. Mac held the shnoodle's muzzle so he wouldn't bark or growl. Then Bertoldi shut the lights off inside the store, and Mac knew he had gone.

McBee leaned back in the paper-covered chair gingerly,

hoping that any inhabitants had vacated long ago. He closed his eyes and listened for the sound of Herr Schnoodle settling down. It felt odd, everything quiet close by, yet the night sounds of the city came alive. Ambulances, fire trucks, kids playing in the streets, the sounds filtered back to him like through a funnel. A cat fight erupted nearby and he quickly grabbed Herr Schnoodle's nose to keep him from barking.

After a while he dozed, waking to the dog's low, menacing growl.

"Shh! It might be the kid. We don't want to scare him off." He patted the shaggy head, and they both waited quietly in the dark. The wavering light from the streetlamp worked its way over the top of the brick building to cast a sullen glare into the backyard. Mac pressed his nose close to the slats in the door and peered through, but nothing moved.

Suddenly, someone stepped into the bunch of piled-up aluminum cans he had set as a trap along the pathway. He heard a yip of pain and strong language. If it came from the Rodriguez boy, the kid was accomplished in cussing in two languages.

Mac waited until the noise stopped and the night settled in again. Putting his hands outside on either side of the lock, he opened the door carefully.

"Wait here, boy. No need scaring him out of the rest of his growth." He couldn't see Herr Schnoodle's expression in the dark, but his snarf of disgust came loud and clear.

Mac crept toward the pile of rags. When he drew close, he made out the small form lying curled in the middle of the pile.

"Jesus. Jesse," he whispered.

The boy galvanized into a ball of action, flinging himself

at Mac's midsection, knocking him down. Before Mac could struggle to his feet, Herr Schnoodle had zipped past and pinned the youngster to the fence, growling his best reincarnated Doberman schtick.

"Good boy," Mac managed, still wheezing from the stomach assault. "Bring him here."

The schnoodle's teeth took hold of the sleeve on the small brown arm and tugged. The boy followed his arm.

Looking at the wiry little ragamuffin, he couldn't decide if this was the ten-year-old Jesse or a twenty-year-old midget.

"Your name Jesus Rodriguez?" He had no idea of how to talk to kids, having diligently avoided the problem all his life.

The boy glared at him with dark, snapping eyes that reminded him a little of Darcy.

"Son, your mother worries about you. She has to go to the hospital, and she can't do it unless she knows you're okay."

"Leave me alone, turkey. My name ain't Rodriguez and I got no mother."

McBee considered for a moment the validity of his statement and then sighed. He couldn't give up that easy.

"Like dogs?" By now Herr Schnoodle had put his chin on the boy's foot to hold him and watched him with sad eyes. Probably begging his forgiveness for scaring him. Some attack hound.

The boy glanced down at the schnoodle, seeming surprised that his leg was still attached to his skinny body. He reached a grubby hand to touch him, receiving a sloppy lick by a long tongue.

"Sometimes I like 'em."

"Well, you made a friend with this one, all right. His

name's Herr Schnoodle. Call him Schnoodle."

The boy laughed at the sound of the name and the twenty-year-old midget disappeared.

"My mom okay?" He tried to sound tough, but the lonely ten-year-old voice come through.

"Sure. Or she will be when she knows you're safe. Why run away?"

Jesse stared at the ground.

"I asked a question. How come you ran away when your mom needed you?"

The youngster scratched through his thick black hair and Mac imagined the scrubbing he was going to get when he went back home. Mrs. Rodriguez would probably scrub him half raw.

"I heard the welfare lady say I have to go to school before they could help my mother. I hate school."

"Hungry?" Mac sat down gingerly on a decrepit car seat across from the boy.

"Nah. Know why?" His expression stayed serious, but his eyes glinted with mischief.

Reluctantly letting go of the dog's collar, Jesse moved into the back of the yard, motioning for Mac to follow.

Away from the buildings, the street light shone unrestricted. A nest of salamis, bread and fruits lay hidden behind broken signs and warped cardboard.

Mac was impressed. "But how did you get all this by that tyrant's nose?"

Jesse wriggled and squirmed, still not trusting.

"Look, we got to give this back. It's stealing. I promise I won't tell how you did it, though, if you let me in on it."

Jesse jumped up on a box, facing him. They stared at one another, eye level, for a long moment. The boy seemed satisfied by what he saw.

"Okay." He jumped down and reached under his treasure trove. He pulled out a long, slender bamboo pole with a rope coming from both ends.

"I still don't get it . . ." Mac began.

Jesse raised the pole expertly and flipped it toward a pile of junk, pulling on the rope at his end. In a second a scrap of unidentifiable obsolescence separated from the rest, and he held it up with triumph.

McBee reached and pulled the end of the pole toward him. The kid had fastened a rusty grappling hook to the end of the cord. That explained why Bertoldi never saw anything. The youth probably waited around the corner of the building until the grocer turned his back and then filched whatever he needed.

"Aren't you tired of salami and bologna?"

Jesse flashed an impish grin and quickly put his small grimy hand in front of his face in a gesture of self-consciousness that dismayed Mac. Two of his front teeth were decayed. Probably had never gone to a dentist in his life.

"My mother, she cooks good." He rubbed his stomach.

Mac patted an abandoned backseat of a car for Jesse to sit down and forgot to spread papers out first. Herr Schnoodle wriggled between them. It was plain to see he was torn between liking the boy and jealous of anyone sitting next to his partner. Mac rubbed him gently up and down the slight indentation above his nose, between his eyes, to calm him down.

"Let me think a minute, Jess. Maybe I can come up with some solution." He had the kid all right and he could drag him back home. But with his attitude, it would be a matter of time until he hit the streets again.

"How would you like to have a job?"

"A real job? Getting paid and everything?" The boy

sounded so eager, he completely discarded his tough-guy role for the moment.

Mr. Steinmetz owed him one, didn't he? What if the old gent feared kids? Time grew short for Treyhune, Mac felt the pressure. If he made this case before Darcy got her mitts on it, he would have a few bucks to give Steinmetz for the boy's so-called salary.

Suddenly things began to fall into shape. He reached to ruffle the boy's hair and before Jesse could take offense, did the same to the schnoodle.

They laughed as the dog grinned from ear to ear.

14

The next day the two sat looking at each other across the kitchen table. Mac spoke between spoonfuls of cereal.

"It's rough, old boy. With Darcy snooping around I haven't had a chance to check with Joe about new jobs. There's only Treyhune to work on. Of course the Rodriguez kid, but that's gratis. Not to worry—we'll do okay."

The dog didn't appear a bit worried. Mac never invited him to eat *on* the table, but he liked to sit across from Mac, keeping him company. Occasionally he jumped off the chair to nibble from his dish next to the refrigerator and hop up again.

"I think I'm ready to put the wraps on this caper. A crying shame. The guy had a good thing going there, guess he overworked it. Got to give him credit for juggling everything. What a schedule!"

Herr Schnoodle made a snarfing noise.

"Go ahead, sneer all you want to, but I hate divorce cases."

He thought of the Count, a caper to make his father proud.

"Know something, Schnoodle? With a pair of glasses and a cigar sticking from your mouth, you're the picture of Uncle Jeff sitting there."

The dog grinned, he could tell when his partner made a joke.

"I'm worried about Apple Sally, though."

The dog barked sharply at the mention of her name.

It was Mac's turn to grin. "Not much of a connoisseur when it comes to women, are you, pal? Darcy R is one sweet-looking doll and you can't stand her."

The schnoodle snarfed again.

Mac chose to ignore it. "Guess we can't agree on everything," he conceded. If he didn't know better, he would have thought Schnoodle was jealous of Darcy. Why would Darcy make the schnoodle jealous and not Apple Sally? But of course, he had no designs whatsoever on the bag lady. While as for Darcy, she was barely ten or twelve years younger, although a generation might as well separate the reporter and himself, so different their thinking.

It took McBee a while to gather his photographs and type the data on Mr. Treyhune. They should have warned him of the paperwork when he took his correspondence course, he might have studied typing, too. This two-finger and thumb business went awfully slow.

Some day he would be able to afford a secretary, a real classy lady like Barnaby Jones or Mannix hired for their offices. Maybe even a computer. Although he couldn't recall any of his heroes pecking away at one. It appeared they always conned someone else to do the paperwork.

He was still stabbing impatient fingers at the typewriter keys when he heard the tap-tapping of Darcy's heels on the stairway. He jerked the paper from the machine, nearly destroying the morning's effort, and shoved it in his desk drawer.

In spite of the ever-present hazard of Darcy's snooping, he was tickled see her. He waited for her knock and the door to push open behind it. She wasn't the patient sort. There never was much time between the knock and the push.

"Hi, McBee," her voice was cheerful. Her bright red lips

looked kissable and he turned away quickly before she caught his stare. He nudged the dog with his foot as Herr Schnoodle growled, paw pressed over a doggie bone.

"Morning," he waved her toward a chair. She looked like morning.

"I could use some coffee, if you have any to spare." She put down her camera case, and Mac was glad to see she no longer snaked her leg around the bag to protect it.

Her blouse was an electric blue, with a chartreuse scarf at her neck and designer jeans that fit as a second skin. He tried to pry his eyes away.

"I thought I heard typing. You're either working on a novel or winding up a case. How come you're so secretive?" She flashed a smile at him that put the static cling back in his socks.

He shrugged, aiming for nonchalance. "What if I admitted to working on a case? Give me a break, I can't share it with you."

She refused to be put off. "You got a job to do, but so do I. Mine is keeping tabs on you—for whatever insane reason the boss has."

They sipped coffee in silence, watching Herr Schnoodle, who never took his eyes off her. The golden dots of his eyebrows raised in constant speculation, his ears flattened to show his disapproval. Mac tried not to laugh, his expression was darned comical, but the dog got his feelings hurt easy.

For once she didn't take time out to laugh at Schnoodle, either.

"You've been following Alfred Treyhune, right?"

McBee almost choked on the sip of coffee just starting down.

"What makes you ask?"

"Numby! I'm probably as good a detective as you. Or

maybe better," she added with her usual lack of modesty.

"Hey, Darcy, girl, this is my big one. If you screw this up on me I'll . . ."

Her dark eyes lit from somewhere inside her head.

"So! I was right. That geezer has a love nest and his old lady wants to clean his clock." She smiled with smug satisfaction, and a pointed little tongue flicked across her full bottom lip like a cat just devouring an expensive canary.

At least she didn't know it all. *A* love nest didn't begin to scratch the surface.

"It's no big deal," was all he could come up with.

She set the cup down and opened her camera bag, fumbling through some papers for a second to drag out a small notebook.

"It's all here, McBee." She tapped the cover with a ballpoint pen. "I've talked to your friend Joe at the station, also your snitch, Sleazy or Smitty—one of the seven dwarfs anyway—at The Cave. They all think you're the nuts, by the way. Maybe you're not as dull and insipid as I thought."

"Thanks a lot. I don't like the idea of you sneaking around behind my back," he said with as much dignity as he could muster.

"Hah! Look who's talking."

"I'm not going to defend my profession. I enjoy it." That was true, it came as a surprise. When did he start to enjoy his work? "Sometimes I even get paid. Like the case I'm on now. First decent paying job I've had," he admitted. "It's my ticket to big time if I pull it off."

"Think the biddy will recommend you to her friends? How's that going to look? Besides, I doubt she has any friends."

He never thought of it that way. It galled him that she knew as much, or more, about the Treyhunes than he did.

"McBee, I can't allow my emotions to rule my head. I need to make a living, too. It's tough getting the boss to notice my work."

If the boss hadn't noticed her by now he had to be over ninety, blind or both.

"When I grew up, we had three ways for a girl in my neighborhood to earn a living." She ticked each off on her long, slender fingers tipped with something that resembled recycled vampire blood.

"One. You began to chippy at fifteen. Two. You married at sixteen to get away from the neighborhood and then your old man turned out to be a pimp. Three. You got away from the street and never looked back." She took another sip of coffee.

"I'm never going back, McBee. I fought for this job, such as it is. I earned everything by the sweat of my brow, not my butt, and I'm going to work for a real paper some day."

He looked at the scarred tabletop, unable to meet the intensity in her expression. What could he do? He couldn't throw Treyhune to the sharks on that paper even if he didn't care about earning a fee. And he did care. Very much.

"Something else, McBee."

His stomach took a nosedive. What else?

"This Apple Sally character? I checked her out. Like I said, she's not a streety. She's hiding something. Something big. I think it's connected to those street murders somehow."

"Oh yeah. Is she part of the Manson gang—the part that got away?"

Darcy shook her head impatiently.

In spite of the troubling words, the anxiety Darcy always

brought into his space, he loved to watch the pale curve of her hair swing gracefully, brushing against her honey-cream cheek.

"Nothing like that. She appeared on the streets all at once, bigger than life. Olson protects her, there's word out nobody should mess with her. A hunk in the karate place downtown taught her for free—there's too much going on with her that I don't understand."

"Maybe they just like her. Ever thought of that? Do you have to have that pretty nose stuck in everything?" He was relieved that the conversation drifted away from his case, but alarmed for Apple Sally. If she didn't want her past known, she must have a reason and he respected that.

"Of course I do," she grinned. "That's what makes me a damned good reporter. I watch for the unusual, the bizarre."

He thought a long moment before speaking. He was still a novice at investigating, as much as he hated to admit it. He had sensed danger surrounding Apple Sally since they first met.

"If I tell you something, give me your word you won't do anything about it until you check with me first?" All his snooping hadn't taken him anywhere, but Darcy's paper had resources across the country. He had a gut feeling that Apple Sally needed help. What made things worse, she didn't seem to realize it.

Darcy studied him for a long moment as if trying to see beyond his words. "Okay, my word's good."

He told her of the explosion and fire. He had discarded Chicago, chosen Boston from little things Apple Sally mentioned. He told her about the family blowing into pieces and admitted that he hadn't found any more clues. Maybe because Apple Sally wouldn't tell him specific dates. He didn't have enough to go on.

"She told me this in strict confidence. I'm trusting you. This woman's hurting; I want to help her."

Darcy reached across the table to punch him lightly on the shoulder. "You old softy. Okay, I promised, didn't I? I'll check on it for you—for us. But if anything comes of it, I get first crack at the story," she warned.

Later Mac wondered if he screwed up. Had he thrown Apple Sally over to protect Treyhune—to sidetrack Darcy? Things were taking a complicated turn. He hated complications. Maybe he should spend a few days goofing off. This job could wait, Treyhune wasn't going anywhere.

Later he would wonder how wrong he could be.

15

Mac climbed gingerly into the Dumpster behind Treyhune's Number-one girl's brownstone. "Yecch! Sometimes this job's a bummer, amigo," his muffled voice rose above the top on a cloud of fumes as he bent to rummage. Honey-boy Treyhune's erratic behavior for the past week bothered him. Even with the odd assortment of households, Treyhune always had a predictability, his ways layered and wrapped in habit.

McBee had assigned numbers to each of the millionaire's girlfriends, keeping a notebook on each. Lady Number One had to be Treyhune's favorite, the only sweetie to own a spanking new Buick and her own condo. She was a tall brunette, may have done modeling in her youth, she had that carriage. Could have been a Rockette even.

Odd, she wasn't the most gorgeous nor the youngest, but Treyhune laughed a lot when they were together and stopped using his silly disguises with her. A sign of carelessness? Too sure of himself?

Aha! Mac dusted off the cigarette ashes with distaste and smoothed the wrinkled bank statement. He had hoped for a break and this was it. If it hadn't had coffee spilled all over, she probably wouldn't have thrown it away.

The statement showed a big deposit recently. He didn't see how even Honey-boy could afford such generosity to all his lovelies.

Mac scrounged around in the remaining papers a few minutes more, but his disgust soon overpowered his

113

curiosity. Now that he found the statement, he could go home and take a hot shower. What was happening here? He sensed a climax threatening, but what sort?

If it hadn't been for Darcy breathing down his neck he might have time to think on it more carefully. Something stranger than usual was going down, and if he wasn't careful he could move too fast or too slow and ruin the whole case.

He couldn't afford to do that now. Not if he wanted to help Jesse with fixing his teeth and give Mr. Steinmetz something to pay the kid's "salary" with.

He thought of how the old man and the boy had taken to each another so fast. The plants in Mr. Steinmetz's home had entranced Jesse. Maybe it might start him thinking along those lines. Florists made good money in the city.

Ah, hell, when a PI lost his sharp edges, he turned soft and mushy. His dad and grandpop would have laughed at him as usual—wouldn't they? He couldn't be sure, this time.

The sound of a window sliding open drew Mac abruptly back to the present. He ducked his head down past the lip of the Dumpster and hoped he wouldn't have to sneeze. He knew he was allergic to cigarette ashes and smoke. Of course he had always thought he was allergic to pet hair, too. He peered over the edge cautiously. The window above was empty, and he vaulted the side of the Dumpster and grabbed the schnoodle's leash. Better head home and figure this out.

Something had to be done, and soon.

After his long, hot shower, McBee spread the contents of his files on the kitchen table. He stacked the shots of Honey-boy with each of his ladies going to and from night-clubs and their apartments with his hokey disguises. Along with that, he added some discarded bank statements, a receipt for a safety deposit box and various articles that he had scrounged from trash bins. Articles that should stand in court—if it came to that.

He didn't see Treyhune letting it go that far. His wife had the guy by the short hairs this time.

"We'd better haul this stuff to old freezer face before Darcy gets on to us, pal." The dog sounded his agreement.

Yet something continued to nag at him. Something out of timing—out of sync. His instincts told him he had better devote at least another day to snooping. Especially on Lady Number One. Would Darcy hold off long enough?

He left Herr Schnoodle home the next day. He had a few disguises of his own to help solve this case, starting with his Wall Street businessman's cover. If it became necessary to stay close to her, he could change to his telephone repairman or city employee uniform. Both were so much alike that it only took a few Velcro-fastened insignia changes on the sleeve and front of the shirt. He packed the clothing into a briefcase.

Mac waited patiently on the bench in front of the apartment house of Number One. Two busses slowed down for him, but he waved them on. Would she sleep all day? It was nearly 10 a.m., and he didn't know how long his cover would hold at this rate.

Finally he heard the door open and click shut again. Would she take the Buick? If she did, he washed out. The bank statement showed the bank a few blocks away and he counted on her walking. Maybe she wasn't thinking of the bank this morning.

His luck held. The woman turned up the collar on her fur coat and headed in the direction of the bank with long, purposeful strides. He moved off the bench and blended in with several people behind her on the sidewalk. Piece of cake, she never looked back.

He followed her through the heavy brass doors of the First National Bank, waiting by the writing stand and pretending to study some bank deposit slips. He sure didn't want anyone to notice him loitering. This wasn't the bank for that sort of behavior.

Her transaction didn't take long. She put an envelope in her leather handbag and then unexpectedly she turned around to look straight at him, their stares colliding in midair.

Damn! Now he would have to be extra careful. She was no dummy. Had she recognized his face as someone possibly following her? Mac regarded her as a cut above Honey-boy's other lady loves. She had taken on a personality to him, as none of the others had.

Mac recalled the old boy taking Number One on shopping sprees while he had watched them, disguised as a garment worker. A neat idea, too, until that union hardnose demanded to see his papers. He almost received a cement jacket for his trouble that time. Not even a PI messes with the garment union.

Brought back to the present by her motions, he hurried outside just as she raised her hand for a taxi. The soft breeze blew the long brunette hair from her neck, blending with the rich color of the fur coat. She was some picture.

He hailed a cab behind hers.

Ever since he graduated he longed to yell, "Follow that cab, here's an extra fin if you don't lose it." Did people know what a fin was anymore? Barnaby Jones sure did. He settled for a simple "Follow that cab," feeling too short of breath from his fast walk to offer an extra tip.

On the way he changed into his telephone repairman's outfit. If the cabby wondered about all the motion in his backseat, he ignored it.

By the time Mac finished his struggle of changing, they had arrived behind the other taxi. It puzzled him to recognize the airport. Did she close the bank account to take a hike? Surely Treyhune wasn't so besotted to trust her implicitly.

Mac paid off the cab driver and followed at a decent pace. She headed toward a locker, inserting her key and removing a large suitcase. Heavy by the looks of it. If he had guessed her destination he could have used his porter disguise. That would be a neat little trick, but then the porter's union would have probably nailed him.

How come they never did that to Rockford?

Number One walked toward a row of seats and Mac's eyes widened to see Treyhune come forward, his face one big smile—a kid on Christmas morning. He took Number One's hand and motioned for a porter to take the luggage.

This was the climax then. The couple prepared to make the Big Exit, probably to Tahiti.

Mac ran for a phone to call Mrs. T. By the time he located the bank of phones he had to stand in line. Finally a male voice answered, probably the butler, informing him that the madam was not at home and should return in an hour. That was a lie. She never left the premises; she was an absolute recluse.

He turned and ran outside for a taxi, hoping to have time to reach the office for the file and then to the Treyhune house before the stuff hit the fan. All the way home he looked out the back window for that sleek head of pale, creamy hair.

Darcy might have tailed him to the airport. If she did, she would recognize Treyhune for sure. Then it was finished. The news would be out before he had time to get to Mrs. Treyhune with the file. The old biddy wouldn't pay him a dime and might sue.

He raced up the stairs, barely speaking to the schnoodle who tangled in his legs trying for attention and then retreated to the couch with an offended sigh. Mac grabbed the file, ruffled through it to make sure he had it all and then tore toward the door.

He could feel reproachful eyes branding against his back as he skidded to a halt and touched the doorknob. He turned.

"Aw, come on, amigo. Don't look so sad. I'll be back in a flash with the cash." He grinned at the dog, waiting for an appreciative grin at his poetic wit under stress, but the dog stared ahead in lofty dignity.

Big deal or no, he couldn't walk on a buddy in such a black mood. No telling what the schnoodle might do to retaliate. Mac walked to the couch and sat down beside him.

"Hey fella, this is big time, see? We're talking mega bucks if I pull this thing off but timing is crit-i-cal." He drew the word out to be sure the pooch understood. "We *need* this one and I can't take you with me. I gotta hurry—besides Mrs. Treyhune hates anything smaller than herself."

Herr Schnoodle pretended to be indignant for a dot longer and then laid his wiry head along Mac's shoulder. He understood, his round yellowish eyes said.

Mac patted him and made for the door. If he opened it and saw Darcy . . . it was all over.

The hallway was empty. He raced into the street. No time for economy today—he yelled for a cab. This better pay off, three cabs in one day was not an exhilarating experience. Any kind of meter made him nervous.

Jumping from the cab in front of the fancy entrance to

the Treyhune condo, Mac showed his ID at the door. He had come up with a butler's phony union card for visiting her, since Mrs. T didn't even want the doorman to know she had hired a PI. The doorman buzzed, spoke a moment in low whispers and then motioned for Mac to go on up.

He took the elevator to the penthouse and the maid let him in. The door swooshed closed behind with the familiar feeling of being hermetically sealed in a complete microworld. From rumors and what he pieced together, Mrs. T hadn't left the premises in years.

Everything in the place solidified into polished perfection. Old—but perfect. Rare antiques that would have made Southeby's drool with pleasure. Rich paintings of soft, voluptuously overfed women lined the walls. There was probably half an art gallery in here. Mac became more uneasy by the minute. Where was the woman?

He heard a rustling sound from behind and turned to see her long, silk gown trailing behind her on the Persian carpet. A wonder the woman didn't electrocute herself with all the static she dragged along with her.

"Mr. McBee?" She looked over the little oblong glasses perching on the tip of her narrow nose. She said the name like someone flicking a piece of spaghetti from a lapel.

"Mrs. Treyhune," he acknowledged politely. She gestured toward a loveseat that didn't look as if it would hold up under a mosquito landing. He sat down carefully and spread his files on the teakwood coffee table before him.

"Here's all the proof necessary for—whatever you had in mind."

"Indeed?" She threw him a searching glare and although she didn't wear a lorgnette, he imagined it perched on the end of her nose. She didn't bother to glance inside the file, but snapped it closed tightly as if it offended her. She rang a little silver bell and her maid hurried in, as if she had stationed herself outside the door.

"I assume a personal check will be acceptable." Without waiting for his answer she motioned for the maid to bring the checkbook and then dismissed the young woman peremptorily. Mrs. T wrote out the check and then ripped it in precise little movements from the large book on the coffee table.

He returned her stare until she looked away first.

"If that is all, you may go."

No, it wasn't all. He hadn't told her of Treyhune's appearance at the airport which signaled his immediate and possibly final departure.

It was then McBee made one of his irrevocable decisions.

He wasn't going to tell her. He had done his job by squealing on the other love nests. Done his job so well that Mrs. T could claim a big chunk of her husband's financial empire. That should be enough to satisfy her.

Darcy would gain the fallout after the stuff hit the fan, which would happen when Mr. Treyhune's corporations and holdings discovered he skipped town.

"Thanks, it has been a pleasure." He lied. Clicking his heels together in his best Peter Gunn manner, he beat it out the door with his check before she of the frozen face could change her mind. He wouldn't be happy until he ran to her bank to cash it.

On the way home from the bank he bought two steaks. Tomorrow he'd go to Mr. Steinmetz and pay what he could toward keeping Jesse Rodriguez busy. He especially hoped to convince the boy he should get his teeth taken care of.

After that, a couple of payments toward the Spaceman's room and board, and oh, what the hey—maybe he should ask Smitty about helping Mrs. Rodriguez with her operation. It was only money—wasn't it?

Mac winced at the treachery of his thoughts.

He stopped for a moment and tallied up. He had nearly spent the big fee before he even got home. Jeez, he was getting soft, no doubt. But so what? He could spend it on only so much foolishness, such as rent and food. He tilted his head and laughed at the murky sky above.

What a good day to be alive.

Apple Sally came to mind along with an urge to search for her to share their celebration. No, he was tired of conversation, tired of people. He wanted to take off his shoes and tie and collapse—a quiet evening with the schnoodle was all he asked. The puzzle of Apple Sally would have to wait for another day.

16

Mac was sipping his third cup of black coffee when Darcy pushed through the front door without knocking. The mug twisted spastically in his hand and he set it on the table.

"Morning." He motioned to the coffeepot on the hot plate, but she shook her head. She appeared ticked off.

"Finished your gig with Treyhune?" she asked.

"How'd you know?" No use to deny it. Too late for that now.

"You're a shit, McBee. A real shit." She threw her shoulder bag toward the couch and missed. It landed in a heap on the floor.

"Don't do that!" he shouted. Too late. Herr Schnoodle moved as fast as lightning when he had a mission. He sat back with a happy grin while Mac dabbed at the dripping case with a paper towel.

"Bad dog! Shame on you," Mac scolded.

"Never mind the damn dog. I wanted to know what you were working on, but no, you couldn't level with me. I should have guessed a holdout, but didn't figure you had that much smarts. This would have been the story of my career."

"Hey, I'm sorry. I had a job to do, too. No way Treyhune's wife was going to pay for their life story splattered all over the front page of your paper."

"Well, maybe . . ." she conceded, still obviously miffed.

"How'd you find out?" he asked again.

She grinned, white teeth setting off her tawny complexion. "Hey, hey, hey. Does a reporter reveal her sources?" She laughed at his puzzled expression.

"I'm kidding. I've got a contact who owns that building Treyhune's girlfriend lives in—lived in," she corrected. "I finally uncovered who you were tailing and put two and two together. But I was too late. That doesn't happen to me often."

Darcy couldn't have been aware of Treyhune's other girlfriends or she'd still have her story. Maybe Number One didn't know about them, either. He considered dropping the information in Darcy's lap and then decided not to. It pleased him to think of Albert Treyhune and Number One forsaking all others and living happily ever after. It might not happen that way, but it wouldn't be his fault.

He was getting soft.

"What are you going to do with what you found?" he wanted to know.

She shrugged.

He loved it when she did that, everything under her T-shirt seemed to change positions. He considered asking her out, but decided she might laugh at him.

Drawing a deep breath, he started. "I'll tell you about it—at least some. Come to dinner one night."

She fielded his move and sidestepped adroitly. "By now the boss has probably changed his mind about spying on you and forgot to mention it to me."

He hoped not. Sometimes she could be a pain with her snooping, but he would miss her. "About Apple Sally . . . I think you'd better back off, you're beginning to bug her."

"Great! That's how I get the juiciest stories. Stir people up, catch them off guard and things begin to move."

He'd better keep that in mind. "Yeah, but she's getting peeved. You said yourself she's got connections."

"I know, I know." Darcy waved a slim hand with long, lacquered nails. "The mafia and all that jazz. That's exactly what intrigues me. How did a loser like Apple Sally come by the Swede's protection?"

The schnoodle had raised his head, interest piquing when the name Apple Sally came up. His head turned from Mac to Darcy, like a spectator at a tennis match.

"Cool it, little buddy. You'll get terminal whiplash by keeping that up," Mac cautioned. "As for you, your Ladyship, I don't regard her as a loser. All of us have been down on our luck a time or two."

Herr Schnoodle laid his head on the couch and put one paw over his nose and ear as if shutting off their voices.

Even Darcy laughed at that one. "Yeah, that was uncalled for."

"Is it too much to imagine that there probably isn't a shred of mystery in the woman? I mean, this Olson character probably felt sorry for her and . . ."

"Yeah, and I'm nominated for a Pulitzer, too."

Such cynicism in one so young.

"What else have you uncovered so far—if anything?"

She pursed her lips and he tried to look away, but couldn't. He imagined their soft fullness beneath a warm kiss. It boggled the mind.

"I'll let you know," she promised casually. "I may need help."

What a switch. He grew heady with success and neglected his usual caution. "Want to go to dinner?" he asked again. "Tonight?"

Herr Schnoodle growled.

She turned her gaze to meet his for a long minute, and he felt like he was drowning in a sea of coffee. Black coffee with the merest hint of cream, the color of her eyes. He looked away first.

"Can't. Not tonight."

He got up and poured another cup. He hadn't left the hot plate on and the coffee was cold, but he put it to his lips, pretending.

"How's tomorrow night?" she offered.

He looked away, striving to hide the boyish elation he felt surge through his body. Come on now, he scolded himself. What's the biggie about a dinner date?

It was then he remembered his appointment to show Apple Sally the new park he'd found while he was on the Treyhune case. Damn! He had no idea how long that would take. She may want to put down her blanket and have a picnic. He couldn't take a chance on being late to meet Darcy. He knew better than to ever welch on a date with her. Better to cancel up front.

What if Darcy never gave him another chance? All he asked for—dreamed of—was one date. One date to see if she could possibly find something of interest in him. He planned to pull out all the stops—be his debonair best, the whole *schmegegga*. He'd take her to one of those overpriced steak houses, not the usual pizza place. He didn't owe Apple Sally anything—did he?

He pictured Apple Sally standing on that corner tomorrow, waiting. A tough corner, but she was used to the streets, wasn't she?

She was also used to getting dumped on by the world.

"Ah . . . I'm afraid that's impossible," he heard himself say. "Got an appointment I can't break." He hoped his eyes didn't reflect his torment while he waited, holding his heartbeat to a steady thousand beats a minute by sheer willpower.

"Okay. Next evening. How's that?"

He breathed a sigh that lifted him out of his loafers.

"Fine. Want me to pick you up somewhere?"

She shook her head, the fine, silky hair fell across her

face and she brushed it back impatiently. "No, I don't think so. Buses don't run by my house."

It wasn't until the door closed behind her that he realized she got the parting shot.

"Damn, Schnoodle! I let her zing me on that one. I'm slipping."

The dog turned away, disapproval showing in every hair of his body, making McBee grateful that Herr Schnoodle couldn't talk.

That afternoon he took the schnoodle to the park to get away from looking at four walls and the boob tube. Mac leaned back on the park bench and regarded the people passing.

"A strange assortment in a city, eh boy?" He patted the dog on the bench next to him. Looking at the schnoodle, he broke into laughter. "If I found a beat-up hat and stuck a cigar in your mouth, you'd give some morning wino quite a turn, sitting there like King Fruit." Herr Schnoodle's teeth showed briefly under the mop of whiskers, and for a wild moment Mac imagined that he understood every word and laughed, too.

Any minute Mac expected to hear Apple Sally's cart squealing down the pathway. The dog sat alert, waiting.

"I wonder what Darcy's got up her sleeve?" He spoke aloud to the dog, and only a few people passing turned their heads to look. That's why he loved the city. Small-towners claimed it was a cold, callous place, but he knew better. It was full of people going their own way and minding their own business. They didn't break stride to see him talking to his dog on a park bench.

"Which is only right, what say, old boy?"

The schnoodle regarded Mac with crazy, gold-dotted

eyebrows raised and a foolish expression of happiness. Mac dug a bone from his jacket pocket.

They had chili dogs for lunch, Schnoodle didn't fancy the sauerkraut. They both had Cokes. "No beers in public. There's probably some law against it," he explained in the face of Herr Schnoodle's indignation.

"We could go to The Cave this afternoon. Tomorrow we don't know how long we'll be with your little friend." Mac didn't want to say the name Apple Sally out loud, thinking of all the flying pigeon fallout. Recalling his conversation with Darcy, excitement stirred him. Gads, he felt like a teenager on his first date. If he didn't cool it, he'd never make any points with her.

He had a difficult time sleeping that night, so he stayed up late watching reruns of *Magnum P.I.*

The next afternoon Mac and the schnoodle walked toward the corner where Apple Sally was to meet them. She was already there. Herr Schnoodle bounded up, nearly bowling her over. McBee was relieved to see she'd left her cart.

"You bums are late. I figured you'd changed your mind. This is a lousy corner to wait on. I nearly got picked up three times."

By what? The garbage truck? He wanted to tease but then felt ashamed. What gave him the right to be judgmental? She always seemed clean in spite of the array of garments she covered herself with. Today she wore her usual boots and he caught a glimpse of jeans-clad legs beneath her long dresses. Funny how he forgot to look around and check out if anyone watched them anymore.

After she knelt on the pavement and cuddled the dog, they began their walk.

17

For the next couple of weeks McBee decided to take it easy. "We earned a rest from this hectic schedule of ours, didn't we, boy?"

Herr Schnoodle sniffed pointedly, as if reminding his master that weeks before he had bemoaned the monotony of his PI career.

Mac frowned and put more syrup on his pancakes. They came frozen and ready to pop in the toaster, but they weren't half bad. Sort of like maple-flavored sawdust.

"I wonder what happened to Apple Sally?"

As usual the mention of her name made the dog raise his dots of gold eyebrows and bark.

Teasing a little, Mac continued, "We don't know where Darcy is, either. Doesn't that bother you?"

The dog jumped from his chair across the table from Mac, plopping on the floor and crossing his two paws in front of him. He laid his chin in the middle of his paws and glared up reproachfully. "Go on, spoil my day," his look said.

Mac laughed at Herr Schnoodle's familiar reaction to Darcy's name. "You're jealous, amigo. No need to be. She wouldn't notice me if I was an ice-cream cone in the middle of the Sahara. Our date is a pity date, I'm sure of that."

Someone knocked on the door. Since it didn't push in, he felt a fledgling disappointment. It wasn't Darcy.

"Come in, it's not locked."

Before the door cracked, Herr Schnoodle began barking

and prancing as if the building were on fire. He hurled himself against the door, and Apple Sally's laugh echoed in the hallway.

"I can't open it."

Mac lifted the dog away from the door long enough to let Apple Sally push through. The schnoodle turned himself inside out for attention, twining around her legs, tripping her.

Finally, she gave up and sprawled in the middle of the floor, her long dress spread out, the crazy hat askew from the dog's knocking against her. She grabbed and held his wriggling form while patting and talking gently, calming him. At last the dog settled between her knees and closed his eyes with a satisfied grin on his face.

"Well! Quite a greeting," Mac said. "I admit a small twinge of jealousy." More than a twinge—a stab in the heart with a rusty butter knife.

"Aw, no need for that. Dogs and kids take to me for some reason."

He hadn't seen her for a couple of weeks and didn't realize how much he missed her. The flood of relief at her being alive and in one piece was totally unexpected.

"You haven't been around. I've—I've been worried."

She took off her hat and tossed it on the couch. "Mind if I get up, pard?" she addressed the dog. "This is undignified to say the least."

Mac agreed, but kept it to himself. He tried to picture Darcy R sitting in the middle of the floor and letting Herr Schnoodle maul her with sloppy kisses.

Impossible to even imagine.

She stood, brushing her thick bunch of clothing as if it were tailored linen. "Mind if I sit?" She pointed to the couch where her hat lay.

" 'Course not. Want some breakfast? Got some left."

She looked pointedly at the discarded box of brown-and-serve pancakes still sitting on the table. "No thanks. Bet the box is tastier, why not eat that?"

"Oh yeah, I forgot you're such a health addict." He hated it when she turned out right.

"Let's not quarrel, Alexander. I came to ask a favor."

"Sure. What's on your mind?" She had expertly changed the subject of where she'd been, but he was onto her now and let it go.

"This Darcy person who works for that awful gossip paper? The one who wears her clothes as if she grew out of them before puberty?"

"What about her, and don't be catty."

"Yeah, I suppose that was a cheap shot. Anyway, I want you to make her get off my case. I'm going to have to stuff that woman in a shopping cart and send her over the edge of the pier if she doesn't quit snooping around and following me. What's the dame want? Did you tell her anything?"

"Hold on a minute," Mac protested, stalling for time to marshal his thoughts. He'd never been a good liar. He pushed away from the table and moved behind his desk. It offered a modicum of protection if she became violent. Right now her face was the same color as her hair, and she looked ready to explode.

He visualized hundreds of wiry red corkscrews of hair scattering around his office mixed with the ton of material that she wore as clothing. No, he couldn't let her detonate in here, they would suffocate. He grinned at the picture.

"What's so damned funny?" she snarled.

"Nothing personal," he hastened to assure her. "An odd notion crossed my mind."

He wondered if it was possible to get through to her

when she was in such a belligerent mood.

"I wouldn't put a hand on Darcy, if I were you," he cautioned. "She's streetwise and can handle herself pretty good, I'd imagine."

"Oh sure, defend her, I knew it."

"I don't think she's following you." Another lie. Not fair. "That's the most ridiculous, egocentric idea I've ever heard." Go ahead, pile it on. "Anyway, I don't have a thing to say about what this reporter does. She and I are barely on speaking terms. Not that I wouldn't like to change that," he couldn't resist adding.

"I bet!" She began to pleat the hem of the cloth jacket she wore, her fingers folding and unfolding the material in an agitated manner.

"What makes you suspect she's tailing you?"

She patted the dog who gravitated between the two of them, changing positions every few minutes. "Could I have a drink of water?"

She sounded so pathetic, he hastened to get it before she burst into tears.

After she gulped it down she brushed the back of her hand across her lips and sighed. "The woman asks all kinds of questions behind my back. They tell me. They don't like it much, either."

"They" meaning her fellow streeties, he imagined.

"She asks a lot of questions. She followed me around for weeks," Mac hedged.

"But why is she interested in *me?*"

He shrugged. "She mentioned once that she thought you weren't a real street person. I guess she's curious."

"That's none of her damn business!" She hit a small fist into a sofa pillow as if it had been Darcy's nose. "There's no mystery—absolutely none. I am what I am. Period."

"I don't think so," Mac said quietly. He watched the expressions moving across her face. "She got me thinking in that direction—that you're no street person. You're hiding something. If you've got a problem, maybe we could help."

"*I* have a problem?" she shouted. "I don't have a problem—*you* have one. It's called 'Darcy-itus.' She's pushy and nosy and you want to impress her. No one gives a damn about me."

He flushed. She always cut to the chase.

"You sure know how to hurt a guy."

Apple Sally grinned, a small dimple showing in her smooth cheek.

He stared. Dimples had always been his weakness, strangely erotic. He thought of that lack in Darcy's golden cheek, the only flaw in otherwise perfection.

"Well? Did I leave some lunch on the tip of my nose or what?" she demanded.

So much for that. "Does it matter?" he retorted. They couldn't see eye to eye over the alphabet, why did he bother talking to her?

"Alexander, I don't have a problem. Believe me, I'm . . . I'm happy the way my life is going. I don't have a care in the world. My husband is dead, my stepson is dead—my life's an open book. I'm not hiding anything."

"Maybe," he conceded. The more she talked, the more he was convinced along with Darcy that something didn't wash here. He hesitated—ashamed to admit to her that he finally discovered she came from Boston.

She'd spoken once when they first met of the park they sat in as being nice—just like Franklin Park—and the wharves nearby, and then he'd caught her mention of somewhere called Logan. That seemed like a long time ago, but he'd tucked it away in his memory as not important at the time. Franklin Park, waterfront, Logan Airport were in Boston according to Darcy.

He watched Apple Sally playing with Schnoodle. Mac's thoughts wandered back two days when he had Joe and his buddy Earl check with the police computer at the precinct.

They had rolled it back until they discovered an entry for a year ago. An explosion and fire, two deaths reported although there had been questions. Only charred body parts had been found, and the deaths could not be confirmed. One female, name of Selena Duvall, had been sent to Boston General Hospital with a concussion and possible internal injuries.

Darcy had volunteered to go to Boston to check with the hospital and newspaper records. McBee might have done it, but how could he leave Herr Schnoodle? Never mind that he'd never left New York and had never wanted to. He wasn't afraid, he told himself over and over. It was just that he and his father had agreed on something. With everything right here in the city, why go anywhere else?

True to her word, Darcy had brought back copies of the microfilmed records from the newspaper. Not much, a paragraph on a back page and dated two days later —two brief obituaries.

Mac and Darcy had sat looking over the papers, Mac getting as close to her as possible with the table leg in the way of his chair. He liked the way the fallout from the lightbulb hanging over the table glinted off her cream-colored hair.

Looking at the old records in the paper, there were still a lot of questions that remained unanswered. Odd there were no traces of the boy. Police identified a partial dental plate as the husband's. It was made of a special alloy found in Europe, nearly indestructible. Also they found a man's gold medallion buried under a pile of debris, protecting it from meltdown. Police blamed the lack of residue on the extent of the explosion, but it was most unusual.

How did the woman get to the front yard before the house exploded?

Mac had already checked all the insurance companies in the area; he dreaded to think of his phone bill next month. No insurance policies issued to any Duvall. Darcy suggested he trace the real estate agent who closed the deal on the house. The agent did remember the family, he remembered reading of the explosion afterward, too. They had barely moved into the house, paid cash for it. No strings leading back to their past whatsoever.

Apple Sally demanded his attention, jerking McBee back to the present.

"What? My mind wandered, sorry."

"That happens a lot with you, Alexander. Too soon for your second childhood."

"Yeah, I guess." He had to get his thoughts away from the subject. It wasn't time to confront her with the information he and Darcy had dug up. Not until he had all the facts. Darcy had better keep her word and not print anything until they all had a talk.

"I want you to meet a friend of mine." Spur of the moment ideas seldom worked. He rarely made a habit of it.

"Who and why?" Her voice reeked of suspicion.

"Aw, I dunno. I might contact some white-slave traders and lure you into their clutches. Then they could spirit you off to some Arab's harem where you could drive him nuts instead of me."

She brushed a stray lock of wiry hair back from her cheek and grinned. "Okay, I'm sorry. Who do I meet?"

"I hoped you and Mr. Steinmetz might hit if off. He's a

gentleman. One of the endangered species. With a fascinating collection of plants he looks upon as his family and
furnishings any museum would be tickled to own. You'd
like him."

She fidgeted. "Well, could be—sometime. I didn't say I
needed any more friends, did I? Right now, I'm . . . I'm too
busy." She lifted her small, pointed chin in the air and
glared at him.

"Hey! Don't get your back up. Would it hurt to take
time from your busy schedule to pay a lonely, old man a
visit?"

He tried to keep the feeling of satisfaction at bay as she
gave a sigh that seemed to come all the way from her toes.

"I suppose I could," she said ungraciously. "When?"

"How's tomorrow? Me and the schnoodle here, we
closed a real case a while back, we even got paid." He ruffled the dog's ears gently.

"Wow! And you're celebrating with frozen pancakes? A
real sport, Alexander."

He flushed and loosened his tie and collar.

"Why wear those gizmos?" she asked. "If I were a man I
wouldn't be caught dead in one." She pointed to his tie.

He raised an eyebrow and gazed at her with barely con-
cealed distaste. "There are undoubtedly a lot of things you
wouldn't be caught dead wearing," he said.

It was her turn to blush. "We always manage to end up
biting each other's heads off, don't we? Why's that, I wonder?"

"I don't know. Let's call a truce for now. I could send
for a pizza."

"No thanks." She made a wry face. "I think it's time I
moved on. We might meet tomorrow. Where?"

He mentioned a corner downtown and she nodded. "Do
we have to take a bus?"

"Why? Won't they allow your shopping cart on?"

Apple Sally stood and straightened her skirts. "Smart-ass! I hoped Herr Schnoodle could come with us."

"We need a chaperone?" He moved closer, looking down at the top of her head. Darcy's velvet-brown eyes were on the same level as his. Why did he compare the two women?

"No, we won't need a bus, if you don't mind a little walking. Are you watching your back?" He tried to keep his voice steady, but a thread of worry was unwinding in his chest, making his throat tight.

She hit him lightly on the shoulder with her fist. "Aw, you're a real worrywart, Alexander. The last killing was way out in Queens, or so I heard."

"Another red-headed street person," he reminded her.

Apple Sally leaned up on tiptoe and kissed his cheek, such a brief contact he thought afterward he'd imagined it. "She was wearing a wig, that didn't count," she retorted.

After she left, he sat a long time staring into space with the dog curled up next to him. He tried to call forth his usual daydreams that included Darcy's face, but Apple Sally kept getting in the way.

Damn women, anyway. He should know enough by now to let them alone. His father hadn't married his mother until in his late thirties, his uncle Jeff never had married, no wonder bachelorhood came so easy. Who needed a woman around to complicate things, spend money on and generally cause problems?

18

The day was as bright as the city haze permitted when they walked up to Apple Sally. Herr Schnoodle tried to sniff every tree, flower and weed he came to. Since there weren't that many on a city street, he nearly turned himself inside out when he did find something.

To tell the truth she looked pretty good. She still wore a hat, a Sunday version of her Wyatt Earp special. Her hair was patted down, somewhat neat underneath and she seemed thinner, dainty almost. As if she'd removed a few layers of clothing. The top layer was always clean. He couldn't fault her for that.

"You look great," he said truthfully.

"Thanks. So do you. Especially without that tie; I like that. Looks more human."

His eyebrow quirked upward in amusement. How could he ever know with this one if he received a compliment or not?

"Your dog isn't particular where he spreads his wealth, is he?" Apple Sally giggled.

"No. Quantity versus quality was never a big decision with the schnoodle."

They stopped by Mr. Bertoldi's and Mac started to introduce them and paused in confusion. What should he call her? He felt ridiculous.

"How's everything?" he stalled for time, thinking.

"Everyting fine," the paunchy storekeeper boomed. "You bring a sweetheart?" His whisper loud enough to be heard in Jersey.

"No. She's just a friend." He wondered at the funny look he caught on her face.

She walked closer to the grocer, looked up at him and offered her hand. "I'm called Apple Sally. I'm a bag lady," she said proudly. She leaned back to look at Bertoldi.

"Bee-utiful . . . a little skinny . . . but bee-utiful."

He sounded like a scratchy 78 record. This was the phony who claimed to hate street people.

"How's Jesse working out?" Mac asked in order to pry him away from devouring Apple Sally with his eyes. Okay, so Bertoldi was a widower and all that, but did he have to drool? Mac decided not to mention it. He'd seen the grocer step in to catch a kid swiping an apple—never had he seen raw bulk move at such speed. He edged back; his thoughts might be too transparent.

"What? Oh, the kid. Fine. Good. Mr. Steinmetz, he loves the kid." He never took his stricken gaze from Apple Sally.

"I guess we'd better move along. We're going to pay them a visit. I want to show my friend here some of the plants and antiques."

"So soon? You just got here. How about a good red apple? I find one the same color as your hair." He blew his breath on one and shined it with his apron, handing it to her as if it had been a diamond.

"Thank you, Mr. Bertoldi. That's very sweet." She smiled and dipped a little curtsy.

"No!" he protested. "Call me Rudolfo, please." He turned to glare at Mac, daring him to laugh.

"That's a wonderful name, Mr. . . . ah, Rudolfo. I'll bet your mother adored Valentino when you were born."

"See?" He turned in triumph toward McBee. "Dis girl, she's no dummy. First person ever figured that out. Mama, she love the movies."

Funny, he'd never regarded Bertoldi as having a mama or even a first name.

"Excuse yourself and let's go before he asks you to marry him," Mac whispered in her ear. She smelled good up close, not perfumey, but clean, like some kind of soap or shampoo.

On the street again, she put the apple in her skirt pocket.

"That's quite a conquest. I've never seen Bertoldi—pardon me—Rudolfo, act so . . ."

"Oh, Alexander, you make me tired! Don't joke about him, he's first-rate."

"Yeah? Everyone on the street calls him Mr. Mean and Ugly. That's when they're being kind. He's a tyrant and terrifies all the kids."

"That's silly. Notice how many kids came into his store while we were there? They wouldn't do that if they were afraid of him. They'd find another store."

How'd she know so much? She was right and he knew it. Her observations made him see another side of the grocer, and it disturbed him that she'd seen it and he hadn't. She always could cut right to center, not hiding behind sarcasm like most people.

He wondered what Darcy would think about Rudolfo Bertoldi. He had to stop that. Why did he always compare the two women?

"When are you going to tell me more about yourself? Where you were born and where you went to school, any brothers and sisters . . ."

"Hold it, Alexander. You sound like a cop."

He grinned, pleased. "My pop and grandpop were. Why should that bother you? On the Ten Most Wanted List, are you?"

"Nutso!" She nudged him lightly in the ribs with her

elbow. "I thought I'd seen the city, but I've never walked in this part before."

No one did, unless he had a very good reason for being here.

As usual she switched subjects abruptly. He pretended not to notice.

"Oh! How quaint!" She stopped to look up at the hanging geraniums and orchids in front of the ancient brownstone.

Mr. Steinmetz had placed the bright flowers along the shabby fence. McBee thought he'd better have a talk with Jesse; that fence should have been painted by now.

"I never pictured it as quaint," he admitted. "It's unique, though. So's Mr. Steinmetz." They climbed the steps. "At first I wanted to keep the schnoodle outside. I'm always afraid his tail will rearrange the furniture some day, but the old man won't hear of it."

"A man after my own heart," she said. "Someone might steal him out here all alone."

"Mr. McBee! And Herr Schnoodle! Come in, come in!" Mr. Steinmetz met them at the door, his face folding into tiny pleats of pleasure.

"Ah, Mr. Steinmetz, good to see you again. I want to introduce a friend of mine—ah—Apple Sally." He wasn't going to worry because of her dumb name, if she wanted it to stick with her, welcome to it.

She took the huge, shiny apple out of her handbag and offered it to Steinmetz. He laughed.

McBee had never heard him laugh before. It sounded squeaky, like a rusty gate opening.

Herr Schnoodle sat in a corner, seeming to know his tail endangered everything in the crowded room, including Mr. Steinmetz.

"How's Jesse doing?" Mac managed to suppress a grin as he watched Apple Sally. She had removed her hat. Her hair sprang around her head—a burning brush fire. She really was a dead ringer for Orphan Annie.

He had to walk away, holding back the laughter, when the old man said, "I'm certain I know you from somewhere. You look so familiar."

"Jesse?" Mac prompted when he regained composure.

"Oh, the boy is so much help. He's with his mother now. She had her operation and it came out fine. Thanks to you, Jesse is getting his teeth fixed. Mr. Bertoldi went with him to the dentist, what you might say an enforcer."

Both Apple Sally and Mac laughed at his attempt to use street terminology.

"I'm sure Mrs. Rodriguez made a bead for you on her rosary," Mr. Steinmetz said.

From the corner of his eye Mac caught Apple Sally's puzzled look and hurried to change the subject. If the word got around that he was a soft touch, no telling who would put the bite on him next.

Mr. Steinmetz gave them the grand tour. The rooms were pleasant once a person conquered the overwhelming feeling of being a hostage captured by terrorist plant life and extinct furniture. Mac listened to Steinmetz and Apple Sally talk and realized with some shock that they discussed paintings and music as if they had been friends for years.

He and the schnoodle went outside and sat on the steps. It was another half hour before the pair missed them. By then Mr. Steinmetz had cookies and tea ready, and Apple Sally poured as if she were the queen.

"I'm glad you enjoy each other's company," Mac said dryly.

"Oh, I'm so tickled you brought me here. He reminds

me of my grandfather so much it's uncanny. He died when I was seven." A look of wonder came across her face.

A chink in her armor? Well, well.

They ate their cookies, drank the tea, and afterwards Mac struggled out of the couch. "The schnoodle and I have got to be moving along. Joe wants to see me at the precinct house. Maybe he's got another case."

"So soon?" Mr. Steinmetz looked around at his clocks as if they had all betrayed him. "Time moves so quickly. It seems as if you had just arrived."

"Run along, Alexander. I'll stay here and visit a while longer."

"Sure you'll be okay when you leave?"

She blew her lips together in annoyance, the little sound speaking volumes. "I'll be fine."

He was glad to escape.

As long as he was in the neighborhood, might as well go to the Y and pay a couple of months' rent for the Spaceman. It wasn't that the fellow couldn't be trusted, but handling money was not his strong suit.

"He'll come up with some tidbit of gossip when I need it someday," Mac told the schnoodle. "I'm not getting soft, don't think it for a minute. This is strictly business."

The next day he awoke thinking of Darcy and their date. He went out for donuts and when he returned he saw the red light flashing on his answering machine. There was a call from Joe and one from Darcy. She couldn't make it, something came up and she asked for a rain check.

"Damn, Schnoodle! It's not fair. I've waited half a life to go out with a girl like that. I bet it's never going to happen." Mac read the last five editions of the evening paper that he had tossed aside. He dozed off and woke up in the afternoon with Herr Schnoodle licking his hand. The dog grinned at him and ran toward the refrigerator. He wanted a beer and lunch, easy to tell.

"I guess we could drown our sorrows." Mac popped a top, pouring the schnoodle's half in a widemouthed glass clipped from The Cave. He brought out a cold piece of pizza and they munched on it. He had stayed up too late last night watching a *Harry O* special with three episodes back to back. He loved *Harry O* almost as much as *Barnaby Jones* and *Peter Gunn*.

Women, who needed them?

As soon as Mac finished eating, he hightailed it over to the station. Joe seemed glad to see him.

"You're a hard man to get hold of," Joe shook hands with McBee and gestured toward a chair. "Mac, I got a problem. The captain says it's okay to use a private investigator if I trust him. Discreet—if you know what I mean. We gotta use finesse." He rolled the word around experimentally along the length of his tongue and sifted it through his big teeth.

Easy to guess the word came directly from the captain, not words Joe might choose.

"So, tell me about it." Mac settled back, figuring the tale would take a long time.

19

It took longer than McBee imagined to get the entire story pried out of Joe.

"I always wanted to say this, but isn't this a job for the FBI?"

"Nah, Mac, the corporation thinks this employee is stealing secret documents and selling them. The company doesn't want to call in the Feds unless it has to, stockholders and all that, ya know. We maybe could do the job with an undercover team, but I recommended you to the captain. The word is no publicity. I mean zilch."

The captain was usually a hog for publicity.

"We're talking about one of those big corporations. Megabucks—know what I mean?" Joe skirted close to the point he was making for a change, giving McBee an idea of how agitated he must be.

"The corporation don't want their guts spread all over the city, and they don't forget about the stockholders, no siree. Besides, our undercovers know all about dealing with pimps and pushers, not computer crooks. It's way out of our league."

He handed McBee a crumpled envelope.

"Our men tailed the suspect to a post office in Queens, and when he threw this away our guys grabbed it. Then the captain hauled our butts off the case. The corporation ought to give a big bonus for this if you help them solve the case. The guy's name is Quentin Royal."

McBee looked at the envelope postmarked Japan. He

couldn't make out the city and there was no return address. Someone probably had addressed it to Quentin Royal at his post office box in Queens. Part of the address label with the box number had been torn off.

"Know where this Quentin Royal lives?"

"Yep," Joe said, handing him a paper from inside his jacket pocket.

"Thanks, I appreciate your putting the captain on to me. Hang loose while I map my strategy and I'll call you, okay?" McBee said.

"This is a killer, Schnoodle," Mac confided to the dog later as they took a bench at the park. "This Quentin Royal geek works at the one of the biggest corporations in the city— in the United States. They think he's siphoning information off the main computer and sending it to a contact in Japan. Can you believe that? I thought we were stealing from *them*."

He leaned back and cracked three peanuts. One for the mutt, one for the pigeons and one for him.

"The way I see it, we can follow this Royal character all over the city—which could turn out darned expensive. Or we could wait until he picks up a drop at his post office. At least the undercovers got that much on him."

He considered a moment. "Joe says Royal probably rented a box under an assumed name because the cops have a warrant to check the post office and there's no box for Quentin Royal."

The schnoodle banged his tail on the bench in enthusiasm. He loved new cases. He snuggled against Mac's thigh, looking for another peanut. When it was not forthcoming, he barked sharply at a pigeon who strutted a little too close. The whole flock took off in a burst of feathers and flapping wings.

"I wish you wouldn't do that," McBee complained. "All that feather dust and whatnot flying through the air. Yech!"

Herr Schnoodle looked inordinately pleased with himself.

They spent the next five days waiting for the suspect to fold into a definite pattern, which he did—terminal dull. McBee's notes stated that the suspect went to work, caught the midtown bus home and stayed inside his apartment all night. Probably watching public television. Fridays he treated himself to a cab ride home.

Quentin Royal was a young, balding, three-piece-suited executive, with nothing to distinguish himself from the hundreds of others in the streets at rush hour. It was like watching an army of robots, all with the same bored expression, carrying their briefcases tucked under their arms or swinging them at their sides.

No wonder the poor nerd filched secret plans. Maybe he learned how to clone himself—churning out another several hundred business executives to set down on the streets, blending in even more. Holograms. McBee laughed at the idea and then sobered. It wasn't humorous, only sad. Really sad.

Quentin Royal, what a name. Sounded like Jell-O. The name fit him to a T.

"Joe says Royal usually goes to the post office on a Wednesday," Mac told the dog as they waited on a bench outside Royal's apartment house complex. Would he take a cab or a bus? Would he go on the subway?

It wasn't long before the quarry emerged from the door of his apartment, dressed the same as when he entered the day before, still clutching the briefcase.

Good, he ignored the speeding cabs and waited. A point in his favor, Mac decided.

Quentin sat at the far end of the bench. He eyed Herr

Schnoodle from underneath his lashes, as if the dog wouldn't notice he was being scrutinized. Finally the bus roared up and he hurried toward it.

"Aha! Number 38, Lincoln Park. Verrry interesting." That meant he might take the bus to the Triborough Bridge or to the subway that would take him right to Queens. Mac looked at his watch. "Next time you'll have to stay home so I can follow him." Odd he should check the post office box every week. Did that mean he lifted a little at a time from the computer? Hardly made sense.

Thursday passed and then Friday. Mac almost decided not to tail Quentin over the weekend. The man probably hibernated inside both days, working on his diabolical scheme for getting away with corporate raiding, or whatever they called it.

The guy was odd, simply because he was so unbelievably ordinary. He had to have a chink, a flaw somewhere. It called for more careful scrutiny. On second thought, he'd better devote an entire week on Royal. Herr Schnoodle had to stay home, as the dog did not blend well into the background.

Saturday morning Mac patted the schnoodle a hasty good-bye and hurried uptown. He had an idea Quentin didn't rise early when he wasn't working.

Earlier in the week Mac had noticed a group of gardeners busy around the building. He put on his blue, long-sleeved shirt and jeans and straightened the bright yellow hard hat he had purchased for the job. Strange, even gardeners wore hard hats now. What were they afraid of? Falling leaves heavy with smog and crud from the air? Maybe the union made it a law, so they could charge more.

The suspect strolled into the street around eleven a.m., looking the same as he did during the week, even to his ever-present briefcase.

Too bad Quentin hadn't emerged sooner. To keep his cover, Mac had trimmed a hedge almost down to ground level, replanted some potted flowers that didn't need it and dug around a rose bush until he accidentally cut something that looked suspiciously like a healthy root. He conceded that he might never learn the niceties of gardening.

When he spied Quentin, he laid down his clippers and followed behind the man for a while. No problem, with so many people on the sidewalk. PIs in small towns must have it rough. How do you tail some clown on an empty sidewalk? His correspondence course never went into that.

Quentin walked into a delicatessen while McBee waited outside. The smells tried to draw him inside, but he stayed firm. No need to blow his cover for lack of a Danish. Even this guy would surely notice him after a while. When Mac looked into the window and saw his reflection with the shiny yellow hard hat, he almost choked. He'd forgotten to remove it.

Mac took off the hat hastily and held it under his arm as he settled for a hot dog from a wheeled stand on the curb. He smothered it with sauerkraut and mustard, and then leaned against the building to eat.

In about half an hour Quentin came out, picking at a tooth with a fingernail. Mac felt that he prowled inside the guy's skin by now, figuring him down to his dark blue support hose. All the good PIs operated this way.

He thought of stashing the bright yellow hat under some brush at the apartment house, but frugality won. They soaked him $25.98 for that piece of disguise, darned if he wanted to leave it around so some kid could find it. Anyway, Quentin hadn't picked up on anyone following him.

The thing Mac noticed about impersonating service

people, it was like being invisible. A sad commentary on life, but then he didn't make the rules.

Suddenly Quentin did the unexpected, raising his hand to yell a greeting to someone. The gesture was so out of character that Mac swerved to look. When he turned back, the bus had come and gone—with Quentin on it.

He walked over to the trash can and threw in the yellow hat. "Damn!" he said out loud. "So much for master disguises. I wonder if the jerk knew I tailed him or just got cautious."

People looked at him and veered away to the other side of the walk. He forgot his partner wasn't standing by to listen. Here he stood, talking to himself. In his own neighborhood everyone did it, but apparently not here.

Bet the schnoodle wouldn't have fallen for this sophomoric trick.

He hadn't seen if his quarry boarded the #38 or not. Some detective. "A defective detective," the little voice sneered. He hadn't heard that inner voice nor suffered the self-inflicted wounds since Schnoodle came into his life.

Maybe it wasn't such a big deal, losing the fellow. After all it was Saturday, not Wednesday. It wasn't Quentin's day for making a drop or checking his box. His destination could be some park to play chess or a museum. With or without the voice, Mac knew his mistake was in being too smug and sure of himself, thinking he knew the fellow like the inside of his closet in only a week's time.

A grudging respect grew inside Mac as he thought of Quentin's unexpected street savvy. Did working with the schnoodle dull his own instincts as he grew to depend on the dog more and more?

"Nah," he said, kicking the side of the wire trash container. "A major fluke. I did the Treyhune case all alone, didn't I?" He turned an embarrassed grin at a couple of teenagers walking by who shot him odd looks.

He took a bus home. Over the pizza and beer he talked about it with Herr Schnoodle. It didn't add up. No way that guy spotted him. Why would he pull that stunt? Could it be his guilty conscience? For Joe's sake, he hoped so. He didn't want to mess this up.

"We could go to The Cave tonight. Smitty will be there and maybe the Spaceman, too." He threw Herr Schnoodle's plastic pork chop across the room so he could retrieve it. The dog zipped over the wooden floor, sliding on a rug.

Good thing there was only an empty warehouse beneath them. The dog sounded like a herd of buffalo running across the wooden floor. When he brought it back, he didn't relinquish the toy but lay close to McBee with his paws across it.

No, he'd pass on The Cave tonight. The idea of both Smitty and the Spaceman under the same roof was too much in his present mood.

He went to bed early, determined that the next week would be better. He would leave Quentin Royal alone for a day. Coming up with a Sunday disguise floored him.

He might try dressing as a priest, he'd never thought of that, then laughed at the thought.

"Anyway, I'd bet my last chance with Darcy that this one sleeps in all day and reads the *New York Times* from front to back. He probably works the crossword puzzle with a red pen, too."

The next morning McBee and Herr Schnoodle went to the park. McBee hoped to see Apple Sally, but she didn't show. He hoped the boss hadn't reassigned Darcy. He felt abandoned.

"Hey, old buddy, there's a *Thin Man* movie on TV this afternoon. Wanna see it?" He looked at the dog, the toothy grin was his answer. What a buddy, always ready to go along with a fellow's mood.

On Monday Mac started early in his natty insurance salesman suit, hat and dark glasses, blending in with all the junior executives headed for work. He oozed behind Quentin as he boarded the bus.

Mac melted in the crowd of swaying passengers, standing near the back door and pretending to read his folded paper. He hurried off at the same stop and watched his quarry open a heavy bronze door. The sign in gold leaf on the window stated the building to belong to the Computer Technological Enterprises. Mac followed, letting the door whoosh close behind his heels.

The lobby was huge and circular, with computers tucked into every available space. Men and women clicked the keys—robots, engrossed in their work. Nobody glanced in his direction. Monday morning was hectic everywhere in the city. He had counted on that.

He watched as a suited man nodded to the receptionist and removed a plastic credit card from his wallet.

No, it wasn't a credit card, Mac corrected his first impression. It fit into a slot in front of a bank of elevators, letting the door open for him. He disappeared inside while Mac watched the eleventh-floor indicator light.

"May I help you?" The receptionist finally noticed him, calling from across the room. He turned and she focused an absentminded almost-smile in his direction. He wondered if she really was a robot. He shook his head and left.

Well, no problem there. The guy went to work Monday morning, as did all the thousands of other computer experts. He could try to finagle some way to get inside, but why bother? If the insiders had watched and were unable to catch him at his spying, then he had to go for another angle.

The post office drop had to be the best gamble.

20

To avoid the chance of a confrontation, McBee waited until Wednesday to follow Quentin Royal again. The schnoodle wriggled with glee when he saw Mac putting on his undercover clothes. He knew a case when he saw the disguise and clearly wanted in on it.

Mac tugged at the greasy-looking wig and shrugged his shoulders into a worn leather jacket. He looked in the mirror and as a last thought, tied a blue kerchief as a band across his forehead. He straightened his reflective, rimless sunglasses and studied his image, undecided if he resembled a punk Willie Nelson or a member of the Bushwacker gang, which is what he aimed for. The penned cross in the web between his thumb and forefinger was a neat touch, a Bushwacker tattoo.

He turned to the dog. "How about it, mutt? Don't I look like a member of the gang?"

The schnoodle barked in answer.

"Do you always have to get in the last word?" Mac chided as he tugged on the brim of his cap.

Maybe he did present an over-the-hill Bushwacker, but the wig and glasses made a darned unique disguise, he consoled his image.

"Don't be persnickety, it doesn't become you," he scolded the dog. "I'll pass inspection as long as no one gets too close."

He patted the schnoodle's head. "Guess I'll have to solve this on my own, old buddy. No way I can take you along without someone spotting me. The guy's a lot smarter than we gave him credit for."

He closed the door firmly behind him, trying not to notice the dog's crestfallen look. No one he had ever met could have perfected that look of disappointment better than the schnoodle.

The late-afternoon traffic thinned by the time he reached the bus stop. He glanced at his watch, hoping he hadn't misjudged the man again. Quentin lived his life by some inner time schedule, completely precise in his movements. He caught the three p.m. bus last Wednesday, and it followed he would this Wednesday.

Sure enough, he stepped out of his apartment building, the briefcase in his grasp. Could be he didn't trust leaving it behind? Did that mean he suspected someone watched him? It would explain a lot. Maybe he carried the stolen computer stuff in the case and mailed it a little at a time to his source in Japan, getting paid for it as he went along.

Mac sat in the rear of the bus, several seats behind Quentin. The coach was crowded, but nobody chose the seat next to him. Of course—who would dare sit that close to a Bushwacker? He leaned back and sprawled over both seats, warming to his cover.

At the mall, Quentin left by the front door as Mac dropped from the rear. Mac sauntered along behind Quentin, blending in as best he could. This was plainly not a Bushwacker's bailiwick, and he felt like a Doberman at a poodle show.

Wrong disguise—but how could he have known? When you think of Queens, you think Bushwacker.

Quentin headed right for the row of boxes inside the post office. Mac lagged well behind, feeling that his disguise made him more and more conspicuous.

Quentin stood behind a tall section of boxes, making it

impossible to see which row, never mind which box number, only that it was close to the floor. As he finished and left, Mac hurried over, but all the boxes looked the same. Damn! Now what was he going to do?

Running out the door in time to see his prey crawl into a taxi, Mac sighed in resignation and hailed one right behind. Gads, at least he got to say again those wonderful words every PI on TV mouthed.

"Follow that cab—and don't lose it."

After a while, Mac began to wonder where this impulse would take him. After all, the captain wouldn't pay expenses and the corporation paid a flat fee. This taxi stuff had to stop.

"The gent you're following might be going for the airport," the driver commented.

Oh boy, not yet. He didn't have enough goods to stop him. What if Quentin planned to leave the country?

The cab in front stopped while Mac pondered his options. It wasn't the airport. It was the front gate of Aqueduct Race Track.

How could he tail anyone in that crowd? Sighing, he drew back into the cab and counted his expenses like beads on a rosary. No way was he going to try to connect with buses this far from home. It would take a zillion transfers. The thought had also crossed his mind that he might meet some actual Bushwackers.

Now Mac knew how the fellow spent his ill-gotten gains. Anyone going to Aqueduct on a weekday afternoon—alone—had to be a gambler with a capital G. The bookies had their hooks into him, no doubt of that.

He almost felt sorry for the guy. Almost.

Mac moped around the office all day. Even Herr

Schnoodle couldn't cheer him. When Joe called to ask how things were going, Mac told him okay. Hah! He might as well give up. No use following Quentin on Wednesdays unless he figured some plan to get his box number. Saturday afternoons bugged him. The dude looked the same, briefcase and all.

That was it! Now he knew what bothered him.

Mac closed his eyes and mentally reviewed the briefcase Quentin carried last. They weren't the same. Saturday's was larger, darker, a small, flat *suitcase*.

Maybe he finally cracked the fatal flaw that gave away most criminals. At least his father had worked with this theory.

It was hard to wait for Saturday. This time McBee put on his termite inspection coveralls and pulled the bill of his cap down over his eyes. The fake mustache itched like the dickens, but it changed his looks one hundred percent.

Watching *Magnum* on the tube had tempted Mac once to try to grow a mustache, but in a few weeks he had abandoned that project. The hairs over his lips came out like steel wool and a funny reddish color, part of his Scottish heritage, he supposed. He didn't want to resemble an Airedale.

"It's a shame what they don't include in the correspondence school, old boy," he said, clicking his heels together and standing for inspection.

He felt cheered by the dog's attention. "I got all this disguise business locked down from *Rockford* and those guys. I should have concentrated on them and saved the money from the school."

Herr Schnoodle whined, begging to go.

"Hey, I want to take you, fella. It just isn't possible. This guy's no dummy like we thought. He'd recognize you the second time out. I'll let you in on the next case, I promise."

In spite of the metal canister, hose and nozzle he had to carry, Mac finally reached Quentin's. What was so unusual about an exterminator carrying his equipment on the bus? The riders who didn't stare at him moved well away. He supposed people were always cranky in the mornings—he was.

Mac worked around the apartment slowly, with the empty canister strapped on and the nozzle with the hose pointing down. He circled the apartment twice and still no Quentin. Maybe he already left.

"Hey buddy. What's going on?"

McBee hoped the voice wasn't aimed at him. No such luck.

"I'm the termite man."

"No kidding. I guess that's what it says on your shirt, too." The man facing him wore a baggy pair of trousers and navy blue suspenders over a white T-shirt with his stomach edging over his waistline. He had thrown on a jacket in a hurry to come outside and hadn't bothered to comb his hair.

"You the manager?" If it was the owner, he was sunk.

"Sure as hell am. I didn't call you." The fellow had a belligerent bulldog look.

Mac sized him up as the manager for an absentee owner. He glanced toward the door. To miss Quentin now would mean an entire week wasted.

"No, you didn't call me, but the owner, Mr. . . ." he reached in his shirt pocket and fumbled through his trouser pockets as if looking for his order with the name on it.

"Mr. Golden?"

"Yeah, Mr. Golden decided we should do this regular, every month for a while during the mating and egg-hatching season. Do you know the little buggers multiply by ten thousand in each tiny egg? Increase that by . . ." Mac squinted his eyes and moved his lips as if to figure.

"Never mind, never mind," the manager said in haste. "Go about your business and don't disturb the tenants. Some of 'em sleep late on weekends and we got night workers, too."

"Of course not, Mr. . . ." Mac extended his hand.

"Jamison, Al Jamison," the man finished for him.

"Ah, Mr. Jamison. Al. I'll certainly tell Mr. Golden how cooperative you've been and how well you keep an eye on things around here."

He barely managed to brush away the man's effusive thanks and turn away when Quentin walked out the door.

McBee threw the canister far into the recesses of the previously desecrated hedge and ambled toward the bus stop. This time his target never looked back.

Once aboard, Mac sat in the rear, watching. It wasn't a long ride to the central station. He saw Quentin head for the men's room. Hurrying to a darkened corner, Mac ripped off the Velcro termite company insignias. He rushed to the candy and souvenir stand and paid what he considered an exorbitant price for a Hall of Fame baseball cap with little plastic baseball cards fastened all over. He bought a pair of sunglasses and a cigar, hoping the change was significant.

The trick about following a person, you could almost count on people not noticing others on the street. But this guy turned out to be a little more observant than he looked.

Poking his nose deeper in the city map as a man emerged from the men's room, McBee almost dropped his map and swallowed the unlit cigar stuck in the corner of his mouth.

If he hadn't concentrated so hard on trying to learn all about Quentin, he would never have recognized the man standing there, dressed in a tight-fitting pair of jeans and western shirt with tiny pearl buttons. His hair, without the usual covering of gray felt hat, was slicked down with that just-combed-and-greased look. Quentin had shaved five years off his normal thirty-or-so.

He walked with a jaunty air and signaled a cab. Oh, oh, this is getting odder and odder. Not to mention more expensive. Mac made a note in this little book while waiting for Quentin's taxi to pull over to the curb. He hailed the next one and worried about how long he would have to follow.

To his surprise the cab stopped a few blocks away from the terminal and let his fare off. Mac passed by and noted the house number where he seemed to be heading.

He sure could have used the schnoodle on this caper, but his partner was sort of hard to disguise.

From now on things could get sticky. The neighborhood was strictly residential and not many places to hide. Paying off the driver, he left the baseball cap and cigar in the backseat for the next customer.

It was early evening and sudden hunger pangs attacked his empty stomach, but he had to stick this out. He found a newspaper on the neighbor's lawn and stretched out on a webbed lawn chair nearby. If someone came out of the house he could always plead light-headedness from a heart problem.

Darkness descended on the quiet neighborhood. The streetlamps spread their glow along the lawns. Mac shifted his chair in the shadow and felt his indecision grow. He could appear a little suspicious now, lounging in a lawn chair after dark. Should he try to look in the windows? Should he leave and come another day to check who lived there?

Should he wait?

The opening of the front door made up his mind for him. A young woman stepped out, with Quentin not far behind. She wore western garb also. This had to be his contact.

Now Mac was getting somewhere. But why the costumes? He had to check who owned the house and the background of the owner. From that it should be easy to find out what secrets the man offered for sale.

He watched the pair pass by. The girl, a pleasantly plump brunette, had no more the look of an industrial spy than Joe. Well, that showed how clever she was, didn't it?

The couple walked several more blocks with Mac skulking far behind. He silently apologized for all the bedded plants and flowers he stepped on that night, trying to avoid the streetlights.

At the corner by a gas station the couple waited, and Mac had the sinking sensation it was for a cab. Sure enough, one pulled to the curb several minutes later and they climbed in.

Damn! He lost them. He noted the cab number in the event he might flimflam some information out of the driver later. Those cabbies were a tough bunch; they expected to be paid for every word they uttered. A twenty-dollar bill could pry open their mouths sometimes. He winced at the thought.

Something niggled at his mind since he first got the case. Even though he didn't know diddly about computers and didn't care, he surmised that Royal could have sent coded messages to his contacts on E-mail instead of using the post office. He must have had his reasons.

It was getting curious and curiouser.

21

Later that night McBee took Herr Schnoodle for a Big Mac to atone for leaving him alone all day and half the night. They sat outside at an umbrella table, enjoying the cool night air. It took two hamburgers before the dog quit pouting and decided to be friendly again.

"I'm going to have to baby-sit Quentin tomorrow, too," McBee pointed out between sips of a milkshake. "Something might turn up on Sunday."

Two nights of sitting at the bus stop down the street from Quentin's apartment until midnight was enough to convince him that Quentin was not a night owl during the week.

His entire perception of the precise, dull, stodgy Quentin had changed drastically.

The dog let loose with one of his shrill barks. Mac jumped and spilled milkshake on his pants.

"Damn, Schnoodle! Can't you learn to lower that range a tad?" Darcy slid next to him on the seat. All Mac could concentrate on was how to escape, get home, and change out of the damp, sticky trousers covered with milkshake.

"My, my, how cozy. I suppose eating outdoors at McDonald's is your idea of a big night." She laughed and touched him lightly on the thigh. "Just kidding, McBee."

As she put her hand on his trouser leg, his blood pressure zinged a few notches, and he looked down to see if his pants were on fire.

"Say, I'm sorry for standing you up the other night. I had

to go clear across town to turn in this story by deadline."

"Hey, hey, no need to apologize. You said you'd give me a rain check. That's good enough."

Her smile dazzled him. "How about Sunday? I haven't planned anything and . . ."

Damn the luck! If he didn't watch Quentin tomorrow he would have to wait another whole week. Maybe next week he wouldn't even meet his contact. Maybe Sunday and Monday were the big days when he might put it all together. He had to track down that cabby before his memory faded, too.

"Aw, gee. That'd be great—except I've . . . well . . ."

"You're working on a case! Oh, swell. The boss didn't exactly say *not* to follow you guys. He probably forgot about ordering me to do it." Her dark eyes smoldered beneath incredibly thick lashes.

"How many times do I have to say it? I'd open my life to you, but a PI's entrusted with confidential . . ."

"Bullpucky! Don't lay that crapola on me, McBee. I recognize a snow job when I see it. Either you've got a date or you're onto something. I'm betting it's not a date."

Jeeze, she knew how to cut to the quick.

"I'm not going to lose a good story like that Treyhune deal."

"Don't you think that's ungrateful? I cut you in on some of it."

She leaped to her feet, hands on hips, glaring down at him. "I knew it! You let me in on your precious Treyhune case, after you decided how much I should have. There was a lot more, wasn't there?"

McBee patted the schnoodle who had moved over on the other side of his leg, away from Darcy. The big phony, some protector. Mac considered his options, stalling for time.

161

He could tell her he was going out with someone, but she could easily discover the truth in that. He could tell her about Quentin Royal, but everyone in the supermarkets would read of it, and Joe would never trust him again.

Maybe she could wring the complete story from Quentin once they arrested him for espionage or whatever. Many criminals spilled their guts to the press that way.

"Okay, I'll level with you. There is this case—an open and shut divorce deal. Blue-collar workers, nobody special, but the fallout can be real messy. No winners, that kind of schtick. Nothing you'd find interesting."

"Are you smokin' me?" She sat close and patted his cheek lightly with two fingers, staring into his eyes.

He felt his temperature rise to meet his blood pressure, and the temptation to kiss those soft, red lips grew almost more than he could resist. So he didn't.

"Hmm. McBee, you're full of surprises," she said lightly, with a funny catch in her voice, not pushing away too far.

Could it be she was drawn to him, too? Hey, how dumb can you get? What would a girl like Darcy see in a beat-up gumshoe? He sometimes thought in his best Mickey Spillane mode.

"Want a burger?" He asked to break the silence.

She shook her head. "No, thanks. I'm on my way over to the paper." She draped her camera bag over her shoulder.

A cloud passed through Mac's thoughts, dimming the electricity of Darcy's presence. "Wait a minute. How about Apple Sally, did you find out anything else?" She could be holding out on him just as he was with her on his cases. He hoped not.

"Nope. Still working on it. You worried?"

"Damn right. Three bag ladies shot or stabbed and two of them redheads. Doesn't look good."

162

"One was a man," Darcy echoed Apple Sally's refrain.

"Yeah, but the killer didn't know that. She's tight with the Swede, think she's connected to the mob someway?"

"Ah, McBee, you been watching your favorite programs again. Tsk. Tsk. I don't see how she's in any danger, but I'm checking her background, cut me some slack."

She stood to go and he watched her move away.

"See ya around," he said low, knowing she couldn't hear. Even her leaving didn't take away the worry about Apple Sally. Some gut feeling told him she was in danger.

He looked at the dog. "See what dedication will do to a guy's love life? I shoulda sacrificed Sunday with Quentin Royal or told her about the case or something. On the other hand, notice how quick she swallowed my line? Very unusual."

Herr Schnoodle licked the last remnants of his sandwich, picked up the Styrofoam container with his teeth and ambled over to the trash to put it in. Several patrons watched and applauded while the dog sauntered back to Mac.

"Show off!" Mac told him. "You forgot to take mine, too, while you're at it." The schnoodle grinned, he loved an audience.

"Come on, fella. *Mannix* is on the late show tonight. It's the episode where he . . . ." The dog took off at an easy lope down the street. Herr Schnoodle loved their exercise period a lot more than Mac did.

The next day Mac waited until past noon to move on Quentin. He had a feeling the guy would sleep late on Sundays—so pathetically predictable. Mac waited across the street, dressed in his guru outfit.

He hated this disguise most of all. He felt ridiculous in the long, flowing white robe tied loosely with a twisted brown tie from a drape.

"You've heard of the Black Muslins? Well, meet one of the White Percales," he confided to some elderly lady walking by who demanded to know his religion. She was not amused. The phony beard itched and the long, scraggly wig fit too tight, making his head feel drawn up into a knot at the top. He wondered if his eyes slanted with an Oriental look. That should help his disguise. Lucky for him he still had a full head of hair. A stunt like this could turn a skimpy head bald in no time.

"Blessings, Sister," he intoned as he gave a passerby a religious pamphlet. Lucky he clipped a stack at the airport once. You never knew when something would come in handy.

Some people took the pamphlets and others walked on lawns to avoid him. He hoped the cops wouldn't roust him. This wasn't exactly the neighborhood for off-beat religions, but it was all he had to work with on Sunday that would let him stay on the sidewalk. Probably in LA nobody would have given him a glance.

Feeling a wave of cold sweat, his heart gave a sudden lurch as he saw Darcy coming toward him. No one else had a walk like that. She peered at the numbers on the apartments. How did she do it? He had been so busy worrying about his tail on Quentin that he never gave a thought to someone following him.

He prayed for a sudden earthquake. A tornado. Anything to remove him from the spot he stood upon. If she recognized him in this ridiculous getup he would never live it down with her. She'd laugh her head off every time she saw him. He suffered humiliation at the idea of discovery until suddenly his sanity returned.

Who could recognize him? The disguise was good. She must have followed him one of the other days. He watched her and realized she wasn't looking for anything specific, just poking around.

She turned, staring right at him.

An electric shock sped through his body, welding all the hairs together from head to toes. He felt naked and looked down to see if his sheet was still there. Then she turned away, jotting something in her notebook as she walked. He was so rattled by now he couldn't even appreciate her trim figure as she blended into the rest of the humanity on the sidewalk.

Whew! Close. Suppose Quentin had chosen that time to emerge from his apartment? Could she identify him by sight or did she guess the location of the stakeout?

Mac stood for a while leaning against the bus bench, gulping breaths of air. He gave handouts recklessly until he was in danger of running out of them. The next step would be to give a long, haranguing sermon, and he knew that would get him pinched for sure.

He began to notice that people were taking his handouts, glancing at them and throwing back the oddest looks. White-robed gurus were a dime a dozen in the village and airports. What were they staring at? He peered at the pamphlets in his hand, checking them out for the first time.

Damn! They were written in Spanish. No wonder people gave him the fish-eye. This was not your typical ethnic neighborhood.

Quentin picked that instant to emerge from his building as a bus drove up. Mac gathered his skirts and made a dash. Just in time he jumped on board, the sack he carried flapping against the door, almost knocking down several people standing close by. Everyone gave him a wide berth as he made his way to the back.

Mac passed Quentin in the narrow aisle. For a second their

glances met. Did his quarry know he was being followed?

It didn't help when the bus arrived at the station and Quentin headed for the john again. What now?

McBee had no idea what to expect when Quentin emerged from the men's room. What he didn't anticipate was this elegant figure in form-hugging, tan gabardine pants with a beige ribbed turtleneck sweater and dark brown designer jacket. That must have set him back at least six hundred smackers for the threads. As before, Quentin was nearly unrecognizable.

Luckily Mac had pulled off the guru outfit and stuffed it away in his bag. He watched while Quentin glanced at the large clock over the terminal door and hurried toward the main part of the bus terminal. No crowds on a Sunday evening and McBee stood back in the shadows, snapping a few pictures while Quentin put some coins in a metered locker, stashing his briefcase inside. He glanced at his watch again, and Mac followed him outside.

They hadn't waited five minutes before a white Olds Cutlass Supreme purred up to the curb and the horn sounded lightly. A knockout lady, maybe ten years older than Quentin, opened the door and waved.

What the hell was going on? Another contact for the stolen computer information? That had to be the answer. Mac resisted the impulse to move closer, sensing the two were well acquainted. Maybe the guy peddled it to several buyers—playing the field.

Quentin sauntered over and climbed into the car, but not before Mac got off a couple of quick shots of them both with his handy-dandy spy camera from the correspondence school. Something fell out of the open door of the car.

As soon as the car pulled away he ran to pick up the red silk handkerchief Quentin had sported in his jacket pocket along with a fresh gum wrapper. He'd never observed Quentin chewing gum. Had the woman thrown it down? Could he be so lucky? He slipped it and the scarf into a plastic bag. The material probably wouldn't hold prints, but the aftershave was unmistakable. He watched the receding taillights of the departing car.

22

Mac hurried home. "As soon as I get this film developed and the gum wrapper dusted for prints, this may be the break we're looking for, old boy. Joe can run Mr. Mata Hari down on the police computer."

He heated two TV turkey dinners for the dog and himself. "The main thing is, Schnoodle, we have to lock Quentin in to that certain post office box so we can take out a search warrant." He showed the plastic bag to the dog.

"Sniff this. He's wearing enough aftershave to blot out the smell of the East River. When Joe puts a twenty-four-hour watch on the box, we'll catch him for sure."

Mac scraped part of the gooey gravy off the stringy turkey, took a bite of the gummy mashed potatoes and pretended that the food tasted good. The image of Apple Sally and her suggestion of warming the container and eating that instead kept intruding.

"Funny, though, it doesn't figure that he should change clothes at the bus station. That beats me. He acted normal, not as if he suspected anyone of spying on him, so why the costume change?" He took a swig of beer and poured a little for Herr Schnoodle.

"You're a damn good partner, old boy. I can spill out my thoughts, and you just look on in approval. Who can top that in a buddy?" He ruffled the dog's ears and Herr Schnoodle laid his chin on Mac's leg.

The next morning when Mac took Schnoodle for a walk

in the park, he spotted Darcy heading his way.

"Ah, top of the morning, sweetheart," he said cheerfully.

"Don't sweetheart me, you louse! This is a barbaric time of day to have to open my eyes or function as a normal human being. I can't trust you anymore, McBee."

They fell into step together while the dog ignored her. A sharp tug on his leash caused the schnoodle to mess up his aim as he lifted his leg toward an elderly lady doddering by in a long fur coat.

They sat on a park bench and he unsnapped the schnoodle's collar. The dog never wandered far. He'd been chased by too many wild-eyed mothers protecting their little darlings from the strange-looking animal.

"Okay, spill it. What's the problem?"

She had never looked so desirable. Her cream-colored hair was windblown, her dark eyes flashed fire.

"Problem! As if you didn't know!" She glared at him. "I'm going to level. I don't expect you to go running to your friend Joe, either. A friend at the same station says you're onto something big. A computer scam involving the feds that's ready to blow sky high. And you said it was a ho-hum divorce case."

He tried to keep his mind off the rise and fall of her sweater. She was steamed this time.

"Well, well. Some kind of summit meeting?"

Apple Sally. He felt relief at the new diversion and hoped it would get Darcy off his back, even temporarily.

"Hello, boy." The schnoodle dashed forward and wriggled around her, turning every which way in delight. Sally knelt and pushed her face in his ear, whispering to him. It sounded as if the pooch giggled in return.

Darcy and Mac watched silently.

"How's it going?" he finally broke the quiet when it

seemed as if Apple Sally would ignore them completely and talk only to the dog.

"Okay, I guess." She stood and smoothed her skirts primly, childlike, as if someone had chastised her for behavior unbecoming in a lady.

Mac got a quick picture of her as a young girl. She had probably been an incorrigible tomboy—the despair of her mother, the pride of her father.

She pushed her cart from the middle of the sidewalk and sat on the other side of McBee.

"Enjoying Mr. Steinmetz's company?" He hoped.

She smiled at him, ignoring Darcy. "Oh, I love him! He's such a fine, old gentleman. We're going to the concert in the park this Saturday."

"Concert? My, my," Darcy commented.

"He wanted us to go to a real one at Radio City Music Hall, but . . ." her fingers worked nervously inside her half glove, making little pleats in the side of her skirt as she always did when nervous.

Surely Mr. Steinmetz had enough money from what McBee left for Jesse to buy her clothes, and he probably had offered. Mac figured now, with Darcy listening, was not a good time to pursue the subject.

Darcy appeared to need an explanation.

"Mr. Steinmetz is a neighborhood gent," Mac offered. "He . . ."

"He takes in stray waifs and orphans," Apple Sally finished his sentence. She turned a speculative look his way, and McBee realized she knew what he had tried to do for her. She hadn't come to grips with it yet, her next question would probably be, why?

"Swell," Darcy said, barely polite. "I've been trying to persuade McBee to share his latest case with me. Do you think a friend would hold out? I think it's damn selfish, myself."

Mac watched uneasily as the two women considered each other, eyeball to eyeball and the silence built into the eye of a hurricane with Mac in the center, waiting for it to explode. It could go either way, but he'd lay odds on Darcy. She was made of strong stuff while Apple Sally was a cupcake under all that camouflage.

What he hadn't counted on was their joining forces against him.

"Well—I can't see what it'd hurt to let you in on a story. 'Course I'm not sure what it's all about, but on general principles, what's the big deal?"

"It's no biggie," Darcy agreed, tapping her long nails against her ever-present camera bag. "Some computer nerd selling inside company information. I don't see what the big deal is, either."

"Hey, wait a darn minute here. It's unbelievable that you two are ganging up on me. This is a confidential case."

"Oh, get off it!" Darcy shot back. "It's only off-limits for my paper. Want to bet the *City Times* will land the story? That's not fair."

He considered the truth to her statement. The city paper seemed to have a direct link with the police departments all over New York.

"McBee, I could have had your tail twice now." She glared at him and blew soft, wispy bangs from her forehead.

"What do you mean?"

Herr Schnoodle nestled between Mac's legs and Apple Sally's skirts, with his chin resting on her knee. Mac patted the dog absentmindedly.

"I might have blown the whistle on Treyhune before you were ready to close in for the kill. I discovered who you're following in this case, too. I could screw it up—but won't," she hastened to add. "All I'm asking is a fair shake here."

He leaned back and sighed. Well, what the hey . . . it couldn't hurt this one time, could it? He felt sure it would make the *Times* anyway.

"Okay, but I'm not giving in because you're threatening me. It's unfair to leave your paper out—even if it is a despicable, gossip-mongering . . ."

"I hate it when you're being subtle." Darcy laughed, and Apple Sally joined in.

He told them of the meeting he planned to stage for Wednesday at the post office. First the dog had to sniff out the right box so they could be ready. He supposed it wouldn't hurt to have a reporter on hand to record the pinch.

"Can't tell much until I talk to Joe. Want to call tomorrow for the details?" he asked.

"Sure thing." Darcy stood and stuck out her hand. "Thanks a lot, McBee. You too, *Apple Sally*." She slung her bag over her shoulder. "By the way," she paused as if considering her words. "Aren't you scared? I'd never go to an open-air concert in the park if I were in your shoes."

"What?" Apple Sally stared at Darcy as if she had dropped in from another planet.

McBee felt the tension building. What was Darcy going to say next? He had tried to warn Apple Sally about the bag-lady killings. That was why he wanted to introduce her to Mr. Steinmetz, so she'd have somewhere to go.

"Surely you read the papers. Don't 'your people' talk about the killings? How do you know you're not going to have your throat slit in some dark alley or stabbed while you're in a crowd at . . . let's say a concert."

Apple Sally leaped off the bench to confront Darcy. They stood toe to toe, with Darcy almost a head taller in her heeled boots. Even so, Apple Sally didn't back down.

"I'm not trying to ruffle your feathers, Ms. Bag Lady," Darcy said. "But you sashay up and down the street like you don't have a care in the world. Some pervert in the city doesn't like bag ladies. Is that too far-fetched to get through to you?"

"I've tried to tell her all that," McBee said in an effort to diffuse the situation. He hated confrontations.

Darcy tilted her chin in the air and spun around on her heels. "Don't say I didn't warn you," she left as a parting shot.

McBee and Apple Sally didn't speak for a moment as she sat back down on the bench.

He thought it a good time to change the subject. He hoped she was digesting what Darcy said.

"How come you joined in with her about the story? I thought she wasn't one of your favorite people."

She took off her hat and began working on the crown as if it wasn't already a hopeless case. The crease on top had probably started to turn crooked in Calamity Jane's day.

Her red hair picked up the sun's rays and reflected on her pale, slightly freckled face. He noticed the hairdo was not quite as unrestrained as usual. She must have combed it or brushed it or used a lawn mower on it.

She saw him staring and clamped the hat back on. "It's hard to say, Alexander. I still don't like her. But fair's fair. If the information is going to leak anyway, why should the *Times* have it sooner than her paper? At least that's the way I look at it."

He scratched the schnoodle and the dog grinned at him. "Wonder why he dislikes her?" he said half to himself.

Apple Sally raised a quizzical eyebrow. "You can be really dense. For one thing, she plainly doesn't care for dogs, but for another, he's jealous. How does that sound, boy?" She scratched Schnoodle's other ear, careful to avoid touching Mac's hand.

"He's not jealous of you," Mac pointed out.

She made a face, and her eyes had a hidden, withdrawn look. "Why should he be jealous of me?"

True, so true. He was smart enough not to express the idea out loud.

"In all fairness, maybe it isn't so much that she dislikes dogs—she probably prefers cats. Doesn't she seem to be a cat person?"

He considered. "Suppose so. Bet you like both cats and dogs."

She shrugged. "Yep. But then, I'm rather odd."

It was a comment that didn't call for an answer.

"Want to get breakfast somewhere?" He had planned to ask Darcy before Apple Sally turned up.

She shrugged. "Guess we could. Where?"

"You pick." He hoped he wouldn't regret that decision.

"One Eyed Jack's?"

He tried to hide the wince, but she caught it.

She gave in gracefully. "We can't take him inside anywhere else, and we can't leave him outside. Let's buy donuts and coffee and come back here."

He wanted to tell her she was being very considerate. He admitted that if he had asked Darcy they would probably have gone to some fancy place without a thought to Herr Schnoodle.

"You? Eating donuts?"

She grinned. "Oh, I climb off my high horse sometimes. Doesn't pay to live too healthy—a body needs friendly bacteria to fight with the unfriendly type."

Just what he needed, a medical reason to eat donuts.

"Okay, wait here and I'll bring the stuff back. We'll have a picnic."

Suddenly he felt good about the case, about Darcy, about the morning. He sauntered away, whistling off-key. When he returned with the breakfast, Apple Sally had taken a blanket from her shopping cart to spread on the lawn. The sun was warm against the lingering early morning chill.

Life was getting better and better. If only the niggling worry about the murdered street women didn't intrude at the oddest times. Maybe Apple Sally was more worried than she let on. Could be she even listened to Darcy's warning.

But it didn't seem so right at the moment.

23

He watched as Apple Sally drank her coffee and, like a kid, she had trouble deciding which donut to choose.

"I like you, Apple Sally." His simple admission surprised them both.

She studied him, green eyes narrowed over the steam of the coffee she held to her lips. "Hmm? Thanks."

"No, I'm not snowing you. You're a . . . a fine human being. But I'm getting a little tired of saying that ridiculous name."

"Why?" She bit into a donut.

He reached to wipe the powdered sugar from the tip of her nose.

"I'm used to it. It suits me."

"And it's something to hide behind?"

He broke a plain donut in half for the mutt who really preferred jelly ones. Mac ignored Apple Sally's frown.

"Are you going to start with me again, Alexander?"

"Aren't we friends? You have to see by now I'm not harboring any dark, ulterior motives. You strike me as a very unhappy lady. I want to help."

"Maybe you should have become a social worker. Mr. Steinmetz said how you helped him out of a jam and the Rodriguez boy thinks you're the greatest. How many others are you donating to? Here I thought of you as cheap as yesterday's newspaper."

He was wise to the way she switched the subject from herself around to him and wasn't going to fall for that again. He waited patiently until she ran down.

She crumbled part of her donut and threw it toward some pigeons. The schnoodle barked with jealousy and she hushed him gently.

"I'm going to say something and if that bleached barracuda hears of it, I'll . . ." she gulped and continued. ". . . I'll catch a bus out of town and never come back."

He knew she would. Her legs curled under her long skirts, comfortable as a tabby before the fireplace.

Now that the moment of truth seemed to be at hand he wondered why he wanted to pry into it. Pandora's box— remember what happened to the poor woman who opened the gift from Zeus?

When would he lay the truth on her about his prying so far and what he found in Boston?

He wasn't sure anything told to him would ever be safe from Darcy if she wanted to wring it from him. He felt help-less under the spell of her ripe plum mouth.

"Okay. I promise never to say a word to anyone." That should keep him from temptation, for it suddenly came to him what a hole would open up in the center of his life if Apple Sally took off for parts unknown.

Her face twisted and tears edged from the corners of her eyes. She wiped at them with her sleeve in angry impa-tience. "See what you do? I don't *want* to think of it!" She gazed up, her eyes brilliant from the unshed tears. "I can't remember, Alexander. Honest to God, I can't remember anything before New York."

He felt stunned, expecting anything but this. Recovering quickly, he sat straighter. "Amnesia? You've got amnesia? But you spoke of your husband and son and the fire . . ."

She nodded and tore pieces out of the empty Styrofoam cup. "I know. That's all I do remember. I've tried to picture my husband's face and the boy—they're people I can't even recognize. As if I never knew them. Flashes come to me now and again, sometimes dreams. I woke outside in the front yard in my nightgown—maybe they told me that at the hospital—I don't know."

"And you don't remember where you lived? What city or state?" Now he had painted himself into a corner. He couldn't admit he had checked on her. Not now, not yet. "What about the hospital? Somewhere there's a hospital with records."

"I guess so. It's possible that I grabbed my—some clothes—and sneaked away. Bits and pieces of that have returned. I had nowhere to go, but felt I had to get away from there. There was some kind of danger involved. Ahh, I just don't know."

"Okay, that's a start. You woke up in your nightgown in your front yard with the house exploded. You were taken to a hospital and then you ran away. What next?"

"I had to have started out hitching a ride. The hospital gave me some clothes, or I swiped them from someone there. But I probably didn't have a dime to my name. I faintly recall hitching a ride on a big truck because the driver gave me his cattle prod."

McBee didn't know what to say. He felt an urge to hold the little body close to his chest, to protect her. Against what? They sat silently for a few minutes. He could tell her he tracked her to Boston, but that would admit to Darcy's role.

He took a deep breath. As much as he hated confrontations, he had to get it said. "What if Darcy is right? What if you are in danger? Someone is killing bag ladies and you know it. What if your past is catching up on you?"

"Alexander, do you have any idea how hokey that sounds? I'm only one of thousands on the streets. In the first place, whatever my past was, how could anyone know me now?"

Things were beginning to click into place. Was that why she hid under the disguise, without really knowing why she did it? It had to be very effective. Was someone on to her but unable to tell one street woman from another? He sure as hell wouldn't have seen any difference in them before getting to know Apple Sally.

McBee glanced at his watch and the intensity of the moment broke into shards. Things moved too fast, the situation was too much, too close. He felt the familiar urge to back away—at least for a while.

"Say, got to give this some thought. Maybe there's a way to help."

She began gathering the refuse and the leftover donuts. "I know. You have to go. Don't say anything, huh?"

He nodded. Darcy would have been invaluable in tracking this down, and he couldn't for the life of him see why the two women formed such an instant mutual dislike. Maybe he'd be able to convince Apple Sally later to let Darcy help.

"Anyway, can I call you Sally, without the Apple?"

She managed a weak smile. "Sally-without-the-Apple?" She shook her head. "I'd rather not. I'm sure my name isn't Sally. It's something close, but not Sally, and I don't feel comfortable using the name unless the Apple part comes with it. Does that make sense at all?"

It did and it didn't. Mac pondered on it all the way to the midtown police station.

Joe met McBee in the coffee room, clapping him on the back like he hadn't seen him in years. His big hand nearly knocked McBee off his feet.

"I knew you could do it, Mac! You're a chip off the old block, you know? I ever tell you that your old man wanted to get into the detective unit? He would have been darn good at it except, in the end, he reneged. Thought it would be too dangerous."

At Mac's puzzled look, Joe hastened on. "Oh, not for himself, God no! Your pop wasn't afraid of the devil. No, he got to thinking that you might be left alone. 'Course any police work's got danger, but detectives don't last too long, especially when they go undercover."

Boy, what a day for revelations. Mac thought all along that his father had gladly petrified into his job and never thought of anything else.

"Joe, I didn't wrap up the case yet. Hold your credits, it's bad luck. Anything could go wrong at the last minute." Mac began to tell Joe about the meetings and the strange disguises Quentin Royal affected. "Did you get anything off the gum wrapper?"

"Naw. They dusted for prints, but a tire had rolled over it."

"Too bad. She looked suspicious, had a good cover. Probably some kind of foreign agent."

"Ya think? Say, this is gettin' interesting. You're good at what you do, Mac, real good."

McBee basked in Joe's approval.

"How'd you find out which was his post office box with the rows and rows to pick from?" Joe asked. "We sent an undercover out there for a week and he couldn't find out. This Quentin Royal, he's no dummy."

McBee and the schnoodle hadn't really discovered the exact box yet, but it would only complicate matters to tell him that now.

"I got that all under control, Joe. I think Wednesday's a go. The suspect always leaves after work to go to Queens. I'll get there ahead of time—you have some of your boys there, too. I'll point out the box."

When Wednesday rolled around, McBee developed but-
terflies in his stomach. He and the dog got out of the taxi at
the post office. They were plenty early, but this might take a
little time. He wasn't sorry he let Darcy in on the kill, but
he hoped she wouldn't screw it up by coming too early.

It was important that he shine in front of her for a
change, but it could go the other way too, and she'd have a
big yuk at his expense.

Snapping the extra short leash on the dog's collar,
McBee put on his sunglasses and tapped the white cane on
the sidewalk experimentally, walking slowly forward.

At the post office door, he pushed past the large red sign
saying NO DOGS PERMITTED. SEEING EYE DOGS
ONLY.

He and the schnoodle tap-tapped over to the writing
desk. No one paid him any attention. He took the baggie
from his pocket and untwisting the tie, knelt down and
shoved the silk handkerchief under the dog's nose.

"Get a good whiff, old boy. Can you help me here?" He
noticed that some of the boxes were shoulder high. Would
that hinder the schnoodle?

Herr Schnoodle wrinkled his nose into the handkerchief,
sneezed and gave one of his ear-piercing barks.

"Shh! They'll kick us out of here!" McBee put a finger to
his lips. He straightened up and the dog almost jerked the
leash out of his hands in excitement. Following him as
quickly as possible, Mac remembered to tap the floor once
in a while when he noticed someone staring.

The schnoodle went up and down, around and around
the banks of boxes. On the second pass, the dog paused and
snarfed against the bottom row along the floor. Mac won-

dered with increasing uneasiness if he was looking for a likely spot to pee.

Before he had time to consider this option and pull Schnoodle away, the dog came to a point much as any good bird dog would have. He looked up at McBee with a satisfied air as if to say, "Boy, that was easy, what's next?"

McBee came closer to kneel on the cold tile. "Which one, boy? Can you zero in a little closer than the whole row?"

Herr Schnoodle looked scornful, pushed his nose along the round brass handles of several boxes and then stopped. McBee knew that was the one.

"Old 943, eh?" He made a note on his pad and ruffled the dog's ears. "You did good, boy. You did good."

Now all he had to do was wait and tell Joe's men. He didn't even have to be in on the capture. They could take care of it all now. He had a lot of unsatisfied curiosity left about Quentin Royal, though.

Mac decided to stick it out to the end.

He and the schnoodle went outside to sit on a bench on the post office lawn to wait.

The bus roared up and McBee glared at his watch as if it lied. "My God! It's Quentin and he's early! What do we do now? Joe's men aren't due for at least fifteen minutes. Maybe the guy suspects something and is on the lam. We could lose it all." He leaped to his feet, snapped the leash on the dog's collar and adjusted his sunglasses.

"Well, here we go, boy." He lifted his cane toward the sky. "It's do or die, now or never, anything for God and country." He grinned down at the dog.

"Sorry, got carried away." For the life of him, he couldn't think of what one of his own heroes would have said just about now.

They trailed into the post office behind Quentin.

24

Once inside, McBee leaned against the wall and took out his handy-dandy spy camera. He waited until Quentin knelt to work the combination and got off a quick shot. Enlarged about a million times that one should even show the number on the box.

Of course he didn't dare use a flash, but the school recommended extra fast film for times like these. His smug satisfaction didn't last long.

Quentin must have felt something odd. He didn't open his box right away, but moved off to the side as if forgetting which one was his. Suddenly he turned and stared squarely at McBee.

Darcy picked that time to enter, with Joe's men hot on her heels. She stood aside while they surged forward before the startled Quentin could move. A cop grabbed him on each side and shoved him over to the wall. The third began checking him for weapons.

"He didn't get his mail yet. It's box 943." Mac walked up to the men and jerked off his glasses with a dramatic flair, knowing Darcy watched.

Quentin appeared startled, his mouth tightened but he didn't speak. He must have known what was going down or he would have yelled his head off for a lawyer. Poor jerk, why'd he have to get mixed up in something like this? He could be sent to Leavenworth. Did they still send federal criminals there or were they all getting VIP treatment now?

"How about opening your box, buddy?" one of the

cops asked in a reasonable voice.

Quentin shook his head.

The cop shrugged. "So, we get a court order. No biggie. One's on the way now—it'll take a while—and make things worse for you." The officer poked his face filled with menacing authority as close to Quentin's as their noses would permit.

Quentin sagged visibly. "I had no idea it was this serious. I mean I—I only . . . Sure, I'll open the box."

McBee felt a twinge of sympathy and steeled himself against it. After all, the guy was stealing information from the corporation and passing it on to a foreign government, wasn't he?

"You don't have to say anything," he told Quentin. He couldn't keep still. "Did you guys forget something?"

The cops looked embarrassed for a moment and then the one in charge grinned. "You're right. Good thing you reminded us." They read Quentin his rights. When they opened the post office box, Mac looked over the officer's shoulder and caught a glimpse of foreign postmarks and stamps on several envelopes.

Darcy, close by, whispered into her tape recorder. Beyond the cops' first admiring glances no one paid any attention to her hanging around the fringes.

As they led Quentin Royal away, McBee and Darcy followed outside and sat on the lawn. She scribbled on a notepad briefly, then stopped, turning toward him.

"That was very clever, using the guide dog as a cover. How'd you manage to come up with it?"

He grinned, appreciating her half-praise. How come women were so good at that? No way was he telling her it had been one of Rockford's better scams.

"Wonder what the poor schlemiel will get?"

She shrugged. "I suppose it depends on what information he stole. Why?"

"Aw, I dunno—a feeling. Like maybe he got roped into it or something."

"That's dumb, McBee. Well, I gotta get down to the station and verify all this before I turn it in. The boss'll love it. I owe you one."

He grinned. "I'll hold you to it."

She leaned forward and wrapping her long fingers around his neck, pulled him close and kissed him.

It was a good kiss, he kissed her back, expecting explosions and fireworks, but something was wrong.

He wondered when the feeling of elation—of "job well done" would come along. All the way home something nagged at him, telling him there was more to this case than he knew.

He was right.

When he checked his telephone recorder, Joe had left an urgent call.

"What's up?" he called as soon as he poured a cup of coffee.

"Can you come down here?" Joe sounded harried.

At the station, they ushered him into a room holding both Joe and Quentin. Joe began without his usual rambling preambles.

"This case's gone crazy at the last minute. Mr. Royal here demanded I call you in as a witness."

"*Me?* A witness?" McBee looked quizzically at Quentin. That didn't make sense.

Joe had McBee's photos spread on his desk. He stabbed a short, beefy finger at them. "This guy hasn't stolen any industrial plans at all. Truth is, CTE doesn't know what to do with him. They refuse to press charges."

"What?"

Joe's brows shot together, and he looked at the limit of a short fuse as he glared at Quentin. "Tell him," he commanded between clenched teeth.

Quentin looked flustered, apologetic. His tie was askew, his jacket wrinkled and stained.

"I did take something from the computer at CTE, but it wasn't what everyone thinks. On the net, I plugged into City Wide Data Dating for—for names of ladies who—ah—might interest me."

At McBee's look of stunned surprise, he countered defensively. "I know it wasn't exactly legal, using their equipment and my working time and all—but I was embarrassed to go to that place in person. If anyone at work found out . . ."

"Is that why you met those women at the bus station? Why the disguises?"

Quentin flushed. "They weren't exactly meant to be disguises. I picked dates who were into dancing. You know, line dancing, square dancing, ballroom, jive—I love to dance."

"But why did you have to sneak out of your apartment and dress in the bus station washroom?"

"Everyone in my apartment building knows everyone else's business. They are such a bunch of gossips. I didn't want them talking about my dates."

The pieces of the puzzle were falling into place.

"Wouldn't it have been easier to get your own computer?" Mac couldn't help the whine in his voice. This was supposed to be his showcase caper. Even though this man explained everything, it shouldn't have been so simple.

Quentin looked even more embarrassed if that were possible. "I joined WWWA. They forbid the use of home computers."

"WWWA?"

"World Wide Web Anonymous. It's like AA or Gambler's

Anonymous. I got hooked on the Web and didn't come down for three days, no sleeping or eating. The company paid for my rehabilitation. I couldn't let anyone know I'd tapped into it again. I only used it for the dating service," he added defensively.

All McBee's perceptions about the guy went up in smoke like a tenement fire. The guy was a born *nebbish.* Shy and bookish, he probably didn't even know how to talk to a female. With this computer dating he was able to assume a different, more forceful personality each time, hiding behind a mask and becoming anyone he wanted to be.

Mac took the super spy camera from his pocket and dumped out the film shot at the post office. "Well, what's he going to do now—sue us all for false arrest?"

Joe grimaced, shaking his head. For once he seemed short on words. Then he wound up. "Nah. Mr. Royal here did a no-no. He's lucky the company doesn't fire his butt. Besides which, he inconvenienced the entire downtown and midtown precincts. Made us all look foolish." Joe's pointed affability seemed to make Quentin all the more uncomfortable, and Joe's indirect warning wasn't lost on him.

Mac hit his forehead with the palm of his hand. "Foolish! Darcy! Oh, my God! Where's your phone?" Darcy was on her way to turn in her story to the editor. If she printed this, Quentin could sue, she would come off irresponsible to her boss and might never speak to him again.

Joe looked bewildered at Mac's sudden outburst. "Go ahead, if it's that important."

"In private?" It would never do to let Joe know he'd leaked a story to a paper—that paper, especially.

"Oh, hell. Go next door. It's Crazy Al's office and he hates anyone to step foot in there, but chances are he won't come in until later."

With a name like that, Mac hoped not. He dialed Darcy's phone at work. It rang several times. Just as panic began to take over, he heard her breathy voice.

"Kill the story! It's turned sour—all mixed up and not what we thought."

"McBee, is this your idea of a joke? It's not funny. I bet you've had second thoughts."

"No! Hey, sweetheart, I'm at Joe's precinct now and I can't talk forever. If Crazy Al gets back . . . Anyway, I promise it's no snow job. Come over tonight and I'll explain. If you run it anyway, the *Union Globe* will get sued for sure. 'Course that's no biggie, everyone sues that rag sooner or later. I just didn't think you'd want your byline on it."

"Oh, all right. But if this is some kind of McBee scam, I'm warning you . . ."

He hung up and sighed with relief. Close. What a mess if she had run the story. Retractions all the way around, Quentin would have sued, cops looking like bungling idiots, Darcy fired and he would have been at the bottom of the pyramid, squashed like a bug.

Mac hurried back to face Joe and Quentin. "I'll bring the other negatives in tomorrow and you can destroy them yourself," he said to Joe. He turned to Quentin, holding out his hand.

"No hard feelings? I hope you find the right person one of these days." Mac tried not to think of the dough he'd spent on bus fare, taxis and disguises. Of course it was good experience, he could take it off expenses if he ever made enough to pay taxes.

Quentin stuck out his hand and they shook. "No, I'm relieved it's all over. You're pretty good at what you do. Rough in places, but an all around smooth detective. I suspected you of following me a couple of times, but couldn't be sure. That trick with the white cane and dog was masterful."

McBee felt a glow. It wasn't often a guy you tried to nail returned such a compliment.

"I still don't get it, why you had to be so secretive."

Quentin Royal would have blushed, if his complexion hadn't been sallow to begin with.

"Did you follow me to the race track?"

McBee nodded. So much for that disguise.

"I thought so. I thought it might have been my—ah—" Quentin darted a look toward Joe, but he had turned away for a moment to talk to another cop. "I thought it was my bookie. He's a little impatient, but I've got that under control."

McBee was dubious. Quentin obviously had been enjoying his life to the hilt, but control was not in the picture. "One more question. The envelope the cops found postmarked Japan. That's what started this whole spy idea. What was that all about?"

Quentin squirmed. "I thought to try a—a foreign market for dating. Maybe start easy, like with a pen pal, but I could see from the first that was too slow and no dancing."

Joe clamped a hard grip around McBee's shoulder.

"Mr. Royal, you got caught by one of the best. Mac here's like my own son, I'm proud of his work." The squeeze Joe gave his shoulder made him wince, and Mac wondered if he wasn't upset by the way things turned out after all.

For instance, if Mac was so damned good, why hadn't he realized before the end that Quentin was no spy? Maybe Joe had a mind to ask him about that when he caught him alone. McBee planned not to let that happen for a while, at least until this caper became ancient history.

He rode the bus home and stopped off for a bottle of

decent wine. That might make a good impression on Darcy, if she showed up.

She must have been really ticked off; she never did show. He wondered why that didn't bother him like it should have.

25

For the next few weeks McBee enjoyed loafing. He sat in the park with Herr Schnoodle and watched the people and pigeons. He spent a couple of evenings at The Cave, practicing his cool with Smitty and the denizens of the Bottleneck.

He still couldn't say he felt at home walking in that neighborhood, but he no longer feared for his life.

When the Spaceman appeared, McBee steeled himself for a barrage of gratitude since the dude wouldn't have to worry about a place to lay his head for a month or two. The big man walked up to Mac perched on a stool and slung his arm around his shoulder with bone-crushing enthusiasm. That was the end of it.

That was enough, Mac reflected, glaring at the dog for being so absorbed in his beer and pretzels. The fellow could have broken something—some watchdog.

Mac needed time alone to sort some things out. Apple Sally, for instance. How could he help her without recruiting Darcy? Digging up information on Apple Sally's past should be a snap for a reporter, with the contacts available from her paper.

He tried not to wonder why it was so important that Apple Sally not disappear from his life.

What did he care, after all? People came and went—in and out of life—he wasn't going to make the mistake of trying to hold on. It never did any good. Yet he worried over the unknown danger she might be in.

"Trouble is, I do care, Schnoodle, old boy." The dog sat

on the next stool. "I'm not sure, but I could be getting short-circuited here." Mac slid his glass around slowly, watching the circles form beneath the beaded moisture on the dark wood.

The dog munched a pretzel, watching him with one ear at attention, the other at half-mast.

Mac grinned and took a sip. "I don't know if I can handle the new Alexander McBee. It scares hell out of me. I liked living alone—without friends and other encumbrances. My life was A-OK—before I met you—and Darcy and Apple Sally and Mr. Steinmetz and . . ."

He swirled the beer inside the glass, slopping it over the sides. "Damn! See what I mean? Everything is out of control." He stared at the mirrored wall and took a good look for a change instead of letting his glance slide off sideways. A lock of thick, sandy-colored hair slid down over his forehead. He raked it aside with impatient fingers. See, even his hair didn't behave in a rational manner anymore. He was glad to see the cowlick in back was still there, that never changed. Maybe he should try a new barber, or stop trimming his own hair in between visits.

There was something about his look now that defied description. His blue eyes snapped with spirit. His expression was unbland. Damn funny, a guy looked into the bathroom mirror every day to shave and never noticed his looks until he sat in a bar staring at his hazy reflection.

Herr Schnoodle took a lap of beer and belched delicately. He leaned his head, foam mustache and all, against Mac's arm, looking up at him with round, brown eyes.

Mac ruffled his ears. "I know you try to understand. I never imagined I'd ever say this to a—a dog—but you're a dandy friend, the best I've ever had." He squinted against the smoky haze and his own failure to focus. Was he drunk? Nah.

What he said was true, all right. He'd had a few beers and he might be getting awash with sentiment. He tried to picture life without the schnoodle and failed.

Mac swiveled on his stool, looking around. Same old bunch. If they permitted dancing, at least he could watch that and not grow maudlin in his suds. He grinned at the idea of this crowd dancing.

The denizens were made up of mostly men. Men who had never touched foot on anything as frivolous as a dance floor. This place was meant for serious drinking and negotiating deals he didn't even want to think about.

He turned back around on his stool before someone decided to take offense at his staring. "The mobs probably send out their hit men from this place," he confided into the dog's up ear.

During the days that followed, Mac felt a strange, enervating depression. He received several calls on his answering machine but nothing made him feel any better. One call came from a disgruntled father who wanted him to check on his daughter.

"Nothing good ever comes from those family problems," he confided to his image in the bathroom mirror. He gave his chin another run with the razor and then rinsed it off. As usual, Herr Schnoodle lay on the bathroom threshold, watching every move.

"Don't ever start shaving, old boy. I'm warning you, it's something you have to keep up once you start." He rubbed his face with the towel and then combed his hair.

"What do you want to do today? We could go to the park, but I'd better haul in another job soon or it's bean sandwiches for us again. 'Course I realize I could have taken that father–daughter thing but we can still afford to be a little choosy, can't we?"

The phone rang, but he didn't feel like talking to anyone. He let the machine pick it up, not bothering to listen.

Once at the park, he decided he didn't want to be there, either. What was the matter with him? He half listened for the squeal of Apple Sally's cart but only yelling children and the coo of pigeons sifted their way into his consciousness.

"Hi, McBee." Darcy moved up to the bench and put her boot up on it next to his leg. She leaned her elbow on her knee and gazed into his eyes.

"Hi, Darcy." The sun backlit her hair, radiating around her head.

"Haven't seen you around."

Her dark eyes locked into his and he stared, hypnotized, then forced himself to break the spell.

"Been busy, I guess."

"New case?"

He ignored the mild sarcasm in her voice. "You never give up, do you, Doll? No, I'm not working on anything now."

She made a little face, her pink tongue skittering nervously over her bright red lips.

He swallowed, remembering how that soft mouth felt under his.

"About your little friend Apple Sally . . ." she began.

At the mention of her name, the schnoodle's ears popped up as if on puppet strings. Mac and Darcy laughed.

"He sure likes her, doesn't he?"

"What's not to like?" McBee countered, wondering why he was defensive.

Darcy shrugged. He loved her shrugs.

"Nothing, I suppose. Aren't you the least bit jealous of your buddy's infatuation?"

"Yeah, guess I am. But hey, there's enough affection in the schnoodle to go around and then some." He tugged gently at the thick ruff of the dog's neck.

"By the way, thanks for calling me to kill that story about that poor computer jerk. What was his name? Royal Jell-O or something like that."

McBee laughed. "You mean Quentin Royal. Turned out to be a bummer, that case. I invested a lot of time and money. He did wrong, but he's going to get off clean if CTE doesn't press charges. I'm not sorry about it, I kinda liked the guy."

"Too bad," she said, as if she hadn't been listening. Her face was turned as she watched kids playing on the grass.

"So what about Apple Sally?" Mac prompted.

"Well—I've come up with something and wanted to run it by you. Get another perspective."

He nodded. "Shoot."

She took out her notebook and flipped through the pages. When she turned her million-watt eyes on him he felt his soles melt into the pavement. How embarrassing— welded to the spot for life.

"I've checked fire deaths in major cities to come up with a definite Boston. It's taken a while. I never imagined so many people died that way." She paced in front of his bench as she spoke, her energy lighting her tawny skin from inside out.

"There was a fire in Boston around the time she claimed to have arrived in New York."

"How could Apple Sally know the time? She has amnesia and can't recall anything before the hospital," he blurted.

"Ah! So that's the missing element." She sat down beside him, their shoulders touched.

"You tricked me!" Mac accused. How did she manage so easily? He never meant to mention the amnesia.

"Come on, McBee. Get serious. I'm trying to give you a hand to figure this out. She needs help, wouldn't you say?"

"Sure, but . . ." Apple Sally didn't want help, she'd made that plenty clear.

"So that narrows it down," Darcy went on as if he hadn't spoken. She glanced down at her notes. "The house burned to the ground. Records show that cleaning and photographic chemicals caused the explosion—spontaneous combustion— something like that. The husband and small son died instantly and the firemen found the wife—Apple Sally—or Selena Duvall—dazed in the front yard in her nightgown.

"Several days later a little blurb appeared in the paper about the missing amnesia patient. If it hadn't been for the computer sort at the paper, I'd never have found it. If you hadn't mentioned amnesia just now, I wouldn't have remembered it."

"You said her name is Selena Duvall. Doesn't fit her, does it?"

Darcy shrugged. "Not my problem. She's in her thirties and her hair is real."

"I never doubted that for a minute."

Darcy slanted a look at him but didn't say what was on her mind.

"She's from Boston for certain." Mac squinted his eyes into the sun, watching the pigeons sift down after a mad flight. "Let's tell her. Maybe she can go back and pick up where she left off."

Apple Sally—Selena—shouldn't harbor any ill will against them for helping her with her past.

Yet the thought of her leaving the city felt like a valve inside his gut let loose. He would miss her. He didn't want her to go.

Darcy closed the notebook around her fingers, holding

the place. "I don't think it will be so easy for her to just pick up the pieces of her past."

"Okay, out with it. You're holding something back."

"Afraid so." She drew small circles on the pavement with the toe of her shiny boot.

Real leather, probably he and the schnoodle could live a month on what she spent for clothes at one time. She sure knew how to dress, he had to admit. She was class with a capital *C*.

"You see, the papers mentioned that Paul Duvall was wanted . . ."

"Wanted? As in wanted by the police? For what?"

"I'm trying to lay it on you, for God's sake. Give me a chance to talk. The boy who died—he wasn't their son at all. The FBI suspect this Duvall of international kidnapping and extortion."

"What?"

She waved her hand impatiently. "I dunno. There's still a lid on this thing, and my contact at the *Union Trib* couldn't get any more. She only remembered it at all because of the flap between the paper and the FBI. Seemed they were closing in on their case when the stuff hit the fan with the explosion and fire. They didn't want the paper to print anything, but of course, they did anyway."

"Are you telling me that Apple Sally—or whoever she is—was—is a kidnapper?"

"Aw, pull your bug eyes back in your head, McBee. I thought you were a real cool dude. I'm not saying anything of the kind. Of course the authorities'd love to find her and ask some questions."

Mac leaned back, the earth shaking beneath his butt. He almost missed Darcy calling him a real cool dude. He straightened his tie.

"Are you going to let her in on this?" he managed.

She shook her head, the large earrings bouncing against her cheek. "Nope. You'd better do that. We're not exactly bosom buddies, you may have noticed."

How could he not notice? "Me tell her? I wasn't even supposed to tell *you*. How do I explain . . ."

"McBee, you make my ass tired. Can't you improvise? Tell her you discovered it yourself. I don't care."

"Yeah, but what's in it for you, Darcy? You already said you two don't see eye to eye."

"So cynical in one so young," she mocked him with the same words he had thrown at her. "There's a story buried here. I damn well better get a story for my effort. But it's obvious there's more to it, and I'll have to wait until you wring it out of her somehow."

"You're all heart, kiddo." He liked her bare honesty.

"Anyway, you guys are friends, aren't you? She needs a friend right now, McBee. I'll wait."

"That's fair," he conceded. "I'll have to think of how and where to spring it on her."

Apple Sally could become agitated at his prying. He'd already seen her temper out of control. Where were all these confrontations coming from in his life? He'd gone so many years without having to face anyone toe to toe.

"Well, don't take forever, McBee. She's in danger. Someone who knew her husband—some of his connections—they might think she knows too much. The explosion could have been set by the mob. Ever think of that?"

"Then the person or persons stalking bag ladies is really looking for Apple Sally? Damn! We tried to warn her."

"I need a good story. I counted on Quentin Royal and his computer until that fizzled out, and I don't even want to mention Treyhune."

He didn't either. "What'd you do before you found me? Don't you do any of that old-fashioned sniffing on your own anymore?"

"Ye Gods, McBee, I'd do a lot better on my own, for sure. I told you it was the boss' orders."

McBee walked back toward his apartment thinking Darcy acted as if her missed stories were his fault. Well, maybe in a way they were, he conceded. Suddenly he felt flat, as if the street sweeper had rolled over him and left nothing but his rumpled and torn clothing on the dirty pavement.

How was he going to tell Apple Sally, and how would she react? By remembering the rest of the story? He had a gut feeling he didn't *want* her to remember. That was cold. In spite of her so-called connections, she was living on the edge of a precipice, and he was reasonably sure she knew that. Anything could happen to her in the streets even without this lunatic killing bag ladies.

26

The next day, when Mac strolled past the Salvation Army soup kitchen line, he spotted Apple Sally. He stopped and watched for a moment. Strange, she was the shortest person in the line, one of the few women. There were no kids in line. They probably hid somewhere so welfare didn't ask why they weren't in school. He imagined the women returning to their makeshift shelters like mother birds, regurgitating their lunch for their children. Yuck. Where did these crazy thoughts come from?

Apple Sally stood a little off center from the rest, shoulders squared back, chin tilted. The ridiculous hat shielded her face. He sidled up, wondering why he should be embarrassed. Who knew him here?

"Ssst! Apple Sally! How you doing?"

A smile hovered around her lips. "Why are you whispering, Alexander?"

He flushed. "Oh, I hadn't realized I was." The dog already went into his usual raptures, and McBee waited patiently for them to finish their ritual of greeting.

"Want to come with me for lunch?"

"Want to come in with me?" she taunted.

He shifted his weight. "Well—I kinda hoped we'd have a little privacy."

She laughed. "You're a nutcase. I was kidding. I know very well you wouldn't step foot inside unless you could wrap your body in plastic wrap."

He looked sideways at the people in line, hoping no oversized specimens listened. Now was not the time to offend.

"Come on. My treat."

"Why?"

"Oh, for the love of . . . we can go to One Eyed Jack's if you want to."

The line hadn't moved an inch closer to the door.

"Well, I *am* hungry." She slipped into step with him as he turned away and began walking.

At the diner they took a table in back and Herr Schnoodle darted underneath. The dog seemed to know when he was in tail-stomping territory.

After they ordered, Mac wondered how to begin. With Darcy involved, Apple Sally was sure to imagine the worst—that he had told the reporter all about her.

"Something has come up. Remember us talking the other night—you said you couldn't remember any of your past?"

He knew he sounded as if his shoelaces were untied, but he couldn't help it. If she got up and walked out in a huff, he couldn't stop her. He considered her hat perched on the chair next to him. Maybe he could grab it and hold it as hostage to insure her sitting still long enough to hear him out.

"What's the matter, Alexander? You got something to say—spit it out."

He tried to be casual, wiping around the edge of his water glass with a napkin before he took a drink.

"I guess the best way is to start at the end and work back," he said. "We—I—know where you lived before and your real name."

Her already pale face drained of color and the little row of freckles across her nose stood out as if they were painted on. He saw her small hand in the ridiculous glove clutch her napkin.

"Does Selena Duvall strike a familiar chord?" He waited expectantly.

She frowned. "N . . . no. Tell me the rest."

"You came from Boston. The suburbs. You had a husband named Paul, but the son . . ." He shook his head, not sure how to continue.

She took off the glove and rubbed her hand across her forehead. "Wait—wait. Something's coming back. Eric was his name. We were going to adopt him—we didn't have him long."

Mac waited, but she twisted the one remaining button of her bulky sweater and stared into her water glass as if it were a crystal ball.

"Well?" her voice cut into the silence.

He jumped. "Oh, I was waiting for you to finish." He patted the dog under the table and his hand touched hers. She had been petting Herr Schnoodle, too, and she jerked away.

"There's not much more—yet. Dar—I've got to make some more inquiries. This much I can tell you. Your—your husband was under investigation, before the fire."

It didn't feel good, somehow, to picture Apple Sally loving and missing someone like a husband. A husband getting closer and closer to being a real identity.

"Who? Why?" Her voice was a husky whisper, as if her energy had drained.

He fidgeted uncomfortably. "The FBI. Something about kidnapping."

Her eyes grew round. "Kidnapping? Did I . . . did I kidnap someone?"

He shook his head. "No. I couldn't find any active investigation concerning you. Of course, they'd like to talk to you. About your—ah, Paul—and Eric."

The food finally came but neither could eat. They nibbled absentmindedly, most of it going under the table to the dog.

"Well, guess there's nothing more to do but go back to Boston," she said. "You seem to know so much. Any idea of where I start?"

He nodded.

Her eyes narrowed and her mouth tightened with suspicion.

"I'm sure you're a good detective, but tell me—how did you find out all this? Why did you do it when I told you to butt out." She sipped her coffee. "I knew there was a reason I didn't want to remember. Why couldn't you leave it alone?"

"That's something we'll never know for sure now. But you can't crawl back under that rock, can you?"

"I was happy the way things are!" she flared.

"I don't believe that for a minute. The first thing came to my mind when we met was, 'that's a very unhappy lady.' "

"I remember my sister now. We—we don't get along."

Mac waited.

"She wanted me to stay with her and her husband after the fire. I remember thinking they could be in some kind of danger because of me." Sally smoothed the checkered oilcloth with circular movements of her cup.

"Okay. What else comes back?"

She scraped back her chair. "Nothing good. Can we get out of here? The smell of food is making me sick."

He refrained from telling her that One Eyed Jack's always had that effect on him.

Out in the street, they inhaled deeply. "Ah, pure smog. How delightful," she said wryly.

They walked along, quiet for awhile.

Finally she spoke. "You didn't tell me how you found out those things about me."

He deliberately stepped on a big sidewalk crack, but even though something bad surely would have happened when he was a kid if he'd had the nerve to try that, the magic must not work for grownups.

"Well—it wasn't all me. Darcy Rasmussen helped."

She took hold of his arm, pulling him to a halt in mid-stride. "You told *her* what I confided in you?"

He shook his head adamantly. "No! I did not tell her a thing. Oh, maybe she dug the part about the fire out of me."

He couldn't look her in the eyes. Even if she needed help, he had promised not to interfere.

"I knew if anyone could get to the bottom of the puzzle, Darcy could with her contacts," he tried to explain.

"But why is she doing this?"

A logical question. He shrugged. "For the story, what else? She's probably not your basic do-gooder."

"Godalmighty! You're a master of understatement. No one would ever mistake her for a bleeding heart." Apple Sally's voice quavered with suppressed anger.

"I'd think you'd show some gratitude. We're only trying to help." He turned her face toward him with his hand under her pointy chin. "You can't stand there—look me in the eye—and tell me your life is a picnic. Can you?"

"But you miss the point, Alexander. It's *my* life, after all." Her expression softened. "I suppose you did it out of friendship."

"So, let me give you . . ." He held up his hand to stave off her objections. "Okay, I'll rephrase that. Let me *loan* you enough to go back to Boston, check things out for yourself. But contact the FBI first, you need protection."

He picked up her hand and held it between his with a gentleness welling up from deep inside him. He had the gut feeling she might never return and that hurt. He couldn't imagine why it hurt so bad, but he was fed up with examining his feelings to extract reasons. To his surprise she didn't pull away from his touch.

Her eyes closed and he watched the rainbowed lights pool on the tears beneath her auburn lashes. He pulled her close in a hug, disregarding the people skirting around them on the sidewalk.

"Well . . ." She pulled away. "I could accept a loan, maybe. I probably have some money in a checking or savings account there. I guess I wasn't always broke."

"Whatever. Now that's settled, when are you going?"

She straightened her shoulders and tilted her chin up. "As soon as I get my things together—what the hey!" She grinned, mocking his favorite expression. "Who'm I kidding? I don't have anything to pack, do I? I could go today."

"Looking like that?"

She held out her skirts as if she meant to curtsy. "No, I guess they wouldn't even let me in the door of the police station with this getup."

At that moment she did look like Little Orphan Annie with her big eyes and woebegone expression. He didn't dare smile.

He reached for his wallet and handed her some bills. "Here. Go in someplace and get rid of that outfit you're wearing. I'll wait out here if you want."

They walked down the street until she came to a store that suited her. It was one of those bargain-basement department stores where the best stuff is displayed in the window. It wasn't much, but he knew better than to argue.

He sat with Herr Schnoodle on a bus bench to wait.

It took longer than he expected, and he began to wonder if she had slipped out the back door when she finally emerged. If he hadn't known she was going in the store, he would never have recognized her coming out.

"Apple Sally! Is that you?"

She laughed. "Dolt! Close your mouth. How do I look? To tell the truth, I feel naked. And cold."

Without the several layers of calf-length dresses, skirts and sweaters, he supposed so. He could see now that she was small built, with a fragile, porcelain-doll look. Even with the cheap clothing she selected, she held herself with an air of dignity. Almost like a child presenting herself for grownup inspection. The dress she chose was green, trimmed in white with long sleeves. He supposed she would feel exposed, shedding all those garments.

"I'm speechless," he said, stalling for the right words.

Herr Schnoodle ran up and sniffed all around her legs and sat back to look at her.

They laughed at the dog's antics and the spell of unfamiliarity between them was broken.

"I left my clothes in there. The saleswoman is probably spraying the place with Lysol." She giggled. He liked the sound of it.

"I can't bear to throw this away. Keep it for me? Sentimental reasons. I'll be back for it."

"Promise?"

She looked at him with a strange expression before she handed him her cowboy hat. He took it, his fingers touching the silly crease that was worn so smooth it felt like velvet. He put a hand under her elbow and guided her along to a park close by. They sat on a bench. "We gotta stop meeting like this," he teased weakly.

She managed a smile, but he knew her thoughts were on more serious things.

"Alexander, can we say good-bye now? I don't like mushy farewells. I'm not even going to tell my friends on the street I'm leaving. I'll miss you—them. Mr. Steinmetz, Rudolfo, Mr. Olson, the people at the soup kitchen . . ." Her eyes brimmed and she wiped at them with a corner of her blouse sleeve.

Mac handed her a neatly folded paper towel from his back pocket.

She looked puzzled and then laughed. "Oh, I might have known, you'd never use anything like a cloth handkerchief. Thanks."

He was grateful for her attempt at normal sarcasm, easing their mood briefly.

"Will you take my cart back and tell him—tell him . . ." she stared at her shoes.

Who wanted to meet the Swede, much less return something that belonged to him, but for a friend, he'd do it.

Mac touched his thumb under her chin and turned her face so he could look at her. "Hey, now, stop that." He pried the wadded paper towel from her clenched hands and dabbed ineffectively at her tears. "I'll take care of everything. I'll tell them why you couldn't say good-bye."

She had fought hard to keep from having ties. Hadn't he lived that same way before the schnoodle? In different ways, he had been hiding, too. It had become a way of life.

This suddenly came to him, making him glad to be sitting down. His legs felt weak and cold sweat broke out over his forehead as he tried to imagine life without Herr Schnoodle, Mr. Steinmetz, Jesse, Bertoldi and the rest of them.

Especially Darcy and Apple Sally. Amazing.

"Damn! I don't like all this soul-searching. Takes a lot out of you."

"What?" She turned to him, the tears drying on her cheeks.

He grinned. "Excuse me. I'm so used to talking out loud to the schnoodle, they're going to carry me off with nets one of these days."

"I got used to it, too, walking around alone, you end up talking to yourself. When there isn't a soul alive who cares about you, will take time to listen to you, you have to talk to someone, even if it's yourself. Humanity fills the city, and no one truly *sees* you. A funny feeling." She shivered, pulling her sweater closed.

"You won't have to worry about that anymore. You have a sister, a family waiting. You should be able to go back, pick up where you left off. I'm sure you had many friends and people who loved and cared for you."

"Maybe. I wish I could remember. It's scary going back when you don't know what's waiting."

"I'm glad you feel that way. You got to be careful. Check with the police and the FBI before you go strolling around the old neighborhood or contacting your sister." He hoped the murdered bag ladies were just coincidences.

She reached to take his hand. "I'll never forget you, Alexander. I promise. Now be a good fellow. You guys walk away. Please?" Her lips trembled, and he sensed the tight rein she held on her emotions.

He watched as she hugged the dog and then Mac pulled her close and kissed her, a good, long kiss that left him shaken. He didn't even compare it with Darcy's kiss until much later, after he got to thinking about it. He touched the wetness on her cheeks and then moved away, letting her go.

Yet something triggered his gut feeling of apprehension. It was more than just losing her, it was a strong premonition that she was in serious danger. And she had no idea where it would come from.

Pulling on the leash, he and the dog walked away.

27

Mac had just started breakfast one morning, disposing of the cardboard container neatly and dishing up the TV dinner of macaroni and cheese, some on each plate.

"Just what we need to cheer up, eh?" He almost set a fork down for the schnoodle before remembering the dog didn't use one. The ringing of the phone intruded.

The call was from a fancy coin shop uptown.

"I chose you because you have the smallest ad in the yellow pages," Mr. Greening, the owner, admitted.

Mac didn't like the authoritative sound in his voice, but he listened, smelling money.

"Someone has stolen coins from my store. Very valuable coins, I might add."

Of course they were valuable, why else would they be in a coin shop. Mac knew the place, no nickel and dime stuff, only vintage, collectible coins, gold coins in sets, placed on display just so and put away at night leaving an empty velvet black hole in the window.

"I'll be down this morning," Mac said.

Out into the street, the schnoodle stayed close at heel. Sometimes he did that out of the goodness of his heart. Mac grinned at the patrolmen walking by and they returned a salute. Everyone knew the dog by now, and him, too. It felt so odd to be really *looked* at. No more Mr. Invisible.

"It's not a bad day, is it, old boy?" Mac began to whistle in a slightly off key. Ever since Apple Sally left he felt as if she had taken part of their lives with her. Gradually the ache began to dissolve a little at a time along with the sense of loss. This was exactly what he had been trying to avoid, when everyone eventually checked out on him.

The numbness it left behind was welcome. Mac had assumed he was immune to relationships harming him. It angered him to be open to such hurt. After the first loss of a loved one it should be like when you catch smallpox and can't get it again.

He stopped at the doorway of the coin shop.

Mac had always thought of coin stores as tacky little pawn shops, but this one looked like a sister to Cartier's. The carpet sucked up footsteps like quicksand. Soft music played on invisible speakers. Coin sets were displayed along the wall in sleek glass cases, the gold coins flickered in the soft lighting—tiny yellow eyes. Chairs grouped around small tables with green-shaded banker's lights in the center of each table.

Several customers sat at the tables, absorbed in the spread out coins.

"We don't permit animals in here," a voice purred into his ear.

Mac turned to see a tall, cadaverous-looking man staring at him over half glasses.

"Don't worry about it, buddy. I talked to Mr. Greening and he's expecting us."

"Arnold, that will be all." A voice came from a half-open door in the back of the room. "Show Mr. McBee in."

"Don't bother, Arnold. I know the way." Mac walked away from the disapproving look.

Once in the office of the owner, Mac sank into the chair offered while Herr Schnoodle lay at his feet and promptly fell asleep.

Mr. Greening had three chins while his eyes melted into

the folded sagging flesh of his face when he smiled. Which was probably not often.

He told Mac about the problem.

"So that's the way it is, Mr. McBee. I'm missing fifty thousand dollars' worth of gold Olympic coins and it is an absolute impossibility." He leaned back with a sigh.

"Did the police check this out?"

"Of course!" Greening waved an impatient hand. The diamond rings on his fingers seemed to catch fire from the desk lamp. "But I realize they don't have time to investigate this properly—not with all the mayhem that goes on in the streets."

"You're covered by insurance," Mac observed.

"Certainly. I won't be out anything in the long run. But I must understand how it was done! I have to know!" He got to his feet, pounding his fist on the desk with a boom that woke the dog.

McBee considered how quickly the man moved for his size and decided he wouldn't care to have Mr. Greening mad at him. The man was formidable; a nasty Orson Welles.

"I noticed most of your employees are older. Isn't that unusual? I mean, few people hire over-the-hill workers. What if one of them wanted a little extra retirement money."

"Those worms? They wouldn't have the intelligence or the guts!" His full bottom lip curled in disgust, reminding Mac of a slab of raw sirloin.

"Don't mistake me for an easy mark," Greening growled. "My father started this business and his most enduring edict was to hire the handicapped or older worker. They don't have options like normal people but remain completely under control always. It never failed to work over the years."

Mac considered laying a right hook into the pompous ass or dropping the case right then, big fee or not. Only the notion that the owner could be running an insurance scam stopped him. Did Greening protest too much? Mac didn't trust him. Watching the man bark orders on the intercom, Mac imagined how good it would feel to pull the plug on the slug.

Greening showed Mac around the shop. As they stepped under the doorway leading to the employee's lounge and the back storerooms a loud siren went off almost in Mac's ear. The hair on Herr Schnoodle's back raised in ridges and he jumped at least six inches off the carpet—straight up, stiff-legged.

"What the hell?" Mac stepped back from the doorway, pulling the dog with him.

One corner of Greening's perpetually pursed mouth twitched as if a smile wanted out but couldn't quite make it.

"I wanted you to see that we have a security system here second to none. Every employee comes to work with empty pockets or this alarm goes off. I had to dismiss a perfectly good secretary once, too many fillings in her teeth. Very unsettling to have the alarm go off every time she took her break or used the ladies' room."

"I imagine so," McBee struggled for nonchalance and wondered when the schnoodle would try to even up the score.

"So what you're saying is that none of your employees have the guts to do it. How about customers?"

Greening raised an eyebrow that seemed to travel up his bald forehead. "I don't suppose you would have any idea how much fifty thousand dollars' worth of gold coins weighs?"

Mac figured it as a rhetorical question, but the big man

sat waiting for him to answer.

When Mac didn't speak, Greening continued. "In the first place . . ." he held his two index fingers each the size of a cheap cigar, to emphasize the numbers . . . "No one ever turns his back on a customer with merchandise in front of them. It's one of my firmest rules and grounds for immediate dismissal. In the second place, we have cameras on each corner of the room, which you probably haven't noticed."

The edge of sarcasm in Greening's voice did not escape McBee. The truth was, he hadn't had time to observe them in particular.

"The third thing is, a customer would be quite conspicuous carrying out an armload of coins. I'm certain one of my employees might have called it to my attention."

"Mind if I look around? Talk to your people?"

"Are you quite certain that—that animal is necessary?"

"We're a team." Mac was getting used to admitting the team thing out loud. Did he just imagine the gleam of appreciation in the schnoodle's eyes?

Greening refused to look at the dog, as if by ignoring him he ceased to exist. "You come highly recommended, otherwise . . ." he turned and waddled away, back toward his office.

What a crock. McBee hadn't forgotten that Greening picked him out of the phone book because he had the smallest, therefore to Greening's way of thinking, the most discreet advertisement.

Mac explored the employee's lounge. As long as he was through the raucous doorway, he may as well stay on this side of the store. He checked for hiding places, searching—for what he wasn't sure. He couldn't get Herr Schnoodle interested.

"I know what your trouble is, old boy. You don't fool me. This posh joint doesn't have any good, juicy smells.

Why don't you hang out here and guard my hardware while I have a look out front. No lifting legs on anything, you hear?" He emptied his pockets of coins, keys and Swiss Army knife and laid them on a table near the dog.

Mac met the employees, especially liking the elderly secretary, Mrs. Wallace. Gray-haired, roundly plump, someone's grandmother, he wondered how she put up with Greening's day-by-day irascibility.

He spent the next several hours poking into corners and interviewing employees one by one. At first they didn't want to take time from their job to talk, scooting frightened looks toward Greening's door while they tried to be polite.

Mac assured each in turn that it was okay, the boss would not object. Not until then were they willing to speak to him, but they had nothing of interest to say.

He saved Arnold until last.

"Is Arnold your first name or your last?" Mac made notes in his book and sucked on his pencil while he waited.

"I don't see how that is relative, but—it happens to be my last name." He stood at attention, looking like a valued member of Hitler's SS squad.

Mac sighed. "Don't make this any more difficult than it has to be, buddy. I'm a working stiff, same as you. With a job to do, same as you."

Arnold unbent a trifle. "It's just that I've worked with the late Mr. Greening and now with the present one. I've got seniority. I feel I should be above questioning. It's—it's degrading."

"Now, now, no such thing," Mac found himself trying to appease the man. "It's a formality, is all. It's possible to have seen something you didn't realize could make a difference . . . help the case tremendously. That's my job, to put pieces of puzzles together."

It had become depressing when people he wanted to dislike turned out to have redeeming qualities. Where was his old cynicism that had served him so faithfully and so comfortably? At least he felt certain Greening would not be a disappointment. He was a thoroughly disgusting person.

Mac finished questioning Arnold and went back to the schnoodle who hadn't budged from the spot where Mac left him.

"Come on, fella. I've done all I can do for now. I'm going home to check over my notes. Got to chew on it some." They walked through the noisy doorway again, only this time they were expecting the buzzer and Schnoodle barely twitched. Mr. Cool, Mac was proud of his partner.

Once out in the lobby, the dog refused to budge.

"Hold on here, I thought you didn't like this place."

Mac snapped on the leash and pulled, but Herr Schnoodle sat looking like a furry Buddha. Knowing better than to ignore him when he was in one of these moods, Mac unsnapped the leash and patiently waited.

The dog walked slowly to one of two waist-high brass posts that separated the customers from the main coin storage area. A heavy twisted velvet cord hung between the two. Herr Schnoodle sniffed one post, moved across to the other and returned to the first one. Mac watched, ready to pounce if that left leg began to raise even an inch off the carpet. He knew the dog hadn't forgiven Greening for the doorway scare.

The customers and employees stopped to watch, and Mac felt as if he was putting on a floor show. It was embarrassing.

"Come on, boy. Quit showing off and let's go."

The dog gazed up, golden-dotted eyebrows raised with an expression hard to interpret. After a moment of letting Mac discover who was boss, the schnoodle permitted him to fix the leash and they walked out the door.

Later at home, Mac read the box from the frozen pizza while it heated in the toaster oven. He'd cut it in two pieces to fit in which always seemed a sacrilege—like chopping up spaghetti with a fork and knife before you ate it. The list of ingredients made him remember Apple Sally.

Several weeks had gone by, but who was counting? He had tried hard to forget that sudden rush of panic surfacing the first week when he let himself think of her.

He could call Darcy to talk, drain away the loneliness, but the thought of their usual snappy repartee seemed too much trouble. Where was all this going?

28

McBee flipped through his notes while he ate, washing down the tough crust with lukewarm beer he'd forgotten to refrigerate.

"Might as well eat the cardboard box," he confided in the dog. "Apple Sally never missed a chance to say that." He took a small comfort in mentioning her name out loud.

The schnoodle sat up in attention, looking toward the door. When it didn't open, he let loose one of his shrill barks that had the anchovies doing a back stroke on the tomato sauce.

"Sorry I brought it up, old man. No one's out there in our hallway. Here, have some of my beer, you don't care if it's as warm as cat pee, do you?"

Mac tried to hone in on the problem of the coin shop until his eyes glazed.

"There's the real possibility that Greening isn't on the level." He spoke out loud, interrupting the tinny sound of the clock ticking away in the silent room.

Outside, the usual sirens blared up and down the streets. The sounds sifted easily through the closed window. Mac switched on the television, turning the volume down so the low, droning sound erased some of the street noises.

"There's Arnold, he'd be high on a list of suspects. Did you notice his dissatisfaction with his job—with life in general? He doesn't like his boss—but then he'd have to stand in line for that privilege. I'd put my money on the boss or Arnold, or both."

Mac smacked his fist against his open palm in satisfaction. "If there's one thing I pride myself on, it's my ability to judge people. It's my long suit, you have to admit."

The dog was busy lapping up beer, lost in his own doggie world.

Flipping the notebook pages, Mac continued, "Mrs. Wallace, now there's a real lady." He doodled on the page as he pictured the silver-haired secretary. "So dignified, so charmingly old-fashioned. Remember her? She offered to pet you and you wouldn't let her." He glared at the dog with mild reproof. "Just because she's elderly—prejudice doesn't become you."

He was so caught up in his lecture that he barely noticed the fourth beer was almost gone. It probably wouldn't have occurred to him even then, except he was talking more than usual and sometimes his tongue found it hard to negotiate between his teeth.

"Hey, old buddy. Let's tie one on. I got a six pack here, that ought to do it."

He took another swig, no longer caring that it was warm. "Getting back to Mrs. Wallace—you owe that little old lad . . . ." he belched and the dog jumped in surprise, as if he wasn't sure who made the sound.

Mac laughed. "Hah! Never heard me do that before, I don't suppose. I got many hidden talents. I can . . . well, never mind that," he waved his hand in a gesture he imagined breezy. He wobbled away from the table and flopped on the couch. A spring poked up through the material and he yipped.

"As I was shaying, you owe that dear, sweet lady an apology, old man. You were rude, rude, rude." He shook his finger at Herr Schnoodle.

The dog laid his chin on his paws and sighed. "It's

219

gonna be a long night," his expression plainly stated.

Mac sat up and kicked at the throw rug he had nearly tripped on. "Darcy's right. I ought not to be so cheap and put in some carpeting. But then, what the heck would you use as a skateboard to zip around the room when you're excited?"

He patted the couch and the dog leaned his head on Mac's chest, looking at him eye to eye. Mac promptly fell asleep.

The next morning he wasn't any closer to the solution than the night before. He didn't even have a headache to show for his night of debauchery. "I guess I'm not cut out to be impulsive and reckless, am I?" He spoke to the dog as he put two Pop-Tarts in the toaster for their breakfast.

"I'll get Joe to run a check on the employees. Could turn up something, although I doubt it. They'd have to be bonded to the max to suit old Greening. It feels like an inside job."

He had nearly finished shaving when he heard someone knock and push the front door open. His heart missed a beat. He ran the comb through his hair and threw on some aftershave. That could only be Darcy.

Darcy stood inside, waiting. "McBee. You decent?"

"Yep. Care for some breakfast?"

"What? A TV dinner? Leftover pizza? Ah, a Pop-Tart. No thanks." She held out a bag. "I brought fresh cinnamon rolls."

Mac looked at her and already his day was brighter.

She wore a lemon-yellow blouse with the usual jeans. Her hair was pulled up into a ponytail, bangs thick on her forehead. She looked fresh as a dish of sherbet on a hot summer day.

"What's new?" He broke a slightly burned Pop-Tart in

two and fed half to Herr Schnoodle who seemed to think he was getting more that way than if he gave him a whole one at one time. But the schnoodle suddenly wasn't hungry, and sniffing in Darcy's direction, he plopped in a corner, turning his back on them.

"I'm going to have a man to dog talk with him about his rudeness to company," McBee said.

"Ah, don't worry about it. He's jealous. He'll get over it once he gets it through his furry, little brain that I'm not coming on to you."

Mac's day dulled somewhat. "Is that true? You mean my macho virility hasn't gotten to you yet?"

She laughed and the sound lit up the room. "Oh, God! You're about as macho as . . ."

He held up a hand. "Hold on, don't say any more. My ego can only take so much battering early in the morning."

She set aside her coffee mug and gave him a searching look. "McBee, word's out that Apple Sally took a hike. Is that true?"

"Yep. She asked me to say good-bye to her friends, and to you, too. Everyone on the street has stopped me to ask where she is. I'd no idea so many knew her and cared about her, or knew we were friends."

"Did you tell her everything we knew?"

"I think so."

"Telling her what I found could have been good news or bad."

"What do you mean?"

"Didn't we decide the bag-lady killings could have something to do with her? What if someone is tailing her? Wouldn't they know she had lived in Boston before she came here? Wouldn't they be waiting for her to come back?"

McBee frowned. Some detective. He'd told her to be careful, to check with the cops, but he really didn't think . . . Actually he'd been so glad to give Apple Sally-Selena her past back, everything else was incidental.

"Could be we're getting paranoid. She changed out of her street clothes, didn't she?" Darcy asked.

"You bet she did. I got her to buy some new clothes for her trip home. She looked a totally different person."

"That's a help. If there's someone after her, he's a hired gunny looking for a certain bag lady and doesn't care who he offs to get to her."

"Good Lord, Darcy. Have you been watching too many late-night detective shows? You talk like someone from *Miami Vice*."

Darcy laughed. "You're a fine one to talk. Did you tell her I helped find out about her?"

"Had to. She wasn't too happy about it at first, but then she warmed to the idea. I think she was grateful we got to the bottom of it for her."

"She's an okay lady. We never got on for some reason. Clash of personalities, I guess. Maybe *she* was jealous."

"Nah. Nothing like that between us, we're friends. The schnoodle misses her a lot."

Darcy frowned. "McBee, for a detective, you can be dense as a post. Don't you know she's crazy for you?"

"Apple Sally?"

"Whoever she is. Even you couldn't be that dumb—not to see it."

"No. I didn't see it. And you're wrong, for once in your sweet life. We're friends, period."

She stood and stretched.

Mac took a hasty drink of coffee and almost choked.

"I wondered—just curious—do you work out or something? You make Jane Fonda look like yesterday's oatmeal."

Time to take the talk away from Apple Sally. He might as well forget about her, like everything else in his life, she was gone. Kaput.

Darcy grinned. "Nope. Don't have time. I burn it all up because I hardly take time to eat or sleep. You're in pretty good shape yourself."

They were standing toe to toe, eye to eye. With her high-heeled boots, she was nearly as tall as his six feet.

Mac didn't plan it. It was spontaneous combustion he told himself later. They moved together in a clinch and a kiss that lasted until both broke away, breathing hard.

"I've been waiting forever for that one," he managed, ignoring the trifling flutter of disappointment. He *had* waited forever, but the kiss was flat. Could it be that after all this time he expected too much?

She sat on the couch to take out her compact, repairing her lipstick. Neither spoke and the clock tick-tocked to fill the silence.

With a quick decisiveness, she clicked shut the compact and looked up at him.

"I'm kinda sorry that happened, McBee. Can we just forget it? We had—have something good. Romances grow like weeds, one week on, the next week off, but friendship is special. I never had a real friendship with a man before you came along."

He never expected poetry from her. It was hard to speak beyond the lump in his throat.

"Friends are fine. But so's—whatever."

"I'm afraid I couldn't handle any whatevers right now. I've got to concentrate on my career. I paid my dues and I'm ready for bigger things. I won't stay at the *Union Globe* forever. Besides—I get the feeling you were kind of going through the motions."

He didn't understand the relief that surged through his body. As if the vent was taken off a pressure cooker full of steam. Wasn't he always telling Herr Schnoodle that he was happy living alone as he always had?

"Okay. Let's go back to square one. Think we can do that?"

She hadn't protested too much, had she?

Darcy grinned and stuck out her hand. "I'd like that." She slung the camera bag over her shoulder. "Thanks for the coffee. If I get any word in the underground about Apple Sally, I'll let you know. I'm convinced there's a great story there."

When the door closed behind her the room felt old and used up, sucked dry of air.

He ruffled the dog's ears. "Well, guess I blew that all to hell, old boy. *Que sera, sera* as they say. Anyway, I gotta concentrate on the matter at hand here. We'll have to make another trip to the coin shop." He split the one remaining cinnamon bun with the schnoodle.

"I should leave you behind this time. No use taking you there and having the boss or Arnold follow our every step like you'll break out into rabies any minute."

The dog barked shrilly, a definite "no."

"Damn! Okay, come along, but be careful. Those cameras don't miss anything. We're moving up into big time, fella. Our caseload is definitely picking up."

He put on the blue tie that was the same color as his eyes. Apple Sally had mentioned that. Sliding the knot in place under this shirt collar, he spoke to the image in his bathroom mirror.

"You might have blown it with Darcy, old man. She's the kind of doll who shouldn't have a lot of time to think things out. Impulse is the ticket with her." He ran his tongue over his lips, trying to recapture the feel of hers.

He decided to walk to the coin shop rather than take a taxi. "You prefer this, too, don't you?" He asked the dog. Of course he did, hardly missing a fireplug along the way.

Once they spied a shopping cart headed toward them and stopped, waiting. What was the matter with his crazy heart? It nearly pounded out of his chest. It was just the worry about her. What if there really was a hit man after her? Nah, that was too far out.

"False alarm, Schnoodle. It's only the supermarket kid gathering up the carts." They walked on past and the dog would have lifted his leg, but the boy was too fast for him.

The coin shop was empty of customers when they arrived. The employees broke from their clusters, probably feeling guilty for standing around talking instead of shining the cases and dusting or whatever they had to do to look busy. It was clear that the boss was not in. McBee walked around the room as if he knew what he was looking for, with Arnold not far behind.

"When does the boss come in?"

"Elevenish," Arnold said, wiping a glass counter after Mac touched it.

Schnoodle ignored everyone, on his good behavior, sitting in his favorite spot next to that brass pole. Actually he leaned against it, his eyes closed. If he had been a person, Mac would have sworn he was concentrating hard. Nah, he was just dozing off. Like a drunk leaning against a lamp pole. He grinned at the idea.

Mac and Mrs. Wallace had coffee in the employee's lounge. She was so different, without Greening around. All the employees were different. Mac heard them softly laughing and talking out front.

"How long you been here, Mrs. Wallace?" He made

detective noises although he already had her record.

"Nearly six years now, Mr. McBee," she said. "Next to Arnold, I have seniority."

"Hmm. That's swell. You like your job?"

"Oh, of course! Mr. Greening is such a perfect gentleman to work for."

"Yes, I would imagine."

"Not many places hire seniors. Most businesses prefer younger people. Mr. Greening is a real humanitarian."

Mac stirred his coffee, envisioning the spoon melting into the black ooze. Stuff dinosaurs came from, probably leftover from the day before. He returned to the matter at hand.

The little gray lady was pathetic. If she only knew her boss hired seniors because of the control it gave him, and probably because it made him look younger, too.

"Uh, yes, I suppose you could say that," he managed. He asked a few more questions to make it look good, but he knew it wasn't necessary.

She excused herself, looking at her watch like the March Hare in *Alice in Wonderland*.

He interviewed the rest of the employees and then settled back to check his notes. Nothing. Zilch. He drew a big fat blank. Besides, he couldn't keep his mind focused when that darn dog insisted on staying out front alone like that. It was so unlike him. Usually he trailed underfoot, a mere step away at any time.

Mac flipped the notebook shut and put it in his pocket. The thief could be a disgruntled former employee, but the records showed they hadn't had any other employees in a long time. Greening had hired extra help for the Christmas season that could be checked out. It had to be either Greening or Arnold. He wanted it to be Greening. Now came the how and why.

226

In the showroom, he found Herr Schnoodle practically wrapped around one of the brass posts. Had the sound of the alarm scared him so much he didn't want to leave this one spot?

Mac shook the post gently, trying to be nonchalant. The dog nearly went into ecstasy. Moving over to the other one, he watched the schnoodle and got no reaction when he touched it. From the corner of his eye he caught a blur of someone peering through a doorway and then stepping back. Had an employee been watching them?

Something was definitely up, and worth checking. Mac remembered the rain gutter and the Count. He'd better give this some more thought.

"Come on, boy. Let's go to The Cave. We can pick up some news from the boys."

At the mention of the bar, the dog licked his chops and made a move to leave. Then he sniffed the post and growled, a low rumble in the back of his throat.

Mac leaned against the post and watched the schnoodle. As soon as he picked his hand up off the round top of the post, Arnold slithered up behind him and wiped it with his dust cloth.

Mac jumped. "You scared the hell out of me!"

"Brass tarnishes with human perspiration," Arnold said primly. As he worked, the dog growled, menace in his voice. Mac had never heard him do that before.

"That dog is vicious!" Arnold backed away.

"No, he isn't. He doesn't like it, either, when someone sneaks up behind like that." Mac snapped the leash on the schnoodle, pulling him out the front door before Arnold could get angry enough to blab to the boss.

Mac felt anxious to get to The Cave. If the gold coins had surfaced in a local pawn shop or a fence still had them,

Smitty or the Spaceman would know.

Once out into the street, he bent to scold. "What the hell you want to act like that for? What's the matter with you? He's one of our suspects and we don't want to antagonize him—yet."

He pulled the dog along on the leash until he thought the schnoodle properly chastised. Once in a while the dog turned his face up to Mac as if to say, "Is it over? Am I forgiven? I need to stop and pee."

Finally Mac couldn't stand it and unsnapped the leash to let the dog trot by his side. "Oh, come on. I'll quit pouting if you will. Let's have a beer. It's early, but what the hey."

The Cave seemed to have its usual number of inhabitants, as much as he could see in the corners of the shadowy room.

"Ah, Smitty! I was hoping to see you." Mac sat on a stool and watched as the dog leaped onto the one next to him.

"What'll it be, gents? The usual?" Harry walked up from somewhere in the gloom and slapped paper coasters on the bar. Herr Schnoodle looked at peace with the world, knowing what was coming.

"Yeah, beer and pretzels. Fill my buddy's glass, too, whatever he's having."

My buddy? Smitty? Gads, he was falling apart. Smitty raised a thin eyebrow without making a comment. Mr. Cool. The Fonz, like on TV.

Mac considered hollering "FIRE!" just to get Smitty's reaction someday. He could imagine it. The man would probably glance into the mirror in front of them, push his greased pompadour in place and saunter out—after he finished three-quarters of his drink. He was etched in time. The fifties had given birth to this man full grown, and he had never changed from his wide lapels and cheap shiny zoot suit to hair groomed by Penzoil.

"I'm blocked on a case," Mac said out of the corner of his mouth when the bartender left. There was no need for secrecy, but Smitty's demeanor inspired this attitude. Imagining himself like the sturdy tough Mannix, McBee took a breath, sucking in his already flat stomach.

He had always been slender, but since the schnoodle came along he had never eaten so regular nor gotten so much exercise outdoors. Mannix would never get soft, no matter how many dogs came into his life and caused him to fill up on beer and pretzels.

Smitty nodded. "Heard about the case."

Mac waited patiently. The sound of the dog crunching pretzels was loud in spite of a pinball machine dinging away in a dark corner. No blasting arcade games for this place.

"You're working the coin shop." Smitty didn't ask, he knew.

"Yeah. And I'm stumped."

"Gotta be an inside job. Burglar alarms everywhere—video cameras, the whole *smeggegala*."

"Yeah, that's what I figured." How did Smitty learn all this? By dumb luck, he had picked the right snitch.

Mac waited, knowing the man would get to the point when it suited him.

In a few minutes Smitty slid off the stool and, sketching a brief good-bye with two finger to his forehead, he disappeared in the gloom, out the back door.

Good Lord. Was that it?

Schnoodle lapped his beer delicately and crunched away. His expression warned Mac not to rush him.

"So much for help from that guy. We got to get in and snoop alone—after the joint closes. I can't concentrate with

Arnold on my heels wiping up perspiration stains off everything I touch." He nursed his brew and stared moodily at his image in the mirror. He loosened his tie and imagined throwing a jacket across his shoulders in the manner of Harry O.

No way Greening was going to let anyone in there alone.

"You haven't been much help, either, old buddy." He turned toward the schnoodle. "You've lost interest since Apple Sally left. Come on now, shape up. We aren't ever going to see that little munchkin again so come to grips with yourself." He wondered if he was lecturing the dog or himself.

He considered walking over to see Mr. Steinmetz. He'd like to see how Jesse made out at the dentist. Mrs. Rodriguez should be back to work by now, and he hoped things were okay with them.

If only Darcy had left Apple Sally alone, mystery or not. Maybe Steinmetz could have convinced her to move in with him and . . . well, no use thinking about it, life seldom worked out to neat little endings.

On the walk home Mac tried to keep his mind on the coin shop mystery, but somehow he knew all was not right with Apple Sally.

And he couldn't do a darn thing about it.

29

As Mac climbed the stairs of his apartment building the dog leaped ahead, taking three steps at a time.

"Hey, slow down! You're in a heck of a hurry to get home, aren't you?" Mac laughed. "We're having frozen pizza again, no big deal."

"Oh no, you're not." A voice drifted down from the top of the stairs.

"Apple Sally!" Mac stood back and looked at her leaning across the top of the stairway.

"Ever try locking your door? My name's Selena, by the way. You might as well get used to that."

Herr Schnoodle had already wrapped himself around her legs in ecstasy and she knelt to hold him.

When she could catch her breath, she motioned toward the table. "Do you guys mind eating Chinese? It's the closest place for takeouts."

He looked her over. She was dressed in the same combination of Salvation Army specials. Mac tried to quell his disappointment. "I thought that—if we ever saw you again—you'd look different. You're gonna ask for your old hat next."

"Ah! Did you save that for me? Thanks a lot, Alexander."

"I wouldn't have thrown it out for the world," he said, meaning it. The hat lay on top of his desk, so he had to look at it every day.

"Thanks. That was sweet."

"You going to tell me what's happened in your life?"

" 'Course, I've got a long story to tell you. Let's eat first, I'm famished," she said.

The food was good and the schnoodle loved the crunch of fried noodles.

They munched in companionable silence, and when they finished Mac poured out glasses of the wine he had bought for Darcy's visit.

"Well? I can't wait all night to hear. Tell me," he said.

She got up and stretched. A comparison between hers and Darcy's stretches came to mind and he shrugged it off. Apple Sally—Selena—still reminded him of a small rag doll.

She sat on the floor, close to the dog and leaned back against the couch. Mac straddled a chair and waited.

"Oh God, where do I start? It's all such a mess, you wouldn't believe." She patted her hair, which for once laid close against her neck fastened with some kind of clasp.

"Try me. I'm listening."

"Someone was—is trying to kill me," she stated flatly. "I suspected someone was following me a time or two when I walked down an alley or a quiet street."

"Here? You didn't say anything."

"No. In Boston. After Darcy went to Boston to check on me, he picked up my trail from her."

"He?"

"Paul, of course. There's no other answer."

"But isn't he dead?"

"I don't think so. He . . . ah . . . he has connections. He could have planted a body, threw in his partial plate along with his medallion hidden well enough so it wouldn't be burned away. He's capable of that sort of thing."

"And the boy?"

For the first time she smiled. "I'm sure Eric is alive, I

feel that very strongly. I hope—I think, he's home with his family by now."

"His family? But I thought . . ."

She brushed his question away. "Later, there's so much to tell you." She sighed.

Mac wanted to hold her small body, shield her against pain. It hurt to look at her pale, drawn expression.

"The problem is, I haven't any proof of what I believe is the truth. I think he meant to kill me in the explosion and then chickened out at the last minute, knocked me unconscious and dragged me to the front yard."

"Well, he had that much going for him." Mac would have liked to strangle Paul Duvall on the spot. "Why would he want to kill you now, after saving you?"

"You'd have to know Paul. He probably followed or had me followed around for a while, discovered I had amnesia and had taken up the life of a bag lady and left me alone. Then when someone called Boston to check records at the police precinct, he was tipped off that my memory must have come back."

"He's got connections, all right."

"I'm sure he has something to do with those poor women being killed here. He knew how I was hiding and hired a killer. Those poor women, dying like that."

Mac had never thought he could hate anyone like he did Paul Duvall. How could she have married such a creep?

"Then when Darcy started nosing around in Boston, Paul must have felt even more threatened and it convinced him he'd been on the right track killing those poor homeless women. He had to be desperate to be rid of me. Oh God, I just realized, you might be in danger."

"Hey, you've got plenty on your mind without concerning yourself with me. But you're right, he knows you're here, just not where. It's a big city."

"I'm the only one who could mess up—whatever his scam is. The police in Boston are trying to get a handle on this. They and the FBI want me to testify against him and I said I would. Meanwhile, I've started divorce proceedings."

"Good idea. Shouldn't be a problem." The thought of her free of ties to this thug made him feel good. "You sure the boy's alive, too?"

She looked at her hands, spreading her small fingers. "Of course. That's what it's all about. He kidnaps Eric and returns him to his family with ransom paid. At least I pray to God he returned the boy."

"But—I don't understand. How long did you know this character before you married him? Why did he marry you in the first place?"

At her hurt look, he hurried on. "I could put that another way. What I meant . . ."

"Oh, I get what you mean. Paul was the photographer at the modeling agency I worked for."

He tried not to smile. Weren't all models like Darcy?

"It's true. I modeled children's clothing—you don't have to believe it. My specialty was the Orphan Annie look. I polished it to perfection."

Of course she did. He held up his hand. "Okay, okay. I believe you. Stop with the explanations already and go on."

She stretched her legs, crossed them under her long skirt and leaned back on her palms to look at the ceiling.

"Paul swept me off my feet," she admitted. "A spur of the moment deal. We'd only known each other a couple of months. One day he looked right through me—the next he asked to take me to dinner, flowers and the works."

"Didn't you think that strange?"

She lowered her chin toward her chest. "Of course I did.

234

He worked with tons of beautiful women. I suppose I tried not to examine it too closely. Now I realize he wanted someone to help him smuggle Eric to the States. Someone ordinary that no one would notice."

McBee rocked back and forth on the chair. This was getting too bizarre. "Can you hold that thought long enough so's I can put on a pot of coffee?"

When he returned with steaming mugs and handed her one, he pulled the chair closer. "Did you say *smuggle* the boy into the States?"

"Yes. It gets stranger as I go along—hang in there. Please." She patted her skirt and Herr Schnoodle laid his head on her lap, curling against her.

"As I was saying—we went to Europe on our honeymoon." Her expression lost the tight, closed look for a moment as her eyes shone.

Mac felt a surge of jealousy, relieved when the bitter look returned to her eyes.

"I had a wonderful time. There's something else that I found about my past when my memory returned. I was married before Paul came along. We had a child—a boy." She lowered her head and sighed. "The boy died from what they call crib death. I—we were divorced not long afterward. I guess we couldn't cope with it as a couple."

"God, I'm sorry you had all this dumped on you when your memory came back. Must have been overwhelming."

She nodded. "Still is. Anyway, Paul and I traveled through Germany. He said he had to buy some camera equipment there. I never questioned him. When we arrived in Italy, we went to this nunnery—convent—whatever they call it. Everyone knew him. He told me a couple, friends, died in an auto accident and left an orphan—Eric—whom he visited from time to time."

"I don't get it. If he kidnapped the boy and stashed him at the convent, wouldn't the kid tell the nuns?"

She shook her head. "He was four, barely talking and then only German. No one there spoke anything but French. I think his father is some German big shot, politics or an industrialist, something like that. The boy's parents probably had nannies to look after him."

"So Paul kidnapped the kid, stashed him in the convent for safekeeping, and then when he thought of how to do it, went back for him with you?"

"I know. Sounds weird, but so was Paul, I'm learning. The poor little kid, he was a shy, quiet little fellow. I rarely heard a peep from him all the while he stayed with us. No wonder, poor baby. I'd love to see Paul burn in hell for what he put that child through."

Mac sipped coffee and tried to digest some of the surprises she had tossed into the room.

"What escapes me is, why'd he have to marry you? Why did he involve you in the first place?"

"Do I have to spell it out? I suppose he saw that I was gullible and naive enough to swallow everything he dished out." She made a wry face, wrinkling the freckles across her nose. "He needed someone—someone ordinary like me, but we had to be a married couple—we had to have legitimate papers. When we walked into the airport together, customs looked at our papers and didn't even ask for the boy's. A cute family on vacation in Europe. When I carried Eric, he held on to my neck like he was drowning, poor tyke, and I had no idea . . ."

Tears ran down her cheeks and she brushed them away with her fists. "Paul must have been sure they wouldn't bother to check us, but I think he had a forged passport on hand."

Mac got the picture. He saw the happy couple. The well-dressed American businessman, the small, earnest young woman with the blond child clutching her tightly.

"What did *you* think about it?"

She wiped her eyes again. "What was I to think? Paul told me Eric was raised in Germany, his father American, his mother German. He said his old buddy was a retired airline pilot who married a German girl on one of his trips and they settled in Europe. Paul said we could adopt Eric so he wouldn't be an orphan anymore, but we couldn't let the German or French authorities know because it would get complicated and take years."

McBee sensed Selena was closing in with the ending. He could feel the tension build in the room, touching everything and giving the battered furnishings a blurred, surrealistic quality. Even Herr Schnoodle seemed to feel it. The dog stood and shook, his collar and tags rattling loudly. He left Selena and plopped next to Mac.

"Getting back to the part before the fire—our lives began to change. I had been after Paul to petition the courts to make the adoption legal. He turned hateful and ugly. I couldn't reason with him; he became a stranger." She shivered, rubbing her arms as if she were cold.

"Poor Eric was afraid of him. I figured it as natural shyness." She hit her palm against her forehead. "Oh! I was so stupid! So stupid!"

"Ah, come on. You're being too hard on yourself. You couldn't have known any of these things, it all happened too fast. Do you—are you sure Eric didn't die in the fire?"

"I understand Paul, really know him now. I've done a lot of thinking. I'm certain he returned the child to his people and claimed his blood money."

"Are the police looking for Paul?"

"Better than that. The FBI is, too."

"But where did Eric come from? Have you any idea? How come his parents didn't raise holy hell with the police when he was kidnapped and again when they finally got him back?"

"I'm sure Paul threatened them with dire consequences."

"Did the parents come to the States to get the boy?"

She nodded. "I believe so. Paul was on his own turf here, holding all the cards. He couldn't have moved the child out of the US anyway, not alone."

"That brings us the full circle—back to you."

"I know. He's trying to get at me. In Boston, a car nearly ran me down, and my motel room was broken into, and someone left a ticking device. I called the police and luckily they dismantled it before the bomb went off." She smoothed her skirts. "That's why I came back to the city. I figured he'd never find me in a million years as Apple Sally. I needed time to consider my options."

"You didn't think this out, did you? If he doesn't mind having a few random bag ladies offed, what makes you think he's given up trying? If, as you say, he has connections, he could find you here. You do kinda stand out, even with that getup."

"Ah, come on, Alexander. You didn't even want to sit near me until you began to know me. Paul would never recognize me."

"What about the dead bag ladies? Do you suppose they deserved to be mistaken for you?" He was ashamed at her stricken look and waited for her reply.

It was slow in coming.

30

Mac sipped cold coffee, waiting for her answer. When she didn't speak, he had to fill the void.

"You can't stay Apple Sally forever, though, can you?" He almost wished she could. He didn't know what to make of the new Selena identity, but the Apple Sally character fit like a glove.

"You're a detective, aren't you? That's good enough for me. I thought you could help."

He considered for a long moment. This was way beyond his league—kidnapping, arson, attempted murder.

"I'll do what I can. I'm small potatoes, though. What you need is a *real* PI. One with experience and . . ."

"What I need is help from a friend," she said. "You'll do fine."

"With all you've been through, it's time you wised up."

"What are you talking about?" Her chin tilted in the air in that way of hers when she became belligerent.

"You're still trusting everyone. Can't you get it through your head that most people are undependable and untrustworthy?"

She jumped to her feet, hands clenched on her hips, her face as red as her hair. "I don't see nothing of the kind! Anything, I mean." She corrected herself automatically.

It must have been hard for her to slip in and out of the Apple Sally character. It left Selena Duvall out in the cold. Mac felt a weary sadness, hoping the two were the same, afraid they weren't.

"I know it's a cliché, but one rotten Paul doesn't spoil the whole human race," she said. "I can't believe that or life would be pointless. You can't mean it, either, you're all talk."

He played with one of the dog's ears. "I guess you're right. What I'm trying to tell you is, you can't walk around with your guts hanging on the outside like you do. It's . . . it's indecent! This whole episode would have never happened to Darcy Rasmussen for instance."

For a heartbeat he thought he'd finally screwed up good and proper. Her face lost its rosy hue and her lips flattened in anger. Then a grin emerged as she stared him in the eye.

"No. I suppose Darcy would never have been sucked in by any of it." She leaned forward and tapped him on the knee. "But Alexander, Darcy is Darcy and I'm me. Never confuse the issue here. Some day this point may be very important."

She was right.

"Thanks for the shoulder to cry on," she said. "I gotta get going."

"Where?"

"Where do Apple Sallys usually hang out at night? You never asked before."

He shook his head, feeling ashamed. "No, I never did."

"Aha! Most people are the same as you. They see streeties like me—they see us and their eyes jump through or over or around us—instant astigmatism. People don't want to believe that we live and breathe and eat and feel— just like they do."

The truth of her accusation struck home. He winced. "I never thought of it. Anyway, you're one streety that isn't sleeping out there tonight alone. You're going to stay right here with us."

"I'll do no such thing. I could stay with Mr. Steinmetz if

I wanted to stay with anyone. Perhaps even Rudolfo Bertoldi would take me in," she teased.

"And what if Paul does find you? You wouldn't want to involve them, would you?"

She took her hand from the doorknob and turned to him. "Why do *you* want to get involved?"

Her expression was curious, expectant, and he stopped the flip answer that worked toward his lips. He slid back the chair and walked over to stand in front of her. "I can't say, kiddo. I honestly can't say. There's no easy way to go here. What if I say—ah, what the hell—I care what happens to you. I care a lot."

He was close enough to catch a whiff of the fresh, clean smell of soap on her skin. He touched her cheek lightly with his fingers and leaned to kiss the tip of her nose.

She stared into his eyes for a long moment after the kiss and seemed content by what she saw.

"Okay. But only until I learn how things are in the streets. Mr. Olson wasn't well, he may be gone, bless him. Strictly business though, understood? I had money in our bank account in Boston. Paul didn't dare touch it. I can pay my own way and I can pay for your time."

Mac took her arm and led her to the couch. Herr Schnoodle watched their every move. When she sat, the dog went into raptures.

"I swear, if I was a jealous man . . ." Mac grinned.

"But you are. You're just good at hiding it." She laughed and he was relieved to see the lines around her mouth relax for the first time since she entered the room.

"You take the bed," he said. "There's a Murphy bed there on the wall, we just pull it down. I've slept on the couch many times when I fell asleep watching the tube." He shushed her protests.

For awhile Mac couldn't fall asleep with her lying so close, almost close enough to touch the foot of the bed from where he lay on the couch. Finally sleep came to him, but sometime in the middle of the night he leaped from the couch at the sound of her scream. His surroundings were unfamiliar, and for a second he was lost. He tangled in the blanket, bumped his shin against a chair and finally managed to make his way toward the bed.

Flipping on the lights, Mac had a sudden fear that she was gone. Then he saw the small bump under the covers. She was hiding. Herr Schnoodle sat near the bedside, his expression plainly puzzled by all the uproar.

Mac sat on the edge of the bed and spoke to her softly. The bed shimmied with her trembling. He removed the covers from around her, pulled her to his chest and began to soothe her as he would a frightened child.

While her sobs melted into soft hiccups, he held her close and patted her cheeks dry with the corner of the sheet.

"You okay? Have a nightmare?"

She shook her head and pointed to the schnoodle. "He jumped on the bed and I woke up scared."

"You thought that louse broke in here after you." Mac hugged her shoulders with affection. "Schnoodle, see what you did?" Mac scolded. "You're lucky he didn't trigger the closing gizmo and shut you both up into the wall."

Apple Sally giggled. "Don't blame him, he wanted to be close—or maybe he forgot and thought it was you in bed."

She felt fragile inside the curve of his arm. He lifted her chin with a finger and looked into her eyes. It was like diving into a green pool of still water.

She cuddled closer, surprising him. "Stay here with me," she whispered, her breath warm on his cheek.

It hurt like hell to say no.

He kissed each closed eyelid before answering. "Nope. You'd hate yourself in the morning—not to mention me." He felt his own need to make love to her, a throbbing ache that he finally recognized had been with him a long while. It couldn't happen like this, not when she was so defenseless.

She sighed. "You're right. We've got a swell friendship going, why spoil it."

That wasn't what he meant at all, was it? Darcy had said the same words, but it felt different now. He wasn't so sure of what he wanted or didn't want.

She kissed him. "You're a gentleman, Alexander McBee."

His grin was wry. "A gentleman and a damn fool?" He said the words softly, more to himself than to her.

31

The next morning she surprised him by waking first and fixing breakfast. He didn't even hear the squeak of the bed going up into the wall when she got up but the good smells woke him. She'd managed wonders using the two-burner hot plate and digging stuff out of the little square refrigerator he'd hauled home from a street sale.

By the time Mac finished the third cup of coffee he was ready to face the world. "Good breakfast." He leaned back in the chair. "How come you woke up early? I had a hunch you would sleep in."

She laughed. Her hair was restrained by dampness, her face still shiny from a shower.

"I got the habit since I've been here in the city. When I stay at the mission or the Y, you must get out of bed as soon as everyone starts milling around or you don't get breakfast."

"I'm working on a case. A good one." He looked at the schnoodle. "I think I'll have to leave him home. What's cooking with you for today?"

"Ah, Mac, about last night—I put you in a spot and I'm sorry. Thanks for not taking advantage of it—of me." Her pale cheeks suffused with pink and he knew she was embarrassed.

"Hey—don't give it a thought." He brushed away her gratitude, it made him uncomfortable. "You'll be okay here?"

"I'm in no hurry to leave. If it's all right with you, the

schnoodle and I'll watch TV."

"Sounds fine. Keep him away from those soaps, though, I hear they're habit forming and he's developed enough bad habits." They laughed.

In the street Mac felt the worry about Selena weigh heavily on his shoulders. He had to think of a way to draw Paul out into the open so the Feds could catch up with him. There was only one way he could think of, and that wasn't good.

To take his mind off Selena, he thought of the coin shop job. He should search through the front office of the coin shop alone. How? He could wait until night and slip inside the joint. It shouldn't be too tough to turn off the burglar alarm system. He had watched Arnold do it and the salesman didn't realize Mac saw the hidden switch outside that activated the entire business.

That's what he'd do. Wait until dark.

It was lonesome on the street without the schnoodle. When he mumbled to himself people steered away from him. When he talked to the dog, most passersby merely grinned.

"Hey, McBee! Wait up!" Darcy's strident voice carried above the sounds of the traffic. She was a classy lady all right, but he'd heard her whistle for a taxi through her teeth in the best Brooklyn whistle ever. Almost caused a traffic jam.

She walked toward him and he watched her movements with appreciation. She wore a sporty knit dress the color of beach sand with a bright slash of red silk scarf thrown around her shoulders. The color set off her hair and golden skin to perfection.

He made an effort at nonchalance.

"What's going on? I've left messages on your phone

since they invented the damn thing," she said. "Try picking it up once in a while."

He grinned, enjoying the angry sparks in her dark eyes. He had forgotten to check his answering device since Apple Sally-Selena appeared. First time ever.

"I got a lot on my mind. Can we go somewhere and talk?"

She nodded, glancing at her little diamond watch. "Let's have an espresso at Pietro's. I love to sit outdoors and watch the people rush by."

No damn wonder they were rushing by, with what they charged at those kind of places. Mac refrained from commenting.

Apple Sally might have regarded that comment as funny, but Darcy had a short fuse when it came to what she perceived as any form of cheapness. He took her elbow and steered her around a vagrant searching through a litter basket.

They sat and she ordered for both of them. The cute little chairs under the cute little umbrella made him uncomfortable. He moved to the chair facing away from the street. He needed to concentrate on Darcy, it wasn't often she held still this long for him. She reminded him of a multihued dragonfly.

Flit—light—flit—light.

She stirred her cup as she watched him.

"Apple Sally's back. Selena, I mean," Mac said.

Darcy lifted an arched eyebrow. "Hmm. How come? I thought she'd stay in Boston from now on."

He told her the entire story.

"Oh God! This is better than I imagined! I *knew* she had a story to tell." She dropped the silver spoon on the thick white napkin in her excitement.

"You're all heart, kiddo. Never mind that the creep is trying to kill her, but it's sure as hell important that you get a story out of it."

"Ah, McBee, I touched a nerve. Sorry, I didn't mean it that way."

"Okay. But remember, you have no story until this Paul character goes to the slammer. Unless you're planning to write about the red-haired bag lady who gets blown away in some dark alley."

"Hey, I hadn't realized you've grown emotionally involved in this thing."

"Involved, inschmolved! Trouble with you is, you never look at people, do you? You see everything in black and white, like newsprint. A story or no story."

She refused to rise to the bait of his argument.

"Don't be judgmental, McBee. It doesn't wear well on you. I am what I am. Remember that."

This was the second time in the past twenty-four hours that someone reminded him of that. He drank the cloying sweet coffee and tried not to make a face. Next time, damned if he wouldn't take her to One Eyed Jack's. He grinned at the idea.

"Well, now what?" she demanded.

"What?"

"You're grinning like you had good sense. Let me in on your joke."

He waved the idea away. "Nah, it's nothing special. Getting back to the matter at hand—I haven't a clue how to nail this creep."

"It's simple. Leave it alone. He'll find her. Where's she staying? Maybe he'll spot her in the soup line at the Salvation Army."

"Very amusing," he frowned. "She's at my place."

"Jeee—sus, McBee! You are an imbecile!" She jumped to her feet and caught the edge of the tablecloth. He had visions of hundred-dollar dishes crashing to the floor.

"Shh! Sit! Everyone's looking at us."

"I don't give a . . ." she glanced around and slid into her chair. "That's insane. You know? This guy is ruthless, with nothing to lose. I've checked it out and that's when I tried to call you. He's also worked as an outside hit man for the mob." She reached across the table to put her hand on his. It felt like warm silk. "This is no penny-ante game of cards you've dealt yourself into, McBee. This is way over your head."

He looked at the slender, golden hand on top of his. Her fingernails were long and covered with a wine-colored, iridescent polish. She wore one ring with a large square-cut topaz. He stared in fascination for a long moment, half expecting it to squirt water. He must have grinned at the idea.

She snatched her hand away. "What the hell you staring at? Can't you be serious—for once?"

He looked at her and finally her words sunk in. He tried to keep the elation from his voice. Darcy cared about him! For the first time since he met her, there was a chink in that armor.

"Someone has to help her. She's all alone," Mac defended his position.

"Big deal. She's been alone since she came to the city. There's her tie-in with the Swede. Can't he help her? What do you know from detecting?"

That hurt. He felt a rush of resentment. Only hours before he was thinking along the same lines, but that was no excuse. Apple Sally thought he could help her, she trusted him.

Darcy must have seen his anger and backed up a little.

"Oh hell! Don't go prima donna on me, you know what I mean. I'm not trying to put down what you do, but it's like trying to play a game of marbles when all the big boys want to play hockey. I mean, he'll use you for the puck. You get it?"

"Thanks for the confidence," Mac said dryly. He shook his head when the waiter came with refills.

She accepted hers and sat back to consider.

"Okay, okay." She raised her palms toward him in a gesture of surrender. "What do we do?"

"We don't do anything. It's up to me to figure something, I guess."

Darcy regarded him over the rim of her cup, then set it down with a quick, decisive movement.

"It's like I told you before. I know those types. He'll find her if he can. All you do is let him. And stay prepared." She opened her bag and rummaged for her lipstick.

"Easy for you to say."

She smiled. Her teeth were white against the gold of her skin. "Nothing to it. Set a trap is all."

He considered the idea. She was right, of course, and he had been considering that very thing. It was the only way to get rid of Paul once and for all.

"I'm sure I have a few days to work it all out. He won't track her right away."

"Maybe. Do you think it wise for her to stay at your place? I mean . . . it could be dangerous . . . for all of you."

Was she jealous? Who in the hell you kidding? He laughed at his wishful thinking. Darcy? Jealous? He fell to earth with a thud.

"She needed a place and a friend last night. Maybe tonight she might decide different." He studied the pattern of the spoon in his hand. "I gotta go. Working on a case and . . ."

"Oh?" She perked up. "What kind of case?" She put her elbows on the table and leaned her chin against her knuckles.

He shrugged. "Nothing you'd find interesting. An insurance scam, I believe."

"Oh." She reached for her camera bag. "Then we'd better shove off. Want to go Dutch on this?"

He considered briefly and then frowned at her grin as he realized she'd been teasing. He pretended not to have noticed. "Hey, no way." He took her elbow, steering her past the cashier and paid the bill.

Once outside, she reached and touched him lightly on the shoulder. "Keep in touch, McBee. Will ya?"

He frowned.

"I'm not talking story-wise. I'm talking . . . well, anyway, like I said, keep in touch. Answer your damn phone." She turned and walked away.

He watched her leave—the slim, straight back, the feisty tilt to her head, as if she owned the world. He wished he could have been so sure of himself.

When he returned to the office, Herr Schnoodle greeted him with reproachful eyes. It was his "Why did you leave me alone?" look.

"Where's our guest?" he said after he bent and patted the dog.

He spied a note under the telephone with small, neat handwriting. She was returning to the streets and would contact him later.

"Didn't you even try to stop her?" he asked Herr Schnoodle. The schnoodle still wore his reproachful look.

Mac felt Selena was shying off from feelings that had erupted between them. He didn't blame her, she had enough on her mind. She didn't want to depend on anyone, he respected that—admired it. Hadn't she come to a strange city alone, under the worst possible circumstances, and survived? Sure he'd worry, but she was entitled to take her life down any road she chose.

Besides, as long as he was attracted to Darcy, things would only become more and more complicated.

As soon as it grew dark, he began to make his plans for breaking into the coin shop.

32

"Shh!" Mac put his finger to his lips in an instinctive gesture, even though you couldn't have seen a fluorescent cat in the dark alley behind the coin shop.

Herr Schnoodle, walking beside him, had rattled over a large piece of tin lying close to the Dumpster.

Mac wore black from head to toe, including a cheap, black-knitted stocking cap he bought at a sporting good store. Problem was, he saw some bum trying the caps on just after he bought it. Even after washing the cap in hot soapy water with a liberal dose of Lysol, he still didn't care for the feel of it on his head.

Probably had nothing to do with the fact that the wool cap shrank several sizes, too. When PIs had to push against the boundaries of rules sometimes, they always wore a getup like this. He had seen it done a dozen times on television.

He found the switch. Arnold had not intentionally let him know of its whereabouts. It slipped out in the conversation when he was trying hard to make an impression with how much Mr. Greening trusted him. Gosh, he was getting the knack of this PI thing, putting two and two together and coming up with right answers, he congratulated himself. Nothing to it.

Mac hoped he remembered right about the janitor's working between seven p.m. and nine p.m. He glanced at the luminous dial on his watch. It was past ten—should be okay.

He opened the back door and they crept inside. Mac

walked through the metal-detector doorway, heart in his throat, expecting any minute to have his ears blasted into orbit. Nothing happened. Smooth as silk. He had been right to assume they cut it off at night so the janitor could work.

A lone fluorescent light burned in one of the displays. He found Greening's desk and rummaged around in the drawers. One was locked and Mac considered springing it, but the big man would know someone had snooped, probably blame an employee. Herr Schnoodle's bark sliced through the silence like a knife.

"Shh! You know better than bark! We're on a case here."

The dog answered with a low growl.

"What's the matter with you? There's likely to be a watchman wandering around outside." He rushed into the main room to see what bothered the schnoodle.

"Damn, boy. You got some kinda fixation on that post," Mac whispered. The brass fixture was nearly as wide around as a fire hydrant or a small tree. "Leave it alone, old buddy. We got to check out the place."

Mac flashed the light away and back again. The mutt hadn't budged. "Hey, you're blocking progress. I got to look in Arnold's locker in the employee's lounge."

Herr Schnoodle sighed and lay against the post with his chin on crossed paws.

"Well—hey—if it's that darned important to you . . ." Mac walked across the room and shook the post. The dog leaped to his feet, alert, as if on point.

Mac leaned over, put his ear to the cold brass and shook again. Sounded like something loose in there. He went around the room shaking each post but they didn't feel or sound the same. He came back to Herr Schnoodle who trembled with excitement. Mac ran his hand over the cap of the post. It had a large ring on top with the velvet rope attached. He wiggled and worked it loose.

"What do you know about that." He removed the brass cap and laid it on the floor. He bent over and stuck his arm in nearly to his shoulder.

The tip of his fingers touched something.

He stretched a little further and pulled up a very heavy cloth bag. Mac sat on the floor and dumped it out, while the dog looked on with interest. Mac wasn't surprised to see the coins tumble onto the carpet.

"Aha! Part of the loot, anyway." He felt the schnoodle's hot breath against the back of his neck. He turned and hugged the dog, ignoring the lolling tongue in his ear. "You're a sweetheart—a great PI. You knew right along something was in here that didn't belong, didn't you? It took me all this time to listen to you. Will I ever learn?"

He switched off his flashlight and sat in the semidarkness a few minutes, thinking of his next step. This proved it had to be Arnold or Greening, an inside job for sure. If Greening did it, though, why stick the coins in the hollow post? Surely he, of all people, could come and go any time of the day or night without question.

Arnold, on the other hand, would have to play it closer to the vest. Take the loot when he got the chance. But didn't that mean he had an accomplice? The janitor! Of course.

"How about that, boy? Got any more clues for me? You seem to make the most headway anyhow." He stood and brushed lint from his trousers. "We're going to take a sample of coins with us and . . ." He suddenly remembered the closed-circuit cameras in each corner of the room, their cyclops eyes dark and shuttered.

"That's it! I got it! The cameras start working when the lights come on, but there's a switch that can turn them off.

I watched Greening do it once at closing time. The alarm company is so sure of their protection outside that they don't require the cameras turned on at night."

Lucky for him, since he had overlooked them.

He forgot to whisper in his excitement of discovery.

"I'll make sure the cameras are left on every night. I can re-activate the switch without anyone knowing. We'll catch whoever comes to pick this stuff up."

He removed a roll from the heap on the floor and slipped it into his jacket pocket. "We'll need this to play the game I got planned for these crooks."

"Here, fella. Smell this and tell me you'll remember it." He pushed the bag of coins under Herr Schnoodle's nose. The dog sniffed it from end to end. Mac shaped the bag to make it slide down into the hiding place again and put the cap on firmly.

"Darn, I sure could use a screwdriver." He opened the nearest desk drawer and flashed his light. His glance fell on a long nail file and he grabbed it.

"Maybe this will do." He walked over to the panel of wall switches and shone the light. "Hmm. Video cameras. There it is." He unscrewed the switch plate and considered the mass of wires. His self-confidence plummeted. "I guess I'd better flip the master switch to make sure I don't wind up with a steel-wool hairdo." But wait. Wouldn't that affect the alarm timing? What he knew about electricity was barely enough for filling in a gnat's hollow tooth, but he did know there should be a reset button.

He sighed. "This PI business is a tough racket, Schnoodle." Speaking in his best Mike Hammer snarl, he mentally crossed his fingers and pulled on the wire closest to him. It was hard to hold the flashlight under his chin while he worked. He undid the black tape gingerly and rewired the lines separately so that the switch would have no effect on the cameras. He flipped the switch. Dead. He grinned, grateful to be alive and unfried.

He didn't dare turn on the overhead lights to check if the cameras were working. He'd have to trust. In a few nights someone would come for the bag and then it was only a matter of running the tapes to nab the conspirators.

The roll of coins he held back would match the contents of the bag. He would worry about explaining how he came by them later. If Greening was the thief then he had no one to answer to anyway.

He let the dog out the door and closed it carefully behind them. When he knelt to flip on the hidden switch for the alarm system a squad car nosed into the alley with a light beaming up and down, searching. Mac squatted close to the ground, praying the dog wouldn't suddenly decide to take offense at this intrusion.

Sweat soaked through his shirt while he waited, holding on to the schnoodle. If they found him and the coins in his pocket, it would take some real explaining. Not only that, Greening would have it made. He could pin the entire robbery on him and get off scot-free.

"Stupid!" he muttered under his breath.

Just as he decided he'd best come out with his hands in the air, the lights swept on by, receding from the alley.

Mac raked the stocking cap off his head and turned down his collar, hitting the street at a run with the dog close by. He inhaled the glow shining from the streetlights, as if the time spent in darkness could be replaced by absorbed light.

"Guess it's a matter of waiting now, Schnoodle. Let's go home."

33

For the next few days while McBee waited for developments at the coin shop, he looked for Apple Sally. He and the dog wandered toward the soup kitchens at meal times. They sat in the park for long stretches.

"I don't mind telling you, I'm worried, fella," he confided as they walked along the street one morning. "Selena could have stopped by to let us know how she is. What if Paul killed her and dumped her in the river? Nobody would know her identity—just another skid row bum. Jane Doe, they'd call her when they fished up the body."

By the time he realized how far they had walked they were close to Mr. Steinmetz's house. "Let's go visit the old gentleman, Schnoodle. That ought to cheer us."

The dog wagged his tail and grinned at Mac. Why not?

He stepped up on the porch and automatically ducked away from the hanging planters, remembering the first time. A small body flung itself at his middle and he almost dove backward off the porch. Schnoodle danced around, barking and jumping.

"Jesse!" Mac laughed and held the boy at arm's length. "How are you, son? Let's see you smile."

"Macabee—look!" His dark face lit as his mouth spread wide to show his teeth.

Mac hugged him. "Beautiful! You could go to Hollywood with a smile like that."

"I don't think my mother would let me," Jesse said, his expression serious.

Mac ruffled the boy's thick black hair. "I'm only kidding. How's your mother?"

Jesse was tugging on his hand and pulling the schnoodle's collar.

"Good. Good. Come in. *El Viejo* will be so glad to see you. Maybe he got a surprise for you."

"Has a surprise," Mac corrected gently.

Jesse nodded. "Yes. I said that." He opened the front door and Mr. Steinmetz rushed to meet them.

"Ah, my favorite person, Mr. McBee." He shook hands and then gave Mac a shy hug. Mac knew there was no use to ask Steinmetz to call him Mac, it wouldn't have worked, the old man was too sweetly formal.

As Mac looked over Steinmetz's shoulder towards the kitchen, his heart did a wheelie when he saw Apple Sally watching from the doorway with that curious, pensive expression she sometimes wore.

He cleared his throat and forced down the lump of happiness. He should be mad at her, she might have let him know. He was—Schnoodle was—worried about her.

"Hi—Selena." Even though he'd been trying to think of her as Selena, still, the name felt funny on his tongue.

"Hello, Alexander." Her voice was subdued.

Mr. Steinmetz offered the usual tea and cookies. McBee watched as she poured the fragrant brew into the paper-thin, antique cups. She wasn't dressed like Apple Sally anymore, but had on a "civilian" outfit as she would have called it. A wool skirt with soft plaids, flaring gracefully around her high-heeled boots and a pale green sweater. He couldn't keep his eyes from her, she looked like a small, perfectly featured doll.

"Close your mouth, Alexander," she grinned at him. "You look a lot like Mr. Steinmetz's Venus flytrap."

Jesse thought this hilarious and he rolled around the carpet with laughter, holding his sides as the dog tried to pounce on him.

Mac winced, thinking of the fragile antique furnishings.

The old man shook his head. "Not to worry, my friend. The boy has never broken anything important yet. Even so—what are mere possession compared with the laughter of a child?"

Mac looked at Mr. Steinmetz as if he couldn't believe his ears. When they first met, the elderly man cared only for his narrow little world of possessions. He had stuffed his rooms to bursting with inanimate objects that he loved without receiving anything in return. Now the room filled with such love it made Mac a little uncomfortable.

"So. How's it going with you?" He looked at Selena. "Why'd you leave so sudden. I . . . we worried about you."

She looked nervous. "I needed time alone—to think."

"Alone? With streets full of people?"

She smiled. "You've no idea how alone you can be out there."

It hadn't been so long ago that Mac remembered feeling the same way.

Selena reached to take Mr. Steinmetz's thin, veined hand in her own. "I don't think I'm endangering anyone. Paul would never think of me coming back here. He won't have any idea which direction I took."

"Mr. S found out she was back," Jesse piped in. His lips pulled open tentatively at first and then he remembered his repaired teeth. At Mac's questioning look, he giggled. "No secrets in the Bottleneck."

"He sent Jesse to find me. Wasn't that something?"

Mac nodded. It was something all right. But for a streetie, which she believed she was, it was incredibly dumb to think Paul couldn't find her if Steinmetz and Jesse had. If the FBI wanted her as a witness when they captured Paul, she would have had to leave her destination with the police in Boston.

What if Paul could track her by having a stoolie in the police department or checking bus or train or plane terminals? To exist as a mob hit man, he had to have reserves to call upon.

He would find her, Mac had no doubts of that. He decided not to rain on their parade, not until he had time to think it over. Maybe Darcy was right. Bait a trap and get it over with once and for all. He took a sip of the honeyed tea and a bite of cookie.

"Hmm. Good. You make these?" He looked at her.

She nodded. "Yep. I love to bake. I'm just a so-so cook, but wait'll you taste one of my pies."

Both Jesse and Mr. Steinmetz protested her modesty. Her cooking was great. Mac leaned back and watched them. It felt good, soaking up the warmth in this room. The uneasiness at being with the new Selena left, and he began to feel comfortable with her again.

He finally managed to get her alone outside on the porch.

"Bet this is the only old-fashioned porch swing in the city," she said, spreading her skirt over her knees.

"Probably. But then there are a lot of onlys in this house. For one thing, I didn't get a chance to tell you before. You look . . . you look gorgeous."

"Why thank you, Alexander," she accepted the compliment gracefully without coquettishness.

He liked that. "Selena, we have a problem. I didn't want to scare anyone in there, but Paul could track you so easy. I'm talking *very* easy. He already knew you were a bag lady.

260

There could be a leak between police departments."

Her eyes widened and her face lost some of its color. The smattering of freckles stood out in spite of the light makeup she wore. "Oh! I would never endanger my friends!"

"Of course you wouldn't. But let's get serious. Paul has contacts in every major city. He would have to, in his line of work. That means it's only a matter of time until he locates you."

Her knuckles whitened as she clenched her fists. "That bastard! How did I ever think I loved him? That he loved me? I've been so stupid."

"Hey, none of that." Mac lifted her chin and looked into her face. Her eyes sparkled with tears which he brushed away at the corners with his thumbs. "He cared for you. As much as a person like that can care. He could have left you to burn in the explosion. Would have saved him a lot of problems."

"I suppose you're right. Probably if I hadn't been dumb enough to help him kidnap Eric he would have found someone else."

Mac wondered about that, but now wasn't the time to bring it up. She needed all the self-confidence she could muster.

"The point is, you gotta stay out of circulation," he said. "No one from the streets would know you dressed this way—except for your hair. Can't get away from that."

She touched her hand to her head. "I could wear a wig," she offered.

"Maybe. Better still—don't go anywhere for a while. There's plenty in this neighborhood to keep you busy if you look. The people in the Bottleneck will protect your privacy, you're one of them now."

"Isn't it odd? As a streetie I never did fit in anywhere and now that I'm Selena I'm part of the streets. I like it. Mrs. Rodriguez wants me to show her how to bake pies. Mr. S and I thought she might be able to sell some at the offices where she cleans."

"Good. Keep you out of mischief." He put his arm around her and she leaned into his shoulder. They rocked gently on the swing for a while, neither wanting to break the silence.

Later, after a light supper, Mac and Schnoodle left.

"I still don't trust this place before dark, old boy. God knows I wouldn't after dark." He rushed along, not letting the pooch pause at every bush and fireplug as he usually did. By the time they reached the full traffic and crowded streets of uptown, the dog was making indignant noises and Mac was grateful he couldn't talk.

He still had a problem of asking Selena to act as bait to catch Paul. Could he do it? Should he? Well, no need to decide tonight. He might come up with another plan in a few more days. Surely he could afford a little more time, couldn't he?

34

The next day, Mac and Herr Schnoodle entered the coin shop near closing time just as the last customer was leaving.

He walked over to the post and shook it with all the nonchalance he could muster. Empty—it felt empty.

Wonderful!

"Wow, I sweated that one, Schnoodle," he whispered, louder than he wanted to because of the canned music playing from every corner of the building. "The thief could have waited a week or two to remove the coins."

"Ah, good afternoon, Mr. McBee. I see you brought along your . . . ah, your animal. I must say, Mr. Greening is becoming rather tolerant lately. He hates pets of any sort. Especially in here." Arnold folded his arms across his chest as if waiting for Mac's reply.

If Greening was newly tolerant and patient, Mac would have hated to have known him years ago when Arnold first came to work. Besides, who was he kidding? Fur-coated women strolled in all the time clutching little fluffy poodles wearing diamond collars and leashes and nobody complained about them.

"It's about closing time, isn't it? I need to use your phone."

"Of course, on both counts. A local call, I presume?"

"Yep." Just then the owner came from the direction of the storeroom.

"Ah, Mr. McBee." Greening pointedly ignored Herr Schnoodle who ignored him right back.

"I'd appreciate it if you'd ask your employees to stay a few minutes after closing. I want to talk to everyone."

"No problem. Of course they'll stay. They haven't finished their work until every single item is accounted for and put away."

Mac grimaced. Ten to one they didn't get paid extra for that, either. He called Joe and told him to come in for the kill, to haul away the thief when he finished talking to the employees.

Arnold finally locked the door.

"People—people!" Greening spoke with his usual cold authority. "We must ask you to cease your work, put it aside for now. Time enough to finish when Mr. McBee has talked to everyone."

Mac watched as Arnold, Mrs. Wallace and several others whose names he didn't recall, looked at him with subdued resentment. No wonder. They would have to work late to make up for this. What they didn't realize was that they would all be out of work if the boss was in on the scam.

Joe told him he might be delayed but start without him.

"I want to see the video tapes for the last two days."

"But . . ." Greening sputtered. "That's ridiculous! The cameras record only when an alarm button is pushed."

Or when the lights came on at night. Mac spread his lips in a tight smile. He felt cool and in command, Peter Gunn had nothing on him today.

"Just indulge me a moment, please. After all, that's what I'm paid for."

"Certainly, certainly," Greening interrupted. He nodded toward Arnold who bustled around getting the proper day's recording. No one spoke. The piped-in music quit at precisely closing time, and the group stood as silent and uncomfortable as Hare Krishnas at a Billy Graham revival.

Everyone turned to watch the monitor when Arnold had it in place. The screen stayed blank, glaring gray with flecks of interstellar rain.

"Are you sure you know what you're doing, young man?" Greening's voice grated into the hushed atmosphere.

"Bear with me. We'll have a lot of film with nothing on it." Mac pointed at the screen. "Okay, it's beginning." He wanted to stand back and watch their faces and the TV screen. That wasn't going to be too easy. He heard a commotion at the door and sighed with relief. Joe had made it.

Everyone turned for a moment to look at the two outsiders. Mac smiled. No matter if Joe wore a suit or a nurse's uniform, he still spelled cop. Glancing at the owner, Mac saw no change of expression, the man looked composed, from his Italian leather shoes to his fifty-dollar haircut.

Mac's pulses began to race as he imagined Greening in handcuffs, his sneering expression crumpled with painful humiliation. This case was nailed down, and it only took careful attention to hunches and a powerful sixth sense to stay a jump ahead of the criminal mind.

And a good partner didn't hurt.

This PI business was a piece of cake.

The monitor drew his attention as he watched an old man in coveralls shuffle around the empty rooms.

"Who's he?" McBee asked.

"Boggs, the janitor. He came with the lease. His father once owned the building." Arnold spoke after waiting first for his boss to speak.

The man in the picture looked old enough to be cleanup detail on Noah's Ark, for gosh sakes. Mac's idea of an accomplice floated away to join the dust motes that poured onto the face of the TV monitor. This man couldn't be a crook. He could barely make it upright each day.

265

Just then he heard a collective hiss of indrawn breaths from the watchers as the janitor unscrewed the top of the brass post and reached deep down inside. His wrinkled face stared absentmindedly at the TV cameras, and his tongue protruded comically in his effort to reach the cloth bag. Suddenly his face creased into smiles as he worked it up and dumped the bag on the carpet.

Mac managed a shrug. So he maybe missed the clue by not interviewing the janitor, but he would have caught on fast. Boggs did have a shifty-looking kisser, no doubt of that.

The janitor didn't bother opening the bag, and when he picked it up he moved out of camera range. A few minutes later he returned and started to use the vacuum cleaner on his normal routine.

McBee reached to push the button turning off the picture. "I guess we've seen enough." He spread his attention between Greening and Arnold, not certain which to watch.

"That's very interesting, but what does it mean? That old Boggs had an eccentric place to hide his lunch?" the owner sneered, thrusting his sharp voice into the cushioned silence.

Reaching in his jacket pocket, Mac let the roll of coins fall on the counter. It made a solid thunk on the glass top. "It means that the bag was filled with these. I took this out when I set the trap with the video cameras."

"But how did Boggs accomplish this? He has no keys to our display cases. He doesn't have the vault combination, no one does but me."

Mac looked at Greening, feeling the moment of triumph draw closer—so close he could taste it on the tip of his tongue.

Joe stood in the background, arms folded across his chest, waiting.

"Mr. Boggs had an accomplice. Right here in this room. I suggest you step forward, it's only a matter of time until the old fellow cracks and tells us everything."

He turned and whistled to the dog. "My partner knows who put that bag in there. He got a good whiff the other night and he's going to walk around among you and . . ." He called the dog over to sniff the coins.

My partner. It didn't embarrass him in the least to acknowledge Herr Schnoodle as his helper, on the contrary, it felt darn good. Mac bluffed—knowing the dog couldn't get a scent from the coins, he had held them too long in his pocket.

The schnoodle politely sniffed everyone's kneecaps as he made a slow circle and came back to stand in front of Mrs. Wallace.

"Come on boy, quit kidding around." Mac walked across the room and nudged the dog away, but the schnoodle growled low in his throat and stood his ground.

Now what was up?

35

Mrs. Wallace's face folded up with the flood of tears. When no one moved or spoke, she stopped crying and dabbed at her eyes with a tissue she fished from the neck of her blouse. She gave a pathetic little hiccup and started to speak.

"We didn't do it for the money. We did it to get even with *him!*" She pointed to Greening.

Joe walked from the back of the room, all cop. "No need to say anything, ma'am. Why not wait for your lawyer. Know what I mean?"

She shook her head. "I understand about reading my rights, God knows I watch television enough. I *want* to tell about it."

She glared at her boss and ground her teeth in hatred. "Do you have any idea how demeaning, how degrading it is to work with someone so despicable—year after year? Boggs is my brother. Our father left us this building and *Mister* Greening and his big-shot attorneys finagled my brother out of it."

"But . . . I don't understand . . ." Greening began.

"You wouldn't!" she retorted. "Boggs sent for me when my husband died, and I decided the way to get back at you was from inside. We waited and planned a long time for this."

"Ah, the old Trojan horse ploy," Mac said.

Mrs. Wallace wiped her eyes again and took a deep breath. "I guess so. I took a job here, suffering his insults and despicable behavior until we figured how best to hurt him."

"By stealing a few coins?" Mac protested.

"Mr. McBee, I appreciate an outsider's ignorance in these matters, but our illustrious superior knows exactly what we did." She walked over to the coins on the counter and opened the roll.

The gold reflected from the overhead neons until she spread them out. The first and last shone softly, the others were a dull nickel color.

"What the . . ." Everyone moved closer to look and Joe pushed to the center.

Mac was hardly listening to her. He was still embarrassed at guessing wrong and angry because he wasn't going to nail Greening.

Mrs. Wallace seemed to enjoy the limelight. "We figured we'd find some way to turn the coins over to the authorities and this—this hateful man—would be suspected of fraud. After all, I processed the claim to the insurance company. I know for a fact he put in double the amount we . . . ah, we stole."

"But nobody counted on Mac getting to the bottom of it, is that it?" Joe said. Mac knew his friend was proud of him for solving the case.

"On the contrary, we had hoped for just that," she said with gracious dignity. "We wanted Mr. McBee to find it, and when it didn't appear that he would we planned to move the bag of coins to a more conspicuous spot. I still don't know how he managed to discover the hiding place."

"Enough! Arrest these felons!" Greening snarled. He glared down his nose and through his rimless glasses at Mrs. Wallace as if he might squash her under his size twelve shoe.

"Not so fast. If what Mrs. Wallace here says is true, looks as if you have some explaining to do as far as the insurance company records and your own little scam," Mac said.

Greening focused his attention on Mac.

"I picked your name from the phone book. You had the smallest ad and the dreariest address. Naturally I looked for some fly-specked hack, content with making a few dollars for expenses and then giving up." His voice was accusing.

"Sorry to disappoint." Mac couldn't resist the smug feeling that crept into his expression as he exchanged looks with Joe. Okay, so he guessed wrong about the thief not being either Arnold or the owner, but what the hey— nobody was perfect, right?

Anyway, he learned a good lesson, don't pick your suspect by which one you most want it to be.

Mac felt a deep satisfaction to the twist of cashing the check from Greening for doing a job, to helping fold him into tiny pieces. The check from the insurance company would soon be on its way. A good job, all in all.

Poetic justice, he congratulated himself as he and the schnoodle walked away from the bank. Greening would be arraigned for defrauding the insurance company, and the swindle he pulled on Mrs. Wallace and her brother would be thoroughly investigated.

Joe assured the worried employees the pair would probably never come to trial when the extenuating circumstances came out. Maybe they would even get their building back when it was over.

Just then Mac heard the tip-tip-tip of heels behind him and turned. "Darcy! I was just thinking about you."

She smiled, lighting the entire corner of the street. "I

bet. How's it going, McBee?" She linked arms with him and they walked along. Herr Schnoodle didn't bother to complain, as if he finally accepted Mac's eccentricity in his choice of friends.

Mac steered her to a sidewalk café. "Cuppa coffee?"

She nodded and folded her long legs as she glided into the chair he pulled out. Apple Sally—Selena—usually collapsed in a puff of clothing, but there he was comparing the two again. After ordering, they sat, watching people pass, lost in thought.

Darcy reached inside her camera bag for a folded copy of the *Union Globe*. "Take a look at the proofs for this week's copy." She spread it on the table.

He stared at the large double photo of Apple Sally—a before and after shot. Darcy caught her pushing a shopping cart in the soup line. The second half showed a fresh-faced, earnest young woman in a plaid skirt and green sweater.

Darcy had followed him to Steinmetz's house. The picture was fuzzy and a little out of focus as if it had been shot with a telephoto from across the street. The caption read "The Double Life of a Mob Witness."

"Good Lord! How could you do this to her? You've just outfitted her for cement shoes, for God's sake."

His voice rose and the dog trembled against his leg.

"It sells papers," she answered.

"How'd you do it in the first place? She'd never let you interview her."

Darcy looked uncomfortable. "Understand how we work. We don't need a whole lot of material. We work with what we can get and skirt around the details. I *did* talk to her, though. She thought parts of her story might help the streeties. Force people to more awareness—something like that. I gotta admit, that's probably the only reason she let me do it."

Reaching across the table, she touched his hand lightly.

Mac waited to feel the familiar rush of pleasure scurry from his soles and work its way to the top of his head. It came finally, but he sensed it was mostly habit and expectation.

"I said it's a proof, McBee. I didn't send it to press yet."

"Then, don't! I'll get you a better story, Darcy, I swear it. If you'll hold this for a while. Paul is going to come looking for her or send for some gunnies to rub her out. With a little luck, we can nail 'em. Wouldn't you prefer to have it all?"

Darcy regarded him for a long moment with speculation, her mouth twitched in a suspicious way as if she tried not to laugh.

"Gunnies? Rub her out? God, you watch too much television. Anyway, it's not as if I want to harm her—or anyone, for that matter."

"I know that." He put the back of his fingers to her cheek. "Please hold off on this. This could be the Big Story to jump off the *Union Globe* onto another paper, but if you don't do what's right . . ."

"Yeah, yeah, okay. I'll cut some slack. But you can't expect me to wait forever."

No, he didn't suppose he could. The question was, would she wait at all?

36

After Mac left Darcy, he thought about her story all the way to his office.

The next morning he dropped in to see Joe.

"An excellent piece of detecting, Mac." The older man clamped his arms around Mac's shoulders in a bear hug. "Your pop would have been proud."

McBee just happened to glance at Herr Schnoodle in time to see the dog look away, as if embarrassed.

Darn! Suppose he really understood? Was this any way to treat a friend? He couldn't have solved this case without the schnoodle and he began to feel like a real phony.

"I couldn't have done it without Herr Schnoodle. He found the right post and almost had to make love to the damn thing to get me to look at it. He's the best partner a fellow could ever ask for." There, he finally admitted it to Joe.

The dog grinned at him as if he understood every word.

"That's great. I never heard of a four-legged partner. Your dad and me always worked alone, ya know? We do have teams of K-9 police dogs. Never understood the need, but guess it's the same idea."

Not the same idea at all, Mac thought, but decided not to pursue it. His father and grandfather weren't into close friends, two-legged or four, for that matter. The crusty old-timers had no room in their lives for attachments. That role had crept in on him and began to settle over his life before the schnoodle came along.

"I gotta ask a favor," he interrupted before Joe could travel down the nostalgia trail of how things used to be.

"Name it, son."

Mac told him about his worry for Apple Sally.

"No problemo. I got a second cousin works in the office at the main precinct of Boston. She'll replace your address for the one your friend left in the files. Let's see, you said the name is Selena Duvall—with two *L*s?"

Mac nodded. "Yeah, she's a witness against Paul Duvall. He's a part-time hit man for the mob. He's trying to trace her, and I'm sure he's got enough leverage to poke into police files. He'll know when the address has been changed and think she's moved. That would only be natural."

Joe shook his head. "This tactic puts a giant bull's-eye on your rear end when he comes looking for her, know what I mean? She staying at your place?"

"Nah. It's a red herring. She's safe for now. I just got to flush him out of the woodwork and end this once and for all."

Joe scratched his balding head. "I dunno, Mac. Dangerous and foolhardy is what I'd call it, ya know? Captain can't send anyone to watch your place, not on spec that the guy *might* show up to get her. Can't you give me more to go on?"

"Sorry, but that's all I have right now. I'll call the minute I hear anything. I have sources on the street."

"Of course you do."

Mac didn't like the way that sounded. Was his friend making fun of the Spaceman and Smitty? Joe knew everything going on in the streets. It would be a sorry day for the citizens when the older cops like him were gone.

Mac spent the next few days in uneasy waiting. He told

himself he was no hero, but it didn't change anything. Someone had to help Selena and he didn't see any other way than bringing it to a head, using his address as bait.

Even Herr Schnoodle became edgy, taking his cue from McBee. He barked at every little noise and followed Mac around the apartment as if he didn't want to get out of his shadow.

"Boy, we're a couple of brave ones, aren't we?"

He tried to keep a straight face at the schnoodle's near-hysteria when the garbage man dropped a can on the street below.

Each time he and the dog went out in the semi-gloom of the hallway and down the stairs, the hairs on Mac's arms and the back of his neck seemed to twist into little animals that marched up and down his skin—a weird feeling.

"We can't even go to The Cave. For sure half the denizens there are from the mob and would kill their own bookie for a fin. Maybe Paul sublet his contract. Maybe he's already checked out that I live here."

Mac couldn't stand it after the third day and they walked over to the Y to talk to the Spaceman. The wild man was glad to take a message to Mr. Steinmetz, that things were okay so far, but Selena must continue to stay off the streets.

When they got home, and moved up the dark stairway, Mac felt the dog tremble and go rigid against his leg. He reached down and touched the hackles on the schnoodle's back.

Man and dog crept up the stairs. When they reached the landing Mac saw the light under the door flick off. Damn that squeaky last step! He'd forgotten it.

He had two choices. Go back to the street and telephone for Joe and backup or brazen it out and push the door open. Guess now that he made some money he should have sprung for a cell phone. Curiosity got the best of apprehension and he moved forward with the dog glued to the side of his leg as if they were permanently attached.

Turning the knob slowly, Mac prepared to duck away from the door.

Herr Schnoodle had his own ideas.

As soon as the door opened a crack, the dog catapulted through. His fierce snarls bounced off the walls and echoed down the stairway.

Mac heard a yell of fear and outrage and ran inside. The dog and a man were rolling on the floor, locked together. Mac dived on top of the thrashing bodies.

Feeling a surge of adrenalin when he found his hands wrapped around the guy's neck, Mac began to tighten his grip while the dog ripped up his clothes.

"Stop! For Chrissake, you're killing me!" The neck beneath McBee's fingers relaxed and the body turned limp.

McBee sat up, keeping his hand firmly grasping the guy's shoulder.

Herr Schnoodle sat back, two furry paws planted in the middle of the stranger's chest, glaring into the man's fear-crazed face as low, menacing growls came from a mouth filled with sharp, white teeth.

The man rolled away. Jerking his body unexpectedly, he swerved around with a gun pointed at the dog's head.

Mac hurled himself forward, attention focused on the inches between the gun barrel and the schnoodle. Panic churned inside his gut, making his legs and arms work together as he smacked into the man and grabbed for the hand holding the gun. The noise of the exploding cylinder ricocheted off the walls, and the dog let out a cry that would have cut through steel.

Mac lost it. He squeezed his eyes closed, dreading what

he would see when he opened them. He tasted a coppery coating in his mouth and felt the cut on his lip when the guy had elbowed him. He tightened his grip on the man's arm, twisting now with a lust to destroy.

"Stop! You and this vicious animal are killing me!" The man's voice sounded muffled, almost in Mac's ear.

McBee opened his eyes cautiously. The schnoodle swiped his big tongue across his cheek and turned to the prone man, growling.

Sighing in relief, McBee grabbed the gun away and jammed it down in his pocket for safekeeping. The dog was safe. Still holding on to the man's arm, Mac rolled sideways and spared a quick glance at the huge hole in his ceiling.

"Come on, Paul Duvall, get up there in the chair." Mac nudged the man with the toe of his shoe and fumbled in a drawer for his handcuffs. He'd never thought he'd get to use them.

"Who the hell are you? How do you know me? Where is she?" Paul snarled as Mac got ready to snap the cuffs on with the chain through the chair arm. Herr Schnoodle stood at his thigh, as if ready to do a job on him, so Paul stopped struggling and subsided in a big sigh.

"You don't need to know, where you're going," Mac said, not wanting to carry on the conversation. The thought of Selena and this bozo together was more than Mac wanted to think about.

In an instant the man lurched to his feet and ran out the open door, heading for the stairs. Mac and Schnoodle tangled together, both of them in hot pursuit. This had to be Paul, judging from Selena's descriptions. If he got away he could disappear and the threat would hang over her head forever. He couldn't let that happen. Neither, apparently could the dog. They both tackled the man just as he reached the top of the stairs, all tumbling and rolling down together. Schnoodle was smaller and could get squashed and broken up, but Mac couldn't push him away as they bumped and bounced downward. The man squealed, a sound so startling that both the dog and Mac loosened their hold for a moment. Kicking and hitting with both fists, Paul slid backward toward the bottom of the stairwell.

This was making enough noise to wake all Manhattan, and half of the Bronx, but either all of the offices were empty or no one was foolhardy enough to venture out.

Paul twisted and gave one last lurch away at the bottom and Mac felt his hands slip off of the man's jacket. Sweat burned in his eyes so that he had a hard time seeing, his shoulder felt battered by the man's last desperate kick, but he couldn't give up. He made a grab as the man got to his knees and crawled toward the double doors and to freedom. That was when the schnoodle leaped upon his back, dug his claws in and grabbed a hank of hair in his teeth. Paul gave a last shriek of unvarnished terror and Mac knew it was all over.

He dragged the swearing Paul up the stairs again, trying not to limp on a sore leg. He didn't want this creep to think he'd inflicted damage. When they went inside, Mac shoved Paul down in the chair. He took the handcuffs off the table and pointing to the growling, intense dog guarding him, the man held out his hands with a huge sigh. Mac dialed up Joe.

Later, when Joe arrived with two black and whites for backup, the office filled with cops. McBee thought Paul Duvall looked relieved to see them.

As soon as the fuss died and they all left, Mac called Darcy. It was late, but he owed her. After telling her what happened and where they took Paul, he hung up feeling finely tuned, unable to relax.

He and the mutt splurged and took a cab to Mr. Steinmetz's house. He couldn't wait until morning to tell Selena. Even if the guy got off on bail, he'd be watched.

She met him in the doorway, her hair tousled, straightening her robe.

"Alexander! Is something wrong?" She opened the door and turned on a lamp. "Shh. Mr. Steinmetz probably didn't hear your knock. We'll let him sleep. So, tell me."

He pushed her shoulder gently until she sank onto the couch. He sat close beside her.

"We caught Paul. We did a number on him that he won't forget soon. Anyway, he's in the slammer without doing any damage. He'll be extradited and on his way to Boston within days—or so Joe tells me."

She kissed his cheek and hugged him. After that she bent over and kissed the top of Herr Schnoodle's head. "You guys . . . what a team. You're something else. But how did you do it?" Suddenly reality set in and her eyes narrowed. "Wait a minute. Where did you catch him?"

Mac wriggled like a schoolboy caught leaving an apple on the teacher's desk. "We caught him at the office—the apartment. He hid there waiting for us and . . ."

She leaped up, hands on her hips. Waiting to hear it all.

He told her of changing her last address to his so Paul could track it easier.

"Oh my God! You used yourself for bait? You took that chance for me? What if he thought it was me coming in the door and shot you?" She turned away, her eyes filled with tears. "I don't know how to thank you. No one's ever . . ."

"Hey, never mind. A friend's a friend and after all, me and the pooch are PIs, aren't we? It's all in a day's work."

She sank down on the sofa, still shaking her head.

"Joe says someone from Boston will be along to escort you back to testify. You still going to?"

She nodded. "Of course. I'd like to see that louse put away for a long time."

It felt good to have her head nestled into his shoulder and he would have liked to stay there all night, but a sense of self-preservation came to his aid. Soon she'd be gone, leaving him, off to her own life.

He moved to his feet. "Well, we got to get going. Don't want to wake the old fellow. I'd hate to have to explain this all again." They laughed.

She stood on tiptoe with her hands on each side of his head, pulling him down for a kiss. A fuzzy feeling enveloped him from his socks up to his eyebrows, his pulse roared in his ears. It was exactly The Reaction he had expected to feel with Darcy and hadn't. They stayed close for a moment before moving apart. She felt as if she belonged in his arms forever.

"There's a reward. It'll give you a new start."

"No," she said. "It's yours, earned fair and square."

He shook his head. "Nope. I want you to have it, a chance to get on your feet."

She touched a finger to his lips. "Okay, okay. Don't come unglued." She looked up at him for a long moment. "I'll be back, Alexander—I'll be back."

He knew she waited for him to say something. Offer encouragement or a hint at commitment.

What could he say to change things? He expected her to leave, it was her right. He had no call to interfere in her life. He touched a finger to his temple in a light salute and turned away, not speaking. Just at the gate, he made the mistake of looking back, seeing her on the porch with a sad, lost expression on her face.

Mac kicked a stone hard as he and the dog moved along, blending with the shadowy streets. He forgot his dread of the neighborhood at night, his mind felt clouded and he struggled to get his breath, like breathing through mud. A feeling of abandonment, of bereavement slammed into his gut.

Why couldn't he commit to a relationship? He'd thought his life had changed, widened, opened, but he was wrong. Oh so wrong. Any changes were only superficial. He *wanted* to tell her—to beg her to come back to him. Why hadn't he spoken?

She'd been through a lot, he told himself. He wanted her to have a full range of choices. He wouldn't feel right if she returned out of gratitude. Months ago it might have been his attraction for Darcy restraining him. Tonight he had forgotten the reporter existed, it was all Apple Sally—Selena. Always had been her.

"Heck, I guess we're just destined to be loners, old pal. I can't make that kind of decision. I wouldn't know how. I should have asked her to come back, could have asked her, wanted to, but I didn't. She won't return, it's a big world out there."

They ambled slowly, the murky gloom sucking up their shadows as they walked between lights.

Leaving nothing behind as they passed.

37

Mac and Herr Schnoodle walked along the dingy board-walk. They had never returned to the wharf since he found the dog. Tonight a restlessness gripped Mac and his feet moved without conscious thought. He listened to the rhythmic slap, slap of the water against the pilings. The dog pressed close to his leg, as if remembering.

Mac reached down to reassure him with a pat. Mem-ories—good and bad—did they ever disappear completely? He looked at a wino huddling in the corner of the wharf, clutching his bottle. Was it the very same wino lying there the night he found Herr Schnoodle? Did anything ever change?

Some things did, he admitted. His PI business was finally taking off with clients coming in on a regular basis. He had friends now, good friends. He could move to a real apartment if he wanted to.

A restless melancholy settled over him. He'd never felt so alone.

"I guess you miss our Apple Sally, too, don't you, old fellow? How long's it been? Too long."

Herr Schnoodle gave one of his sharp barks at the sound of her name and Mac grinned. "She might come back someday. Mr. Steinmetz swears she will, and he's a sharp, old guy."

Mac stood at the edge and looked down at the debris-filled water. He shuddered at the remembrance of hauling the schnoodle up out of that morass. How close he had come to walking away and leaving him down there.

Even after pulling the dog onto the dock, he'd still fought against becoming involved—not wanting to commit to an action without knowing all the consequences in advance.

But life wasn't like that, all sorted like files in a cabinet. Sometimes it wasn't enough to *let* something happen. Sometimes you had to *make* it happen—damn the consequences, full speed ahead.

"Hey. I got a great idea!" Mac knelt and stroked the dog's head. "Let's go back to the apartment and call Apple Sally-Selena Duvall. Never mind the hour, she won't care. Let's tell her we love her and want her to come back to us. We know how this PI stuff works now. If she wants to live somewhere else, we can do that, can't we?" The idea surprised him, having lived his whole life in New York. "We got enough stashed away to get a nice place here, too. Maybe in the 'burbs."

Before Herr Schnoodle, the thought of needing someone as much as he needed this woman to share the rest of his life with would have been impossible to imagine.

The dog shook in wild ecstasy as if he understood every word. He looked at Mac with one eyebrow raised, one ear up and one down. He was ready to go.

They walked away together, their shadows following close behind.

About the Author

P. K PARANYA was born and raised in Phoenix and now lives near Yuma, Arizona.

To start her day she fills all her bird feeders, puts food out for feral cats, fills the hummingbird feeders, feeds her own four cats and her dog Schnoodles. It's her philosophy that if people live longer because of pet companions, she should live to be two hundred.